The Sweepers

David Reynolds-Moreton

sci-fi-cafe.com

The Sweepers
David Reynolds-Moreton

This edition Copyright © 2016 by Oxford eBooks Ltd.
Published under the sci-fi-cafe.com imprint.
www.oxford-ebooks.com
Story Copyright © 1998 by David Reynolds-Moreton

ISBN 978-1-910779-31-6 (Paperback)
ISBN 978-1-908387-50-9 (ePUB)
ASIN B005UHF6NY (Kindle)

sci-fi-cafe.com

One:
The Selection

THE INSTITUTE OF Advancement and Scientific Interest was an impressive complex, and to someone who was seeing it for the first time, it must have been down right awesome.

It was spread out on a small alluvial plain, nestling among green tree-clad rolling hills which in turn were bounded by the snow capped Black Mountains of the Kaulberge range.

A more perfect site for a seat of learning could hardly be imagined, the pristine white buildings with their red brown slate roofs in stark contrast to the pale green of the lawns and the darker greens of the surrounding forests, but blending in beautifully to give an aura of majestic calm.

At any one time there were about two thousand students studying the various subjects which were on offer, having been culled from the top post graduates of the planet's Universities, and invited to join the Institute.

Jassic Koblintz had just taken his finals along with two hundred and eighty one other students, and it had been an intensive and gruelling eight consecutive days of exams, both theory and practical, culminating with a five minute verbal assessment of his attainments and ambitions for the future before the board of examiners.

He knew he had done well, but just how well was to be a surprise, even to him. The celebrations that night resulted in not a few sore heads and unstable limbs next morning, and Jas was no exception. By midday, a degree of orientation had returned and his head had cleared a little, enabling him to remain ambulant without the support of the furniture in his room or cannoning into his fellow students.

All agreed it had been one hell of a bash, and thoroughly justified by the hard work over the years and the extreme pressure of the ensuing exams.

It was three days later, when he was reasonably compos mentis, that he received a request to present himself to the Principle's Office, and as this was not the usual procedure after exams, he wondered if he had failed miserably in one of his subjects.

Very few students knew where the Principle resided, let alone had the honour of a visit to the hallowed inner sanctum, so it was with some trepidation that Jas went to the main reception to ask for directions.

As he walked up to the desk, an usher who had been standing nearby approached him, confirmed who he was, and requested that he follow to visit the Principle.

They used corridors and lifts which Jas didn't even know existed, and soon he was totally disorientated in the huge complex, and hoped that the usher would be around to return him to more familiar territory after the interview.

At last they reached the antechamber to the holiest of holies, and he was asked to be seated and await further instructions, whereupon the usher disappeared into the woodwork, and he was left alone with his thoughts.

He had to admit his heart was beating a little faster than normal and his palms were decidedly sweaty, but to hell with it, he had given the exams his best shot, and after all, he was only going to see another human being, not one of the fire breathing Gods of the ancient legends.

A soft tone sounded, and a well modulated voice said,

'Please enter the door immediately in front of you.' As he could see no other door, apart from the one he had come in by, he thought the announcement was unnecessarily precise.

As Jas approached the doorway, the wooden panel slid back with a barely audible sigh, and before him was the office of the Principle.

It was a medium sized room, sparsely furnished, but business like. The far wall was one large window, giving a magnificent view of the campus below, and the complex of buildings which receded into the distance to merge into the surrounding forest.

Between the window and Jas, stood a massive highly polished wooden desk, behind which sat the Principle and one other, an elderly man with steel grey eyes and hair to match.

'Welcome Jassic Koblintz, please be seated.' said the Principle. It seemed to take forever to traverse the few metres across the floor to the desk, and Jas sat down just before his legs gave way.

'After this interview, my colleague here,' the Principle indicated the grey man beside him, 'would like to speak to you on a matter of some importance and possible interest to you.' The grey man gave a nod of acknowledgement which was so slight that Jas wasn't sure if he had seen it.

'On behalf of the Institute, I would like to offer our congratulations on an outstanding exam result, you gained the second highest mark attained by all the students.'

'Although you didn't come first, I want you to understand that this is no mean achievement, as the top student has attained the highest marks ever recorded here'.

'You must realize that you now qualify for any job you may wish to take in the future, and I'm sure you have already mapped out the area in which your main interests lie.' The Principle looked down at something on his desk before continuing, 'you have one other attribute of which you may not be aware, and that is your psychological profile.

'Although it is not unique, it is quite rare, and is the main reason for my colleague here attending this meeting'.

The Principle glanced at the grey man, who again gave a hardly discernible nod, not having moved since the last one.

'Should you decide to take up the offer which will be made to you, the Institute would consider it a great honour to have contributed towards your acceptance of the appointment, but it is something which you alone must decide upon. I would respectfully request that you give it your utmost consideration, and listen carefully to what my colleague has to say.' The Principle paused again, as if he was judging whether to say his next piece or not, and having made up his mind, went ahead.

'If you decide not to take up the offer, the Institute would be pleased to secure for you the employment of your choice, but as an alternative, and much preferred, we would like to offer you the future position of lecturer in a subject of your choosing.'

The Principle arose from his chair, and extended a hand to Jas, who also got to his feet. As they shook hands the Principle said, 'once again, our congratulations, I'm sure you will make the best choice.' and he left the room.

As Jas sat down again, the grey man looked up and locked eyes with him. It wasn't a stare, just a total confrontation of one being to another.

'I belong to an elite group of people who have perhaps the most important job in the Galactic Confederation. I'm not making a statement about myself, but just stating a fact'. He paused to let any doubt Jas had about the situation to settle.

'We work on the principle of 'the greatest good for the majority' which sometimes means we have to make tough decisions and carry them out ruthlessly, regardless of our own personal feelings.'

'It is a very rewarding job, not only in payment, but in satisfaction when looked upon as a whole. I would assume that this kind of work would appeal to you?' The grey man paused, waiting for Jas to comment.

Not knowing quite what to say, Jas just nodded, ever so slightly. He wasn't going to commit himself to anything he didn't fully understand, and it looked as if there was a whole lot more information on its way, if he just kept quiet.

The grey man's gaze hadn't faulted nor had he blinked once during the time they had been together, and Jas realized this was someone who was totally dedicated to his purpose, and probably unshakeable in his beliefs. By now the room had faded from his vision and he was only aware of the man before him, and those intense grey eyes.

'What do you suppose is the most important thing to maintain in the whole Confederation, bearing in mind the level of science available to all, and the amount of trade which plies between the different worlds?'

Jas thought deeply about the question before replying with,

'I suppose stability among the member planets would be of paramount importance, but we already have that by the very nature of the people involved.'

The faintest of smiles flickered across grey man's face, and then was gone.

'You are of course, correct, but such things do not come about by relying upon nature, or the good auspices of the people concerned. Sometimes a little help is needed to grease the mighty wheels of the Confederation, and sometimes a few faulty parts of the machine need to be replaced or removed,' a pause, 'and that's where we come in.' The grey man waited until he thought Jas had ingested that little offering, and then continued,

'Do you think you might be interested in such an important occupation Jas?' It was the first time his name had been used by the grey man, and immediately he felt the mental distance between them decrease to a more comfortable level.

'It certainly sounds interesting, but what exactly would I be involved in?' Jas asked, hoping more information would be forthcoming.

At this point the grey man leaned back, relaxing in his chair, as an almost inaudible sigh escaped him, or was it the wind outside, brushing against the huge curved window of the Principle's Office.

The silence between them seemed to drag on for ever before the grey man finally spoke.

'There is one constriction which you may find too much to accept. If I tell you any more about the organization I belong to, you will never be able to return to your family or this world. As far as anyone is concerned, you will cease to exist.

'You will appear to have gone away on a project, as far as anyone else is concerned, and we will keep up the pretence for as long as is necessary. Unfortunately you will be forgotten as far as your home world is concerned. For good.'

This was a little more than Jas had expected, and only served to stress the importance of the job, whatever it was.

The idea of belonging to a secret organization which was whizzing about the galaxy and adjusting things here and there for the good of all appealed to him in a way. He recalled the stories and rumours which had gone the rounds as a youngster, which no one gave any serious credence to.

Surely the bizarre tales of his youth were based on myth and legend, but then myths usually had a reason for coming into being in the first place.

'Can you tell me a little more without my committing myself to oblivion?' Jas asked, hopefully.

The faintest of smiles crossed the stern face of the man opposite him, and he leaned forward a little, his gaze never once leaving Jas's face.

'All I can say is that if you accept the offer, you will go through three stages of training and occupational experience before you reach the main job, and if you should fail on any one of them, then that will be the level at which you will stay for the rest of your working life. I wouldn't expect you to have any problems in attaining the final goal, or I wouldn't be here now.

'I can't of course guarantee your success, that's up to you, but I have little doubt that you will make it. Your working life would not be quite so long as is normally expected because of the nature of the job, but retirement would be everything anyone could wish for, should you wish to retire that is.'

'Do I have to decide right now?' asked Jas, not at all happy at the speed with which events had taken place. This wasn't like volunteering for a week to plant trees in order to reclaim a piece of desert, this was a total long term commitment with no going back once it had begun. This time the grey man smiled openly and said, 'you must give the offer some considerable thought, and if you decide to join us, then you must make your peace with your parents and other relatives and friends, such that they think you are going away for an intensive period of training, and won't be back for some considerable time.

We will then take up the pretence on your behalf and take care of a carefully controlled flow of information such that they will feel at ease with what they think you are doing.'

The grey man's last statement had removed the main hurdle to Jas accepting the offer, but he still wasn't happy about something, but couldn't define exactly what it was.

'I will return here in four days, and at the same time. By then you will know what you intend to do. I have told you nothing more than that which you may well have already heard as rumour or fable, so at this stage you are still a free agent, to accept or not, as you choose.'

Jas knew the interview was at an end, and arose from his chair to leave. He didn't reach out to shake the hand of the grey man as courtesy would dictate, somehow feeling it wasn't the right thing to do at this point in time. It almost felt that if he had touched the grey man, he would then be inextricably bound to follow through and join the organization, and he wasn't quite ready for that yet.

The usher was patiently waiting for him in the anteroom, and silently signalled for him to follow, retracing the steps they had taken earlier from Reception.

As there were still several days to go before the Institute closed down for the mid year break, Jas had to ask permission for a couple of days leave, which was granted without question, and on the journey home he mulled over what he would say to his parents. Although he was very fond of them, and they of him, there wasn't the very close knit relationship he had observed in some families, so his going away for training shouldn't be too hard to put across and get agreement upon.

His parents had both retired from official work long ago, being somewhat older than those of his peer group, and were engrossed in their hobby of cataloguing the various forms minerals took due to the different circumstances in which they were formed.

He too, had found it quite fascinating during his breaks from the Institute, and had often given a somewhat amateur hand in the research, but it hadn't resulted in him being any closer to them. His only brother was away as a technician on another world, and was only seen very infrequently, so there were no real family ties as such.

The subject was broached at the main meal of the day, and both his parents thought it was quite an honour for him to be selected for something so grand, not fully understanding what was really entailed in the offer.

As caring and thoughtful as his parents were, Jas couldn't help but think that they were too wrapped up in their own world to realize that he was going to be away for a very long time indeed, and although one day they would wonder where he was, he didn't think they would be too put out if he didn't turn up for several years, and then it would be too late.

With his only concern now fully put to rest, his mind was made up, and he would accept the offer made by the grey man as the unknown had always intrigued him, and just how much more unknown can you get with what he proposed?

The rest of his two days leave passed quietly enough, with hardly a mention of what he intended doing being mentioned by his parents. He told them he was going to take back with him a few of the little odds and ends he had collected over the years, to remind him of home, but in truth these were dumped in the Institute waste disposal unit as soon as he returned.

There was no point in leaving mementoes at home to remind them of their long lost son, should they ever tear themselves away from their interests. He didn't mean this unkindly, it was just a statement of the facts as he saw them.

Having returned to the Institute, he had one more day to wait before he was scheduled to meet with the grey man again, and decided to use that time to find out all he could about the old stories of a secret organization, somewhere among the stars.

None of the tutors gave any credence to the tales, and there was very little in the data library, apart from that which he already knew. One or two of his fellow students elaborated on what they knew just for the sheer fun of it, but generally speaking, he knew no more about it than he did before.

Next day, just before the appointed time Jas went to the reception desk, and there waiting for him was the same usher. Not a word was said as the usher led him through the maze of corridors and lifts again, to arrive at the Principle's Office with just a few seconds to spare. As he went to sit down the tone sounded, and a voice asked him to enter the door ahead of him, as before.

This time the Principle was absent, and the grey man sat alone at the big desk. He nonchalantly waved Jas to a chair without even looking up from the surface of the desk on which were strewn a several pieces of paper. As Jas sat down, the grey man scooped the papers together into a neat pile and looking up, fixed him with the same unblinking gaze of their last meeting.

'You have made your decision and squared it away with your parents?' Jas realized that the question implied that he had decided to accept the offer, and he was a little put out that he hadn't been asked the question in such a way that he could have given his own answer.

'Yes, I have. I would like to accept your offer, but I need to know a little more about it first.' The grey man didn't reply at first, he just looked straight at Jas, unblinking.

'As I said four days ago, I can tell you nothing you don't already know, until you actually join us. Do you still wish to do so?' Jas knew deep down that he did, as nothing else had sparked such an interest in him, and nodded. There was no reaction at all from the grey man, and so Jas blurted out,

'Yes, I wish to join your organization, unreservedly.'

The grey man actually smiled, and then extended his hand across the desk. Jas knew that if he took the offered hand, he was committed for life, there was no going back. Their hands touched, and then clasped firmly. For an instant Jas felt a flow of energy surge between them, or was it just his imagination brought about by the tension of the meeting and the momentous decision to which he had just pledged himself? He wasn't sure.

'Welcome young man, we are pleased to have you join us. Now I can tell you a little more about what you will be called upon to do, and how the whole system works, but that will not be done here. Tomorrow, present yourself at the main reception desk, and you will be contacted. In the meantime, tidy up your affairs and say goodbye to your friends. What you say to them is up to you, but be discreet. I will see you tomorrow. This interview is now terminated.'

Jas knew he was now supposed to arise from his seat and leave the room, which he did.

The usher was waiting in the antechamber, as he expected him to be, and silently they both retraced their way back to the main desk, and parted.

For a brief moment Jas wondered if he should back out of the situation, but deep down knew he couldn't now.

Although nothing had been committed to paper or had been contracted in any way, somehow it didn't seem to matter. He had been accepted, and that was that.

He was intrigued as to what the special qualities were which they had seen in him.

They certainly seemed to have their own way of doing things, he thought, as he emptied his room of all the trivia he had collected over the years. Everything went down the disposal chute, as he somehow knew his body would be the only thing which would be accepted into the 'whatever it was' he was going to be accepted into.

Saying farewell to his friends was a lot easier than he had expected, and they all took it as a matter of course, his abilities throughout the term indicating that he was destined for something special.

He told them he was going to join a research organization, and would be off-planet for some considerable time, but would try and contact them when he returned, knowing full well that could never be.

He slept well that night, much to his surprise, and after breakfast in the main hall, went to his room for the last time. As he entered, he was aware that there was someone in the room already, he froze. It was the Principle, sitting in his bedside chair.

'Please come in and shut the door, Jas.' The Principle got to his feet, and extended his hand. Jas took it for the second time since he had been at the Institute.

'I am very pleased that you have accepted the offer made to you, and it is a great honour for the Institute to have you selected from its ranks of students. Unfortunately we can't put up a plaque in your honour, or even announce your departure for higher things to the other students. But I know, and that is enough.'

Although it didn't worry him, he could see that the Principal was disappointed with the outcome.

Jas had a thousand and one questions he wanted to ask the Principle, but knew he shouldn't, as it would probably be as unproductive as the interview with the grey man.

'The first thing I knew of your selection was two days before you took your final exam. The man who interviewed you came to me and said that he thought you would be eminently suitable to join his organization, and he would like to see you. And so it was. We would very much have liked you to become one of our lecturers, but it would seem that you are destined for greater things, and I just wanted to wish you every success and happiness for the future.'

Their hands parted, and Jas knew that one section of his life had finished, and another was about to begin.

As the Principle left the room, Jas knew there was nothing else to do but go to the main desk, and wait for his escort to appear. Taking one last look around the room which had been his home for so long, but now stripped bare of all the things which had made it his, he turned and left, quietly shutting the door on one phase of his life and then striding off down the corridor to start the next.

He was about to take a seat at Reception when a hand touched his arm.

'Please follow me.' it was the same usher he had seen before, and silently they left the main building to cross the campus and enter the monorail transport terminal.

The sleek shape of the transport cleaved the morning air with a steady hiss as the kilometres sped by, neither of them speaking as Jas didn't know what to say, and the usher seemed to prefer silence anyway. Arriving at the main terminal on the outskirts of the city, Jas was guided to a small building a few blocks away from their arrival point, the door opening as they approached.

The building seemed to be basically just an empty shell, apart from a few packing cases untidily stacked along one wall, but in the middle of the floor was one of the sleekest pod-shaped personal transports he had ever seen. There was little time to stand and admire the graceful machine, as a door quietly slid open and he was guided in by the usher.

With a soft clunk the door regained its former position, and through the forward view screen Jas could see the end wall of the building slide back to reveal a high fenced open yard as the transport slowly moved forward.

The view screen suddenly misted over, obscuring his vision, while at the same time there was a violent surge forward and upwards. Jas was surprised at the upwards acceleration which pressed him firmly back into his seat, as this type of vehicle wasn't supposed to take to the air. As far as he knew.

The flight was over quite quickly. The deceleration forces took effect, and being much stronger than he had anticipated, indicated that the speed of the vehicle had been greatly in excess of what he had expected. There was a dull thump and all motion ceased, while the door of the vehicle slid back with a soft hiss to reveal what he could only assume to be the entry bay of a space ship.

The usher was out first, and gave a steadying hand to a rather shattered Jas, as he climbed from the vehicle. Their footsteps reverberated with a hollow sound as they crossed the metallic floor of the bay and entered a passageway.

They had only gone a few metres when a section of the wall slid back to reveal a small room into which the usher guided Jas by the arm. The usher stepped back, and the section of wall slid back completing the box-like room once again, leaving Jas alone with his confused thoughts.

Before he could turn around, the lift began it's ascent with a degree of acceleration which almost forced him to his knees, then stopping as suddenly as it had begun. A slightly less violent sideways motion took him by surprise as he staggered against the wall of the lift, and then lurched forwards again as the lift stopped. By the time the door had glided open onto the grey man's office, Jas was feeling quite disorientated and not a little annoyed.

'Welcome aboard, as they used to say in the good old days.' The grey man was in a good mood, and smiling.

Jas did his best to walk in a straight line towards the desk, and flopped into the vacant chair in the same instant the grey man asked him to take a seat.

'In order for you to fully understand why we exist and what we do, I shall have to go back into history quite some way. I will give you the bare outlines of what has happened, and if you want the full story, then it can be obtained from the data banks in all it's gory details, complete with pictures should you wish to see them.' Here the grey man paused, as if assessing the maximum rate at which he could transfer data to their latest recruit.

'From what you know of the Galactic Confederation, I am sure that you will agree that everything seems to run smoothly, with regard to information interchange and trade.

'Each planet has basic laws which are shared among all worlds, and in addition to these, there are a some local ones peculiar to those races which need them. There are no wars or crimes, no manufacturing company produces goods which could harm anyone if used in the manner for which they are intended, and no harmful by-products are produced and allowed to escape into the atmosphere or waterways during their manufacture.'

'It all seems very normal and correct. We wouldn't have it any other way.' Again, the grey man paused to let his statement sink in.

'Well yes,' said Jas, 'who would want to change any of that. It is, as you say, normal. So where does the Organization come into the picture?' The grey man smiled, took a deep breath, and lay back in his chair.

'That's how things are now, and have been for a very long time. But they were not always so. Let me explain.'

At long last Jas felt he was going to get somewhere, the old mysteries would be cleared up, and he would know where he was going, or not, as the case may be.

'I will begin as near the beginning as is pertinent for the data which you will need in order to gain a good understanding of the present situation.

'A very long time ago, on a planet near the centre of the galaxy there was a race of people who had developed their science to the point where they could have ripped their world apart, so wiping out all life.

'All it needed was for someone to start another war, and bearing in mind the attitude of the people concerned, the war would have gone on to the bitter end. Long after all human life had been extinguished, the robot controlled devices would still be selecting their pre-programmed targets, and sending the missiles on their way'.

Jas thought he saw a slight flicker of sadness cross the grey man's face, but didn't know why.

'Fortunately for them, and subsequently for us, a small group of men who were terrified about the situation and were fed up with the lies, graft, cheating and general corruption that was prevalent at the time, got together to see if there was a way out of the mess before it was too late.'

'They were small in number, but wealthy and had connections in high places. A research team was set up in secret to find out if the present state of mind exhibited by the general population was the norm, and fixed, or if it could be altered to a more sane and stable state, and how this could be achieved.'

The grey man had a questioning look on his face, and Jas thought he was expected to say something.

'I am with you so far, but I don't understand how they could be so insane as to do the things you mentioned.'

Perhaps the grey man needed the odd interjection to tell him that I'm understanding what he's saying, Jas thought.

'In our journeying among the worlds of this galaxy, we have found two worlds which have been wrecked and are devoid of all but the very simplest forms of life, and no reason for this could be found except that which I mentioned earlier, a massive war.

'The radiation levels were much higher than could be explained by any natural source, and so the conclusion drawn was that they had had a total war situation, and neither side could call a halt to it before it was too late, and possibly with robotics taking over in the end.'

The ill concealed look of disbelief on Jas's face must have registered on the grey man, for he paused a while, allowing Jas to assimilate the full horror of what he had been told.

'I don't understand how a people could let things get to such a state and not be aware of the consequences.' Jas managed to get out.

'It was easy, as you will see later.' replied the grey man,

'Don't forget, you have a knowledge which they didn't have, but the basics of which were about to be discovered by the research team.'

'Anyway, back to our research team. They had come up with the fact that eighty per cent of the general population were reasonably honest, and left to their own devices, would get along with each other quite well, and that included between different races and countries. About fifteen per cent were of a more devious nature with low ethics, and it would seem that only the threat of punishment kept them to the straight and narrow. The remaining five per cent were much more dangerous, being without ethics of any kind, and a small percentage of them were pure evil.

'The five per cents could easily whip up a bit of enthusiasm among the fifteen per cents, who would be promised whatever it was that they wanted, and so they were able to take control of the greater majority with only a small group at the top calling the tune.'

'Why,' asked Jas 'didn't the greater majority just take over, and send the trouble makers packing?'

A sad smile from the grey man.

'So called human nature isn't, or I should say, wasn't, like that. The eighty per cents were basically simple ordinary people, who just wanted to get on with their lives, they weren't leaders of men or people of great ambition.

'The first step towards a more sane world was a little extreme, but would have worked if circumstances had been a little different. Those in charge of the research team had come up with the same concept which we use today, namely 'the greatest good for the greatest number' which salved their consciences to some degree for the dastardly deeds they were about to perpetrate upon their unsuspecting fellow men. Secret hit teams were put together after the targets had been identified as the real trouble makers, and they were then eliminated.'

'For a while this worked quite well, and several potential wars were averted, crime dropped to a new all time low, and a fairer sharing out of the world's resources was achieved. It all sounds too good to be true you might think, and it was. They were lacking a vital piece of knowledge which we now take for granted. They were, as we are, immortal. Spiritual beings, units of awareness, call it what you will. They had not discovered the true 'life-death cycle', mainly, as far as we can tell, because they were so materialistically minded. It was what you had, not what you were, which counted so much to them. They had no concept of the fact that the body would die, they as a being would then take on another body at its birth, a mental shutter would drop blocking out all memories of the past life, and they would start all over again.

'The main difficulty was that some of the deeply imbedded less pleasant attitudes, and evil intentions in some cases, could get restimulated in the next life, so propagating further problems. So, basically the baddies returned in new bodies, and before long the troubles began again. Two main things saved the situation, and gave us the basics of the system we employ to this day. One was the realization of a lot of people that life could be so much better without the troubles, and the other was a rudimentary form of space flight.

'It was crude and very slow compared to what we have now, but it worked. The trouble makers were shipped off to another world which was only just able to support life, and they were too busy trying to survive to bother about trying to get back home.

'I think it's time for some refreshments, don't you Jas?' and with that the grey man got up and walked over to a cabinet in the wall and withdrew two tall glasses.

A pale amber fluid was poured into each glass from a tall jewelled container, and he handed Jas a glass of the liquid.

Courtesy decreed that Jas wait until his host had taken a sip before he could quench his not inconsiderable thirst, and as the grey man raised the glass to his lips, Jas did likewise.

As the ice cold liquid touched his lips, he experienced an explosion of tastes, the main one being .... he wasn't sure, but it was the best thing he had ever tasted. The look on his face must have amused the grey man, prompting him to say with a smile 'An interesting little concoction, isn't it? It works on two levels, mental and physical. A substance in the drink triggers your taste buds, and memories of all the nice things you have ever tasted flash by, the best of them is then restimulated into present time, and that is what you experience.'

'What would happen if you had only tasted unpleasant things?' asked Jas, trying to bring a note of joviality into the conversation.

'I don't know.' replied the grey man, with the hint of a chuckle in his voice,

'That's something we could look into sometime in the future, I suppose.' They sipped their drinks, each enjoying the flavours peculiar to their own memories, and relaxed for a while.

'Right, back to the story. They found that by shipping the criminally insane, for that's what they were, off to another planet solved most of the difficulties they had been having, and life in general improved, slowly but surely. Of course, some people objected, but they were over ruled.

'A reasonable state of stability was not attained until very much later, there being a lot more to be discovered about how the human mind worked, as you will see.'

'A further development of finding out who and what they really were, was that by addressing the past, and by that I don't mean just the current lifetime, they were able to rid some people of the fixed considerations they had, which had been causing them to behave irrationally.

'The really evil ones were shipped off without compunction, for there was little we could do to help them as there was no co-operation on their behalf, whilst those of a lesser degree of troublesomeness were given help to sort themselves out.

'Over a long period of time, sanity returned to the planet, that's if it was ever there in the first place, and we have our doubts about that'.

The grey man paused to sip his drink again, and then continued, 'Feasible space travel was achieved after a while, and other civilizations were found on other worlds. Some were down right hostile, while others wanted to trade, especially for information. The technology of stabilizing a race was also selectively introduced, once the need for it was brought to the attention of those requiring it.

'And so the Galactic Confederation was formed. It was a little different to what we have now, the basic aims being the same, but the method of achieving them having been refined. This is, as I'm sure you can see, the most important job in the galaxy, from our point of view'.

The grey man sat back in his seat and relaxed. Jas wasn't so surprised at the revelations as he thought he might have been.

'Well' said Jas, 'I must admit it all makes very good sense to me, and explains some of the old legends, but is it really true that all races contacted so far, have this mixture of good, bad, and indifferent people in their make up?'

'Yes,' replied the grey man, 'with one possible exception. Recently, we have contacted a civilization on a distant world far from the cluster of planets which make up the Confederation. They seem to have solved the problem, that's if it ever existed in the first place, but do not want to have anything to do with us. They don't wish to trade or exchange information on any subject, and will not tell us very much about themselves.

'They are polite but firm in their refusal to join the Confederation without giving any reason. That of course is their right, and we don't intend to push it, but we are intrigued as to how they have reached the state they are in. They seem to have something we don't, and that is a level of serenity you have to see to believe.

'We hope to establish a more productive contact in the future, but so far we haven't found a means of doing so.'

It was Jas's turn to sit back in his chair, while he mulled over what he had been told. Everything seemed to follow a logical pattern, but there were one or two things which didn't quite gel in his mind.

'Why is it that human beings, whereever you find them, seem to have this self destructive element built in?' asked Jas. 'Animals don't behave like that, in fact they seem to work with nature, not against.'

There was no answer from the grey man, he just sat looking at Jas with those powerful grey eyes, inviting Jas to expound further on the subject.

'Surely, if we go back far enough in time, we will find the point where it all went so horribly wrong, and from that we could find the cause? Obviously it's not a genetic factor or it would run in families, so it must be a mental one, carried on from lifetime to lifetime.'

'Research on those lines is being done at this very moment, but it isn't quite so easy as you might think,' the grey man replied, 'perhaps, in the future, you may have an aptitude and desire to follow that line of work, we shall have to see how things work out.'

The grey man poured out another helping of the amber fluid, and they both relaxed for a few moments in silence, each thinking their own thoughts on what to say or ask next, and enjoying the pleasurable sensations created by their taste buds from the stimulative liquid.

At last the grey man broke the silence,

'You will find out for yourself in time, so I may as well tell you now, you will only be given enough information pertinent to the job you are doing at the time, enabling you to do it efficiently. This is not done to engender a feeling of mysticism into the system, but for two very good reasons.

'It helps to concentrate the mind on the task in hand, and boosts the curiosity factor. Several of our operatives have come up with modifications to the system, and this has benefited us all.'

'When do I begin.' asked Jas, a little impatient to get his teeth into what he thought would be a really worthwhile job, instead of just teaching or doing some research job along with a team of similar minded people.

'Very soon,' replied the grey man, 'you will be given some basic training, and then, for want of a better expression, be apprenticed to an expert in the field. You will observe, ask questions, and generally help out. When your mentor thinks you have gained sufficient experience, you will be allowed to operate on your own, but under strict supervision.

'After that, we shall see if you want to head up your own unit or go into research along the lines just mentioned.'

Jas's impatience must have shown, for the grey man leaned forward and quietly said, 'It may sound a simple introduction to your chosen work, but make no mistake, you will be watched very carefully indeed, and any errors will incur a period of intensive retraining. Not only can we not make any mistakes, we don't make any mistakes, the job is far too important.

'You may think that a period in some college would be the best method of learning, but experience has proven the method we now use is the best, as it encourages you to learn at your own rate, and use your initiative under supervision.'

Jas felt he had almost received a reprimand, and realized he had not acted in a very mature manner over the last question and his reaction to the answer. 'The grey man didn't miss much' he thought to himself, whereupon the grey man gave a slight nod, and Jas wondered for a moment if he could read his thoughts.

'There is one thing you may not like the idea of very much, and that is we shall implant a very small electronic unit into the bone at the base of your skull. It is quite painless and you won't even know it's there, until we need to activate it. The reason for this is, that in an emergency we can communicate with you directly, and we will always know where you are should the need arise. I hope this isn't a problem?'

'Oh, no.' Jas answered, wondering what other surprises were in store for him.

'You are probably aware that you are onboard one of our ships, orbiting your home world. Let's dispel a few myths about that for a start. They are generally known as the 'Dark Ships', as far as the stories go, and the reason for this is that they reflect no light, and so therefore can't be seen in the general sense of the word.'

'This is achieved by the outer layer of the hull being composed of a material which absorbs all light radiation, and that includes most radiation from electronic sensing systems. The only way you would know that one of the ships was there, would be by the star field behind the ship being blanked out, just showing a piece of black sky. But even that is not easily detected, as the ship is very small when viewed from the planet's surface, and the patch of dark sky would be hardly noticeable.'

'But that's impossible,' retorted Jas, 'everything reflects something, or we wouldn't know it was there.'

'Patience, young man. Don't forget, we have recruited the very best people from many worlds into our organization, and therefore are in the forefront of scientific research, and we don't reveal all our discoveries to one and all.

'There's one other thing which we do, as an organization that is, and you may well become involved in it if you show the necessary aptitude and desire so to do.

'We are contacting people on new worlds all the time, not every day of course, but a little more frequently than you might expect. The great majority of them need a little help in stabilizing their worlds, such that we can then bring them into the Confederation safely, and that is where education comes in.'

He paused to pour out another helping of the strange liquor, and they both sipped it in silence for a moment.

'Let me give you an example. Most worlds, but not all, develop somewhat unevenly. There may be one large land mass, or it may be broken up into many islands, but in most cases, one section of the population will be more advanced than some or all of the others, and you can imagine the problems this could cause.'

'This leads to an uneven distribution of the natural and man made resources, and this in turn can lead to war, as one party tries to take from another that which it hasn't got, but desires. The reason some races are a little backward can be attributed to many causes, but the main one is tied up with the old religions, which in turn are founded in myth and legends.'

Here the grey man sat back in his chair, waiting for Jas to catch up mentally with the new ideas with which he was being bombarded.

'Until a civilization realizes that its population is in effect immortal, for all intents and purposes, it will consider that bodies are the most precious things around, and will protect and preserve them to the bitter end. When this gets out of control, which it usually does, they have a problem.

'At birth, genetically damaged bodies are not only allowed to survive, but are encouraged to do so, using any scientific means at the disposal of the medical technicians, who themselves have a vested interest in perpetuating the system.

'These bodies will then reproduce, the offspring duplicating the genetic faults until the race becomes weakened to the point that the resources needed to support them are overwhelmed, and can no longer cope.

'In nature this doesn't happen, the weak and malformed fall by the wayside, only the strong and healthy survive to breed the next generation. You can see how a missing piece of data can have a devastating effect on a race, hindering its progress and eventually reducing the population to a level of poverty the like of which we can't remember.'

Jas nodded, finding it difficult to understand what he took for granted, could so easily be overlooked or totally missed by others.

'There is another concept which is quite difficult to dispel, and that is if a race is impoverished to subsistence level, it will produce as many offspring as possible, the general idea being that some of the children will survive to look after the ageing parents.

'This of course, leads to a population explosion, exacerbating the already worsening living conditions of the race, and weakening it still further. Left to their own devices, a level of stability will usually ensue, but if there is another race which is relatively better off, the tendency is to supply aid in the form of money, food and medical assistance, which only makes the problem worse, as the old ideas of producing as many offspring as possible will persist for a considerable time, unless corrected by education.

'The sustentation of a race can also depend upon its mores and religions. A race of people can be at starvation level, while there might be an abundance of an animal or plant food which for some reason is considered by them to be holy, unclean or just plain inedible.

'Again, education is the answer. So you can see, we are involved at many different levels in our quest to stabilize the worlds we encounter, and it is not through any altruistic reason that we do this.

'We are fairly sure that one day we will come up against another group of beings who may not welcome us with open arms, so to speak, and may be aggressive in the extreme. A strong Confederation of planets, technically advanced, would be more able to survive such an encounter. We hope it will never happen, but if it does, and communication will not resolve the differences, then we would be prepared.'

This was something which Jas hadn't thought of, and added a new importance to the occupation he had chosen.

The grey man smiled at him, 'I have only given you a broad outline of what is involved, there is much more for you to learn in the years ahead. You will find it fascinating work, very rewarding, sometimes a little tough and quite possibly heartbreaking at times.'

Jas somehow felt that the interview was to be concluded at this point, and said 'Thank you for your patience and explaining everything so succinctly, I must admit there were a few surprises, but everything you have said is logically acceptable to me, I just need to realign some of my own data.'

'You are most welcome.' The grey man arose from his chair, extending his hand to Jas. The grip was firm and steady, he was now one of the team.

'You will be escorted to another room where your transponder will be fitted, and then I'll introduce you to your mentor who will accompany you down to the planet's surface. You may not have realized it, but we have been travelling at quite a high velocity for some time now, and are fast approaching your first project world. They are very similar to us, the skin is a little darker, and yours will be adjusted accordingly to match in.' The grey man, with his hand lightly on Jas's shoulder, walked him to the door which swished open to reveal his escort, and then closed behind him.

Together they walked down the long brightly lit corridor, neither of them speaking, used two lifts and several passageways before coming to the medical section. The escort touched a small plate on the wall, and a doorway opened in the facing wall. 'Please go in, I'll be waiting for you.'

The room didn't have much in it, apart from a clinical couch with an overhead operating light.

Jas was trying to figure out why he felt so at ease, when two technicians seemed to appear from nowhere and one of them smilingly indicated with a swing of his arm that Jas should lie upon the couch.

Another surprise was in store for him as he sat on the edge and swung his legs up, he was floating a few centimetres above the surface, but held firmly in place. Before he could say anything, there was a soft 'ping' and oblivion. He was floating somewhere up near the ceiling, looking down on the two technicians who had turned his body over onto its face, and were busy doing something at the back of its neck.

There was the odd flash of surgical steel scalpels, a few quietly muttered words, and then he was back in his body.

One of the technicians swung Jas's legs off the couch and he was back on his feet again, feeling none the worse for the operation.

'Quick, isn't it, we've got it down to a fine art now.' he thought one of the technicians said as he led Jas towards the door.

'It sure is, but how do I know it's working.' asked Jas.

'We just tested it. Did you see either of our lips move just now? That voice came from another room, and you answered it.' Come to think of it, the voice did have a strange quality about it, thought Jas, as he passed through the doorway and into the company of his escort.

'Please follow me, and I will introduce you to your tutor.' the escort said, striding off down the corridor.

'Right, thanks.' Jas replied, hoping to solicit a further verbal outburst from the usually silent escort, but it wasn't forthcoming.

He couldn't help wondering why some of the personal were so friendly, and others so reticent.

Another lift and many metres of corridor brought them to a small room with a large curved window which looked out onto the star field. Jas nearly fell over with the disorienting effect of open space suddenly thrust upon him.

'Please wait here until your tutor arrives.' the disembodied voice said as the door closed behind him, and he was left alone with his thoughts. The curvature and cleanness of the window gave the illusion that there was nothing between him and the bright shining lights outside, and Jas was drawn, zombie like, towards the glass-like material, touching it to see if it really existed. He found the experience of his first journey into space most exhilarating, as it was like nothing he had encountered before, and far better than the campus simulator.

'Please be seated.' a well modulated voice said behind him. The tutor had silently entered the room, and indicated two chairs which Jas hadn't noticed before.

Still observing correct procedure, he waited for the tutor to take a seat first, and then he sat down, extending his legs before him and crossing them at the ankles. Suddenly realizing that this was impolite in senior company, he withdrew his feet until they touched the base of the chair, and wondered if he should apologize for his indiscretion.

'That's fine,' the tutor smilingly said, 'please be comfortable and stretch you legs out if you wish, we're not all that formal here.' Jas relaxed as the tutor looked up at him and opened the conversation with a question.

'Why are you here?'

'Because I did well with my finals, and a man with grey eyes and hair to match, asked me if I would like an interesting job for life.' retorted Jas, a little taken aback with the suddenness and directness of the question.

'All right, please don't feel you have to take up a defensive attitude, I was just curious to know your reasons for dedicating your life to something about which you know so little.' The tutor was still smiling.

'I'm sorry. I didn't mean to appear like that. In answer to your question, I just felt it was right, a gut feeling, intuition, call it what you will, I know it's right for me, even if I don't yet know all the finer points. I needed something with a real purpose behind it, not just a teaching or regular research job.'

'That's good, Grel rarely makes a mistake in choosing new personnel.'

The atmosphere had relaxed a little, and Jas felt he could talk to this man without reservation, and that might mean he could get some of his questions answered.

'Your mentor, who is already on the planet we are orbiting, has been advised of your imminent arrival, but first there are one or two things we need to sort out, so that you will feel better equipped when you begin your work. Let us first look at some definitions'.

The tutor eased himself back into his chair, which remoulded itself to suit his new position. Jas was a little surprised at the chair's reaction, and moved likewise, and to his amazement his chair also readjusted itself.

'Neat, isn't it?' the tutor was enjoying Jas's reaction to the chair, and showed it openly.

'Just one of those little comforts we afford ourselves for all the hard work we do.' he said with a chuckle.

'OK, down to work. How do you define sanity?'

Jas was surprised by the bluntness of the question, and thought long and hard about it, as he hadn't really formulated any ideas on the subject prior to this.

'Well, I suppose it's … well, not doing irrational things.' Jas blurted out, stumped for a better explanation, and feeling somewhat embarrassed at not being as erudite on the subject as he would have liked.

'All right, that's part of it, but we need to define it a little more accurately than that to be of any use. We look upon sanity as 'the pursuit of pro survival activities', in other words, doing things which will enhance the survival of one's self, both as a being and a body, your family, friends, work mates, the group in which you coexist, your fellow country men, and ultimately the whole population of your world and the physical world itself.

'The antonym of which would be doing things to endanger one or all of the above. A simple example will illustrate the point more clearly. Someone discovers some fissionable material, like a deposit of uranium ore. They think 'I could make an explosion with that'. They refine it, and set off a huge blast, destroying for arguments sake, an off-shore island.

'They haven't killed anyone directly, but just consider the radioactive material which has now been released into the atmosphere. It is going to settle somewhere, and that can cause mutations in plants, animals, and his fellow human beings. Just for the fun of blowing something up, or demonstrating how clever he is, he has endangered his world on many different levels. It is a totally irresponsible act, and we would therefore class it as an insane act. The person is a danger to the rest of society.'

Not having looked at the concept as deeply as this before, Jas was surprised how easily it all made sense.

'And I suppose that type of person would have to be removed from society, for the safety of all.' he added.

'Yes, that would be a good idea. You could say that extermination would be justified for the good of all, but there is another difficulty looming up on the horizon. That person is going to pick up another body, and may well cause more problems in the future. So it is the removal of the being that is the answer to the situation, not just the body. Bearing in mind that a being is indestructible, this in itself poses another problem, but we have got over that one, and you will see how later on. For the moment, the identifying of the insane is your main task, what follows later will be in your next assignment.'

'But surely, the person making the atomic device would be observed by others, and could have the dangers pointed out to him and so be persuaded not to make it?' Jas asked.

'That's possible, but not a certainty,' replied the mentor.

'Let me give you another example. This could easily happen, and in fact has happened many times. Imagine a world composed of two main countries. One is small, well advanced in technology, and prosperous. Life is easy and relatively tension free, machines do most of the hard work, and everyone is having a good time of it. The other country is much bigger, hasn't advanced technically, so there is a lot of manual labour involved. Life is tough, there aren't enough of the good things to go around, but they are making progress slowly but surely towards better times.' He paused to see if Jas was following his train of thought.

'Along comes our insane person, who in this example is power hungry. He gathers around himself a few like-minded people, stirs up a degree of discontent among the general populous, and points out that they being the larger country, could easily overwhelm the richer country and take what they want.'

'This is how wars are begun. The ensuing battle impoverishes both sides, wrecking their economies and causing a lot of long term damage in a more subtle form than you may think.'

The mentor paused for his last offering to sink in, and the light of understanding to shine in Jas's eyes.

'Thousands of people will be killed in this kind of situation, and that means a like number of traumas will be recorded in the minds of those who have suffered. As you know, events of a heavy traumatic nature can affect an individual in future lifetimes, causing irrational actions as the events of the past get restimulated into present time and the emotional contents flavour the actions of the persons concerned.

'This is the long term danger which is so damaging to a civilization, not the actual war itself.'

The mentor readjusted his body in the chair, and the chair obligingly adapted itself to the new position.

'I expect Grel introduced you to this,' holding up a familiar looking jewelled bottle, and pouring out two portions.

'Just another little perk for doing such a good job.' he said, smiling.

'This is indeed an amazing beverage.' said Jas, as he allowed the ice cold liquid to swill around his tingling taste buds, all the wonderful flavours of the past flashing into present time, along with the good feelings associated with them. He was warming to his mentor, who seemed a kindly man with a deep compassion for his work, the odd flicker of humour softening the otherwise steel hard character behind the gentle face.

'So you see, any kind of criminal act is a sign of insanity, and if left uncorrected will lead to the downfall of all persons connected or related to the act.'

'There are of course, many degrees of insanity, from the little cheat one might perpetrate to win at a game you are loosing, right up to instigating a full scale war on an international level.

'There are a few terms I would like you to understand with regard to our usage of them. One is known as the 'OBA', Overt, meaning knowingly done, Bad Act. We have refined it to mean a bad act, or to be more precise, a contra survival act committed against self, the group in which you exist, or on a grander scale, the whole world, but which is done knowingly.

'It can also be an admission of something that should be done. An 'OBA' is an insane thing to do, as it damages self and those it is performed against. The term 'OBA' has two other terms associated with it, one leading to the other'.

'These are, the 'WOBA' and the 'MWOBA'. When you commit a bad act, you don't want anyone else to know about it, so you withhold the facts of the action from others, obviously, hence the 'W' of Withheld. Because you know the act was bad thing to do in the first place, the action of withholding it will cause the incident to carry a 'charge' of energy on it when it is stored in the mind. This is why you feel better when you confess to doing a bad act. I use 'you' in the colloquial form, of course.'

Jas nodded in agreement, as the logical sequence of related events fell into place, making sense.

'The other term, 'MWOBA', is the more powerful of the two, and can be very damaging to the person withholding the bad act. The 'missed' part occurs when someone quite innocently does something which makes you wonder if they know what you have done. This leaves you in mystery, not knowing for sure if you have been found out or not.'

'The normal reaction to this can be an aggressive attitude towards that person, keeping them at arms length, in a metaphorical sense, or a disparaging verbal attack on that person's character, in order to lessen their standing in society, so that if they do expose your crime, no one will take much notice of them.

'In extreme cases, this can lead to one person killing another, in order to conceal their crime. So you see, a little insanity can do a lot of harm to a lot of people.'

The mentor paused again, carefully watching Jas's eyes for the look of comprehension before continuing.

'There is one other factor involved here. All these incidents are stored in the mind, to go from lifetime to lifetime. They are 'logged in' as it were, in chains of similar kind, adding to those which are already there, and carrying a mental charge which can be restimulated at any time in the future, with the old feelings brought into present time, causing more havoc.

'Were we once in such a state?' asked Jas, hoping for a denial of what he suspected. The mentor looked him steadily in the eyes before saying, 'yes, we all were, but it was a long time ago.'

Another long pause, the mentor sipping his drink, while Jas realigned the data he had just been given with that which he already knew, and then realizing the complexity of the situation. Although he was well educated, there was much to learn in this new science.

'There are many more pieces of data explaining why people are the way they are, and what can be done about it, but that is for later when you move on to your next post. Suffice it for now to be able to spot those who are a potential threat to a civilization.'

Again the mentor adjusted his sitting position, as though impatient to get on, the chair eerily following suit.

'I had better tell you about the set up down below, as you will need all the data you can get. There is one big land mass with a few islands dotted around the shores. Fortunately for us, there is only one race of people, so that makes matters a little easier to handle.

'There is a main governing body of elected representatives, one from each region, and they are in on our operation. They know who we are and what we do, but few others have access to that knowledge. Their civilization is somewhat behind the one you have just come from, so you will find a lot of the refinements you have been used to will be missing. We will only have to darken your skin a little, as your other features are not too dissimilar.

'They have one very interesting system going for them, and that is their judiciary. Let me explain how it works, you will find it fascinating. For every crime one could commit, there is a set number of points to be earned in order to cancel the debt to society.

'The points are earned in a series of factory prisons where they work nine days out of ten, earning a set number of points per day, after which they then earn some more points to qualify for their food. If they don't work, they don't eat, if they starve to death, that's their choice.

'It's tough but effective. Very few re-offend, which is not surprising. They have a crude form of electronic truth detector, which seems to work very well indeed, as we couldn't fault it when we tried. The person who is caught for the suspected crime is tested with the device, and if it indicates that the person did indeed commit the crime, then the penalty list is checked, and off they go.

'There are no ifs or buts, if you do the crime, then you do the time, it's as simple as that. We checked their statistics, and the crime rate has been steadily falling ever since they introduced the system. Mind you, there was an outcry from some of the population when it was proposed, so they were investigated, and quite a few had something to hide, which was not too surprising.

'The rest of the data you'll need will be released to you as and when you need it by your team supervisor. I expect Grel has told you that we operate down there ostensibly under the guise of a research and survey team. It gives us access to just about anywhere, and as such, no one seems to ask awkward questions. I shan't see you again until you move on to your next post, so I wish you good fortune and a safe stay down there. Oh, by the way, people doing the job you are about to embark upon are generally known as the 'seekers'.

'The actual position title is a long and cumbersome one, so it was shortened a long time ago.' The Mentor leaned back in his chair, the meeting was coming to an end.

'Good luck, young Jas, I shall look forward to our next meeting.' and with that, he arose from his chair, extended his hand grasping Jas's firmly, and then with a slight nod of his head, turned to walk to the back of the room.

As Jas looked at the door he had come in by, it opened, and the escort was standing there waiting for him.

'I will now take you to the shuttle bay, and you will be sent down quite soon as we are approaching the dark side of the planet.' Their footsteps echoed hollowly as they left the normal corridors and dropped to the lower levels where the main drive plant and docking bays were housed. The whole area had an austere feel about it.

The subtle colours and general opulence of the upper levels were in sharp contrast to the more businesslike area they were now in, and Jas wanted to stop and look at some of the equipment, the like of which he hadn't seen before.

'There will be plenty of time for looking around next time you are up here.' the escort said, somewhat testily, and hurried Jas along towards the main shuttle bay. He had no idea just how big the dark ship was, but judging by the time it had taken them to reach the bay area from the interview room, it must have been as big as the bulk transporters he had seen in the Institute lectures, and that was some size.

And how much of the dark ship still lay untraversed by him he didn't know, as he wasn't sure where he had entered.

They skirted around two very sleek and mean looking black craft, and Jas asked what they were.

'They're interceptors.' was all he could squeeze out of the escort, and gave up any further questioning, as it was obvious the man wasn't in a chatty mood. In the far corner of the bay a small streamlined craft lay on its launch rails, and he supposed this was the vehicle which would take him down to the planet's surface.

'Please strap yourself in. There are no controls, the whole thing is automatically guided from here, and later you will be locked into the guide beam from the receiving station. Someone will be there to meet you. Have a good journey.' and he was hustled into the shuttle like a dim witted child.

The door closed with a dull thunk, and immediately he felt a surge of power as his body was pressed into the back of the seat. There was slight noise as the shuttle sped down the launch rails, and then silence. Several times he felt a sideways surge as the shuttle changed course, or did something he was unable to see.

As there were no view ports on the vehicle, he had no idea of where he was going or what the craft was doing, and he didn't like it very much.

Jas was beginning to get a little bit edgy, when the soft sound of rushing air indicated that he had reached the atmosphere of the planet and would soon be landing, he hoped. The noise grew in intensity until it was almost a scream, and then the shuttle dropped its front end with a savage jerk and Jas felt his last meal beginning to rise in his throat.

He swallowed hard, and before he could do anything else, he was thrown forward in his seat with a violence he thought must have been caused by a crash landing. The shuttle gave several little jerks and wriggles before coming to rest, and Jas almost wished he believed in the old gods, so that he could offer up a prayer of thankfulness. There was a slight hiss as the door opened and the pressure inside the shuttle balanced with that of the planet's atmosphere.

'Welcome Jas, I'm sorry about your rather abrupt landing, but we had to dodge an unexpected aircraft. They don't usually fly at night, so we were caught off guard, so to speak. You weren't in any danger really, it just needed a couple of quick manoeuvres to bring you in safely.'

Before him stood a well built jolly looking man, with a dark suntan. His blue eyes twinkled as he smiled his welcome to Jas, and he at once felt at ease. Climbing a little unsteadily out of the shuttle, the man grinned and grabbed his arm to help him regain his balance.

'I can assure you it isn't always like this, sometimes it's worse. Sorry. I'm only joking. Come and have a meal with the rest of the team, and I'll do the introductions at the same time.'

Two:
The Seekers

THE SHUTTLE HAD arrived in a small cell-like room, and was resting on rails as it had been on board the ship, although Jas couldn't see where it had come in. The rails just seemed to stop at the wall, and he began to wonder just how this was achieved. As they approached the blank wall, a door opened automatically, and they passed through into what appeared to be a normally furnished room.

'Sit yourself down, the others will along in a moment or two, it's nearly time for our evening meal. Oh, how rude of me, my name's Col, short for Collnik. We are all on first name terms, as there is little need for formality here.'

The bronzed happy man left the room, and Jas had a chance to look around. There were three view screens on the wall, all staring blankly at him, a couple of desks with their own screens and what looked like a series of filing cabinets along one wall. The rest of the room was obviously for resting and recreation by the look of it, as there were six chairs, a long bench-like seat with a table in front of it, and a series of brightly coloured pictures on the walls. The pictures took his interest at once. The scenes were of the countryside of the planet, he assumed, but they were three dimensional, and with a difference. As he moved past one of the frames, he got a changing view, as if he had actually walked past the scene in real life. It was quite fascinating, and he was still going back and forth when the door opened and Col came back in followed by the rest of the team.

'Clever, isn't it,' said Col, joining Jas at one of the pictures.

'But wait 'til you see this.' He reached forward and adjusted a small slider at the base of the frame which Jas hadn't noticed, and the magnification of the picture increased many fold, showing fine detail of one of the trees.

Pushing the slider along a little further, the picture was now showing just a small section of one of the branches, and then just a single leaf. Soon the leaf filled the frame, and a small crawling insect could be seen. And it was moving.

The insect grew in size until it too filled the frame, and at this point Jas took a step backwards. Col grinned.

'Don't worry, it isn't real, it's just one of those odd creations we picked up somewhere in our travels, and have kept. The amount of detail contained within the structure is truly amazing, and we never tire of looking at them, when there is nothing better to do, that is. Also, none of us have a clue as to how it works, so I can't answer your next obvious question.' he added with a chuckle.

The rest of the team had taken their seats, and that left two empty chairs in the middle of the group to which Col guided a somewhat overwhelmed Jas.

'He's had a bumpy arrival, and I suspect things have been moving a little faster than he's used to, so lets get the intro's done, and we can all relax and get to know each other.'

In turn each of the other five were introduced to Jas and he was pleasantly surprised to find them a very friendly and informal group, compared to that which he had experienced over the last few days. The meal was served, and although the food was different to that which he was accustomed to, it was tasty and filling.

The meal finished with a drink of some kind of exotic perfumed fruit juice, pleasant in taste, but without the surprise of the drink the grey man had served, which gave Jas a chance to add to the conversation.

'Have any of you ever tried the drink which somehow duplicates the most pleasant taste memories you have, and which you experience again when you drink it?'

No one had, but two of the team had heard of it, and Jas thought he had gone up in their estimation as someone privileged enough to have been offered it by the grey man. The rest of the evening was spent swapping favourite tales of exploits past and general conversation, mainly to make him feel welcome.

'We shall be having an early start tomorrow,' said Col 'so I suggest we all get some rest, and we'll meet first thing to set up the next scan.' It was a gentle suggestion, but had the effect of a command as far as the others were concerned, or so it seemed to Jas, who was then left alone with the man who was obviously the boss of the team.

'You have no doubt been briefed on the general method of operation here, so I'll not bore you with that. All you have to do for the time being is to accompany me, and observe all that I do, asking questions where you are not sure what is happening, and so build up your own idea of how things are done. I know this will seem a little different to the more usual methods of learning, but it works very well here. I'll show you your rest room.' and with that they left the recreation area, walked along a softly lit corridor for a short distance, and Jas was shown into his room. It was sparsely furnished, with just a bed, table and two chairs.

'You may add anything else you choose as time goes by, it is your room, and as such is sacrosanct to you. No one else will enter it unless specifically invited by you. Sleep well young man.' and with that, Jas was left alone with his thoughts.

A lot had happened in the last few days, and Jas was only just coming to terms with the new pace of life. Seeing a small recess in one corner, he approached it. Automatically it opened to expose a washing and toilet facility.

Having completed his ablutions, he lay on the block-like bed, which instantly wriggled beneath him, adjusting to his body form, the lights slowly dimmed, and he drifted effortlessly into sleep.

The bed somehow knew when it was time for Jas to awaken, and readjusted itself accordingly to be just a little bit uncomfortable. Jas awoke, just a mite peeved that he had been disturbed from his slumbers by a mere mechanical device, and especially as he had been having a most pleasant dream and he couldn't recall exactly what it was.

The window covering had rolled back to reveal a beautiful view of rolling countryside, gentle hills covered in trees of many shades of green and brown, with clear patches of vivid yellow green grass and multi coloured flowering bushes on their fringes. His ablutions finished, he quickly dressed and made his way to the recreation room, where the rest of the team had already assembled. A chorus of cheerful 'good mornings' greeted him, and he took his place at the long table to have the first meal of the day.

After the meal, Col sent the rest of the team off to their various duties, and then asked Jas to follow him into the operations room. They walked down the corridor in which his room was situated, and at the end the wall suddenly swung back to reveal another room, crammed full of equipment and viewing screens.

'No one but us knows of the existence of this room, and of course, no one must ever find out. The door sensor will be programmed to recognize you, and will therefore open for you in the future, so just stand there a moment.' indicating where Jas should stand. There were a couple of clicks, and Jas had the distinct feeling that something was having a good look at him.

A moment later and Col beckoned him into the room fully.

'This is where we can scan any place where we have been able to plant surveillance optics. We have full sound and scan control over the sensors, so there isn't much that we miss.' Col had seated himself at one of the desks, and indicated that Jas should draw up a chair and join him at the viewing screen.

His fingers flew over the touch controls before him, and the pictures flicked through many scenes, far too fast for Jas to make any sense of what he saw.

'Now that's interesting,' said Col. 'see that man in the dark blue suit? He's going around the crowd giving various people instructions by the look of it, so he's up to something which he doesn't want others present to know about. We'll watch him for a while, and see what transpires.'

Quickly Col's fingers flew over the controls, and another screen came to life with a close-up picture of the blue suited man, now in different garb, but with a complete wealth of script details down the side of the screen.

'We have been keeping our eye on him for some time now, as we suspect he's been trying to cause some upset for the local Control Agency.

'Let me explain, the Control Agency runs everything in its area, from health to work allocation, justice, and the migration of the work force, should anyone want to move to another part of the country. It's not as regimented and harsh as you might think, due consideration is given to all requests, and few are rejected.

'It's just that they like to keep tabs on everything, so they know who is where and doing what. It's really a very benign set-up, and works very well. I wouldn't object to being under its control, and I like my freedom.'

The blue suited man had now climbed upon a box and was addressing the crowd.

'Let's see what he's up to.' said Col, and touched a control. The sound suddenly boomed out, as if the man was in the room with them.

'...and you are all under a lot of unnecessary control, the bureaucrats run your lives as if it were a game to them, telling you what to do and when to do it.' The well placed 'helpers' in the crowd joined in with a chorus of 'yers' and other foreshortened forms of agreement. The main crowd showed signs of agitation, and small groups began arguing among themselves. Having got into his stride, the blue suited man harangued the crowd for all he was worth, whipping up simulated anger from his 'helpers' and inviting others to join in.

'Don't like the look of this.' commented Col, switching to another optical system which showed the view from behind the orator. The lens of the viewing device was positioned high up on something, and gave a good overall view of the speaker and the crowd before him. From this vantage point it was easy to see that the speaker was very precise in directing his attention to the crowd before him, concentrating on those who were already arguing.

'Don't know where he learned his technique, but he's good at it.' commented Col to no one in particular.

'Why do you think he is doing this?' asked Jas, as stirring up trouble still made little real sense to him.

'Well, there can't be a lot in it for him, unless he just craves power as a leader, and he's certainly shaping up that way. Let's take a closer look at this man, he could upset things quite badly if he really gets going, although there is something a lot more sinister behind his motives, I'm sure.'

Jas felt the first surge of excitement he had experienced for some time, apart from his finals, that is.

'I think we'll infiltrate one of our operatives into his little band and see what he is about. Usually, but not always, people like that are loners, and as such are quite easy to handle, but we will first have to establish that he is not connected to any other group, or is a faction of a main organization, which I somehow doubt.'

Once again his fingers flew over the touch keys, the screen to his left lit up, and a cheery face beamed out from it.

'Hi Col, I was just about to call you. You know that chap who has been going on about excessive control by the local Agency, well he's at it again. Like me to go in there and take a look?'

'I'd like you to move in and get all the details you can pertinent to a relocation please.' Col replied.

'On my way, Col. Oh, by the way, I hear we're to have a new boy join us, what's he like?'

Col took Jas's elbow, easing him in front of the screen and said 'Take a look' with an ill concealed chuckle in his voice.

The face at the other end did it's best to hide it's embarrassment by grinning even wider and said 'Hello, welcome to our little club, I'll no doubt meet you later.' and the screen blanked out.

'One of our most subtle operators, although you wouldn't think so after his last offering.' Col commented as he put his attention back on the screen with the blue suited man.

'What will you do with him?' asked Jas, half knowing already.

'Well, it depends what we find out about him. If I'm right, we'll have to find a new home for him, where he can do his thing without causing too much trouble.'

'How we do that depends on what we learn from our man in the field.' Jas realized that he would have to make do with that for the time being, no doubt more would be revealed to him when he needed to know it.

'What I really don't understand is why, if everyone is happy with the system, anyone would want to cause trouble and change it.' stated Jas, really asking a question.

'As you can see, their system is a little more regimented than anything we have, but that being said, they voted the system in, and the great majority like it, or they could throw it out.

'It might seem a very tight set-up, but in fact, there is very little interference with what people want to do, everyone knows what's expected of them, and they're quite happy with their lot in life. Someone like our friend in the blue suit comes along every now and again, and tries to bring about a change which most people don't really want.

'There will always be a few people who will join in the disruption just for the kicks it gives, and then not be able to handle the ensuing mess, so that's where we come in.

'We try to nip this sort of thing in the bud, before it gets out of hand and begins to threaten the stability of society in general.'

Jas thought for a few moments, trying to align everything into one coherent whole, and not getting very far with it.

And then he remembered what the Mentor had said on the Dark Ship.

'Surely we're interfering with the natural progression of a planet full of people, who are of another race to ourselves, and riding roughshod over anyone who isn't in agreement with what we think is right. Do we really have the right to do this to another world and its people?'

Col smiled and continued to play the touch pads like a well practised musician, bringing up new information to the different screens in turn, all of which didn't mean a thing to Jas.

'Two 'no's' and a 'yes', in answer to your triple question. No, we're not interfering with the natural progression of a people. Whoever said that a disruptive influence was a natural thing in the first place? Don't forget, if our friend in the blue suit has a good idea, he only needs to go to the Control Agency and put it to them. If they think it has any merits, they would hold a referendum, after giving the people all the facts on the matter, and they would vote it in or out, the Agency then implementing the result for the good of all. He hasn't done this, by the look of things, so I doubt very much if he has given his audience all the facts anyway.'

He paused, something having caught his attention on one of the screens. A worried face came to life as the static flare on the screen died away,

'Sorry Boss, we've lost the target we cornered earlier down on the peninsular. He saw us coming, guessed the game was up somehow, and did the big exit by throwing himself under a transport. Not much left really.'

The static returned with a vengeance, turning the viewing screen into a multicoloured fireworks display, and then it cleared again.

'OK, you've done your best, close the operation down, clean up any loose ends, and return home. Thanks for a good try anyway.' Col looked disappointed for a moment, and Jas assumed a quizzical look, hoping that the team leader would be forthcoming without having to ask him outright, thus saving another possible awkward 'postponement of data until later'.

'I had better explain what that was all about, as you will have to know sometime, and you may well learn something from it. On the furthest most part of this land mass there is a large mining operation. Not the most interesting or pleasant of jobs, but one that has to be done by someone. At one time, those who had transgressed against society, which includes any form of criminal activity, paid off their debt to the general populace by doing such unpopular work.

'It wasn't long before two things almost wiped out all crime. One was the technology we brought, which tackles the problem from a mental aspect, and the other was the fact that having done a stint at the mine, no one was too keen to qualify for another go, so crime soon disappeared, and the job became vacant again. It's not too difficult to get workers, as they are only there for a short time to make the work seem a little more acceptable.

'This planet's technology isn't quite up to the point where it can automate the mining operation fully, and it would be wrong for us to give them the necessary data, as they should develop it for themselves, it is part of their growing up process, if you see what I mean.'

Jas nodded his acceptance of the explanation, hoping more would follow.

'A particularly unpleasant individual, hell bent on disrupting anything he can get a degree of control over, has been fermenting trouble at the mining site, to a point where he almost closed the place down. It is necessary for this planet's development that the mine continues to produce ore, as it is the only really viable mine discovered so far. He has been approached by the local Control Agency, who tried unsuccessfully to point out to him the error of his ways, and he went 'underground' for a while, still fomenting trouble.'

'Recently he resurfaced, and openly advocated revolt against the system. We were then called in to restore the status quo. The local team had just finished checking him out fully, when it became obvious that he would have to be relocated. Somehow he got wind of the fact that we were about to capture him, in the nicest possible way, of course, and he threw himself under a fast moving transport.

'What's a little worrying, is the possibility that he somehow knew what would happen to him, and avoided it by losing his body, to return later in another one, and one day begin his little game all over again'.

'Was he,' asked Jas 'one of the 'five percents' the grey man told me about?'

'Yes,' replied Col 'and so is the man in the blue suit, by the look of it, but we'll have to check that out a little more to be certain. In fact, this planet is very nearly stable now, and they are making great progress scientifically as their combined responsibility level comes up.

'Pollution levels are down to a minimum, recycling is the 'in thing' and there's a great team spirit among the population. Our work here is nearly done, and then we will only have a very small unit here, just to keep an eye on things for a few years. After that, it's up to them to totally manage their own affairs, and then they can become a full member of the Confederation, with all the benefits which that brings.'

The rest of the morning passed quickly for Jas, as more teams reported in with varying degrees of success or not on their various missions.

By midday, after a few more questions had been answered to his satisfaction, he had grasped a lot more about the functioning of the 'Survey Team' than he thought possible in such a short time.

By mid afternoon the station had acquired a stillness which belied its function. Work was going on in the various rooms, but the soundproofing was so good that Jas could hear nothing of it in his private chamber.

He had been told to take some time off to relax and generally summarize the events which had been taking place of late, and bit by bit he was coming to terms with the somewhat distasteful job of lifting people from the environment, extracting any necessary information from them and then dispatching them to some lonely planet which no one knew about, except the dispatchers.

It was all beginning to make sense to him, although he didn't really like the way it was being done.

But then again, he couldn't come up with another method of doing the job so efficiently, so who was he to criticize? He still didn't like it.

The germ of an idea was beginning to form in his mind, but the thoughts were fleeting and hard to pin down. He somehow sensed that the cause of the problem lay with the mind of the individual, something therein was driving people to do insane things, or so it seemed.

He had to make exceptions for those who were just plain evil and did bad things just for the sake of it, but he felt that most people didn't really want to upset such a well run system. So therefore there must be something making or enticing people to transgress, but what was it?

Jas considered that he was on the edge of a breakthrough, but couldn't quite see the entire picture and so get it all together, but he would one day, he felt sure.

He slept very soundly that night, knowing that soon he would be fully involved in operations, and then he would be exposed to more data, and that was what he needed.

Next morning Jas was feeling refreshed and eager to join in with what ever he could, making himself as useful as possible and trying to understand some of the mysteries of the system which became evident as the day progressed.

In the middle of the afternoon, three operatives arrived with a large collection of boxes marked up with references to a series of surveys. All the boxes bar one, were unceremoniously piled into one of the store rooms, while the lone container was wheeled into another small room which had a secret door like the main control room.

'Now is as good a time as any to introduce you to the heavy end of our little operation,' Col called out to Jas, 'so come along with us, and behold the opening of the present brought in by the team.' All five piled into the little room along with the wheeled box, and the door shut.

Col pushed a small metal blade into a slot in the side of the box, and the lid obligingly opened to reveal the sleeping form of a very angry looking man.

'Have any trouble bringing him in?' asked Col, scrutinizing the recumbent form as if he had never seen a sleeping man before.

'No trouble really, and he checks out as good for relocation, there being no family or relations we can find, and he seems to have few friends who will really miss him. Therefore we've already set the scene for his disappearance from the area.'

'Thanks.' said Col, reaching into a cupboard which had suddenly revealed itself in the wall surface on some hidden command from him, and withdrawing a shiny cylindrical instrument of some kind. He turned it over several times, as if deciding whether to use it or not, and then having made up his mind, pressed a button on its end.

Two of the team had lifted the sleeping man from the box, and placed him in a chair-like device which had also sprung into being from a hidden recess. His arms and legs were somehow held tightly to the structure so that he would only be able to move his head when revived. Col bent over the figure, the silver instrument hummed, and the captive slowly opened his eyes.

'Who the hell are you lot,' was the first angry retort offered, 'and what am I doing here?'

'You aren't doing very much at the moment, just sitting there in a chair. What's more to the point, what have you been doing these last few weeks?' from a very calm Col.

The man glowered at all present, and then clamped his mouth shut. Even Jas could see that this character wasn't going to co-operate, unless suspended by the unmentionables, for a considerable period.

'You may as well tell us what we want to know, because we will get it out of you one way or another.' said Col, and the others nodded sagely.

'You can't make me say anything I don't wish to, I have my rights as laid down in the constitution, and I'll report you lot of bandits to the Control Agency. They'll sort you out, double quick.' Again the thin red mouth clamped shut, with an almost audible snap, and the man tried ineffectively to struggle against the restraints of the chair, almost as if the chair had somehow drained his physical energy. At first he looked surprised, and then fear crept into his features, as he realized there was little he could do about it.

'All right, now that you've said your piece, made your point, and terrified us out of our wits, let's get down to some one to one dialogue.' said Col, and adjusted a control on the silver instrument in his hand.

The chair changed shape very slightly, and the man began to look very uncomfortable.

'We have all the time in the world. You don't. So the sooner you co-operate the better it will be for you.'

The man's eyes blazed pure hatred, and even Jas could feel the pure evil intent which radiated out from him.

'I have my...'

'Shut up.' Col's voice thundered back. It now had a hard cold sound to it, almost as if it had been generated by some mechanical contraption, being devoid of all emotion and feeling.

'You forfeited all your rights when you pushed the site supervisor down the drainage shaft, so don't hold any illusions about justice and rights, you have none.'

The man now looked really frightened, and a few beads of oily sweat broke out on his brow, and glistened on his upper lip.

'Will you co-operate with us?'

Again the surly silence, accompanied by another withering glare to all and sundry.

'May I respectfully remind you sir, that you have a meeting in about half an hour, and then you are due to go on to headquarters.' one of the team said to Col. He nodded, and said 'Set the time lock for a week, cut the light, and let's get on with our work.' and marched out of the room followed by the other three, Jas bringing up the rear and managing to the give the man in the chair a pitying look, quite by accident. The door closed, and became part of the wall again.

'You aren't really going to leave him in there for a whole week without food and water, are you?' was Jas's first words as the door closed.

'Of course not,' replied one of the team with a grin, 'he'll feel that it's a week, due to the chair which has adjusted itself to be as uncomfortable as possible without being too obvious about it, and the fact that we can play a few tricks on his senses while we're at it. When we go in tomorrow, he'll be quite convinced it's been a week, and a very long one at that.'

As far as the team were concerned, the man in the chair didn't exist any more, at least not until tomorrow, and they went about their business as usual. Jas followed Col into the operations room and sat down, a stream of questions boiling away in his head, and wondering if he should ask them, or wait until invited to do so.

He hadn't forgotten the other side of the man, when his voice had changed, and he began to speculate as to which was the real Col.

After a quick check on the live screens and the message terminal, Col turned and said with a serious tone to his voice, 'Now you really are in at the deep end, as far as this unit goes. Let me explain what happens next. We will extract all the information we can from that nasty little man in the other room, and then hand him over to the 'Keepers' as the holding unit is affectionately known among us.

'What happens to him then will be disclosed to you when you move on to your next post, but for now, let's just say he is permanently out of circulation, as far as this world is concerned.'

They spent the rest of the day checking on the results of the various field units, giving advice and data where necessary to help them locate those they were investigating.

'Not everyone gets the seemingly rough treatment doled out to them as our friend in the other room.'

'Some people just need a little guidance, a slight shift of attitude, a reappraisal of what the game of life is all about, and they're fine useful citizens once again. It's only the few who spoil it for the rest of the world, and there aren't too many of them left now, thank goodness.'

Jas got the impression that Col would be rather glad when the job was finished, or perhaps he just wanted a new world to get his teeth into, with the accompanying excitement which that would bring.

Work for the day had finished, and Jas was asked to shut down the control room and then adjourn to the recreation room for a well earned evening meal. The rest of the home base team were already there, along with the three newcomers. After the usual cross table banter, one of the team asked Jas what he though about the unit so far.

'I'm enjoying the work and the team has been more than helpful, but I need a few more questions to be answered before I can give you a really meaningful answer to your question.'

There was silence, as the others around the table looked at each other in turn and then back at Jas, inviting him to add to his comments, but he knew better than to take the bait, and remained silent also. Then Col broke the ice by saying, 'Wisely said young man, you hold your opinions to yourself until you have a little more to go on, and then you will have something interesting to say.' and with that the subject was dropped.

The rest of the evening was spent in a more jovial fashion, recalling amusing incidents, interspersed with the odd joke, some of which Jas didn't get, and then, much to Jas's surprise, they brought out an old fashioned board game of such complexity that he gave up trying to follow it.

But he got his amusement from the expressions on the faces of the players as fortunes and positions seemed to randomly change places in rapid succession.

Next day, Jas was left alone in the control room, scanning the screens for any untoward activity and recording it for future evaluation. The occasional call-in from an operative in the field for information was after a while, handled with ease, as he got used to the data retrieval system.

In mid afternoon, Col entered the room and asked Jas if he would like to be present at the interview with the man in the chair. Jas considered it a command, rather than an invitation, but he wanted to see what would happen anyway.

They all trouped into the secret room to be confronted by the angry man who now looked as if he had indeed been in there a full week, and then some. How they had achieved this effect, he knew not, but was interested to find out.

Gone was the arrogant blustering man of yesterday. Before him Jas saw a broken creature, thoroughly convinced that he was nothing more than a useless piece of rubbish, to be tossed aside at the whim of his captors should they wish.

He seemed to have shrunk, withered up, and slumped in his chair which was still holding him in a vice-like grip. The change quite shattered Jas, and he wondered how they had achieved the effect in so short a time, and without even being present, as far as he knew.

One of the team went up to the figure in the chair, and prodded it with a finger.

'I think it's dead.' he casually commented to Col, who had moved around to the back of the chair.

'Hmm, seems to be, perhaps a week was a little too long, it's dehydrated beyond recovery by the look of it. Better liquidize it and send it down the drain.'

There was a soft whimper from the wretch in the chair and the head lifted a little to stare straight at Jas. He would never forget those eyes. They were full of hate and defiance, right to the bitter end, and then Jas knew what sort of person they were dealing with.

'Oh look, it's still alive,' from one of the other team members, 'perhaps it would like to talk now, and possibly save its skin.'

'I doubt that,' said Col, 'anyway, there is little else we need to know now after the mind probe we did two days ago.'

It was at this point that Jas realized the whole thing was a well rehearsed charade, designed to crack any last bit of resistance.

'Well, I suppose we could question it,' said Col, 'and see if the answers tie in with that which we already know, it might be worth saving, perhaps.'

The questioning began, the team taking it in turns to fire the questions in with such intensity that Jas found himself almost inclined to answer some of them himself.

The inquisition went on relentlessly, the man in the chair driven into such a confused state that he could no longer withhold the answers he didn't want to give, until they had all the names and locations of those involved with his obnoxious scheme.

At long last they had extracted all the information they required, and the pressure lessened as the interview came to a close. The man in the chair was now able to gather his thoughts together, and somehow suspected that he had been duped into revealing all. The old malevolence returned to his eyes and a long string of exceedingly rich expletives issued forth, directed at all and sundry.

'OK, let's wrap it up.' and so saying, Col reached behind the chair and touched something. The restrained man slumped forward as if dead.

'What happens to him now?' asked Jas.

'He will be sent on to the Keepers, who will find a suitable location for him in which he can do little harm, to us that is. He will probably cause chaos to those around him, but they will all be of similar ilk, so in a way, it's a form of justice, don't you think?'

Two of the team lifted the limp body out of the chair and placed it back into its box, securing the lid down with an enthusiasm which indicated their distaste for the incarcerated.

'As I've said before, there is little point in killing him, as he will only return sometime, and someone else will have to go to all the trouble of locating him again. This way he is permanently removed from society, and everyone will be better off for his absence.'

'It would seem so far, that it is the males who are hell bent on causing trouble, do you ever find the female of the species so inclined?' asked Jas, trying to be as objective as possible.

'Oh yes, occasionally,' replied one of the team, 'but the really nasty ones are usually male, odd isn't it? I think it's something to do with the male 'beingness' adopted at the moment of taking on the body, but we're not sure yet.'

'What will happen to the people whose names you extracted from our guest?' asked Jas.

'They will be taken care of' Col replied, 'A couple of outreach teams will be sent to round them up, and they will be taken to a Rehabilitation Centre, where they will be offered help to sort themselves out.'

Those who don't want to co-operate will follow our last visitor on a very long holiday, while those who see the error of their ways will receive help on a mental level, to erase their evil intentions and so make them useful and stable citizens again.'

'People back home would get the shock of their lives if they knew all this,' said Jas, 'was my world like this at one time?'

'Yes, I expect it was, but without going through the records at Central, I couldn't be sure. It seems that most civilizations go through a phase of instability at some stage of their development, the degree of harm caused escalates especially as they advance technically, although if you look carefully at their early years, all the signs of future trouble are there.'

'At what stage do teams like this move in to help?' Jas realized that the information was really flowing now, and he wanted to find out as much as possible.

'Only when they ask for help.' Col replied. 'We make ourselves known to them when we think they are ready to accept the fact that the universe is teeming with life, and they aren't the only people around.

'You'd be surprised how often a newly discovered civilization thinks it's the only one existing, and it can come as quite a shock for them to learn differently. So we give them a little food for thought, so to speak, before showing ourselves. It usually works quite well.'

There was something in Col's manner which indicated that this was the end of general conversation for the time being, and so Jas followed him into the Surveillance room for the day's work.

During the next three days, two more 'public nuisances' were brought in, the blue suited man being the first.

He awakened from his transportation box a little early for some reason, and kicked and screamed abuse at everyone, until he was secured in 'the chair', and that left a very angry and voluble man, yelling obscenities at the team until they gave him the 'week on your own' treatment.

Next day, he was a little more circumspect, having been convinced that they couldn't care less what happened to him. He too, yielded under the pressure of rapid and intensive questioning, and having retrieved all the data they required to clean up the mess he had created, he was unceremoniously dispatched to the Keepers, for keeping.

It took a while, but at long last Jas could fully understand the reasons why the removal of certain persons was vital for the safety and progress of all. It had to become his reality, not just a group of words or a phrase from someone else which he could accept, even if it couldn't be faulted.

Jas had now become quite adept at scanning the screens for the slightest signs of unrest, and brought them to the attention of the team leader.

It was during a time when Col was assessing one of the trouble spots which Jas had located, that he got a chance to question him a little more on the system adopted here for the control of criminality.

'I checked back on the record of crimes committed, and apart from the people we locate, there is very little other trouble now, and the death penalty was dropped from the system a long time ago.'

'That's a statement,' said Col, 'what's your question?'

Jas had difficulty in hiding a grin as he realized he was dealing with a very precise man, and accordingly had to make definitive questions if he was going to get anywhere.

'Sorry Col, I should have added a 'why' to my statement.'

Col paused for a moment as he zoomed in on a still picture of a gathering of some ten people, who were being harangued by a man with bright ginger hair.

'Well done Jas, we've been after this one for some time, but so far he's avoided us. Look at the profile screen. It's the same for the last three lifetimes, and although the physical form is different, it's the same being.'

Col checked the co-ordinates of the picture, his fingers dancing over the touch controls, and another screen lit up. A cheery face beamed out at them, grinning from ear to ear.

'Have you confirmed it's him?' asked the grinning face.

'Yes,' replied Col, 'but how did you know?'

'One of the locals tipped us off that someone was trying to recruit a bunch of dissatisfied youngsters for something, and the pattern of his operation seemed familiar. We sent one of our youngest looking lads out and about to see what he could find, and the rest you know.'

'Well done Jac, have the rest of the team keep an eye on him for now. I'd like you to come in and collect Jas, as it was he who spotted the target in the first place, and it would be beneficial for him to experience a capture at first hand. Is that all right with you?'

'Sure thing, see you tomorrow morning, early.' and with that the screen went blank.

'One of our better operators,' said Col, 'a very able person indeed. Don't be put off by his general geniality and cheerfulness, he's as hard as diamond, and very sharp with it. He's enjoyable company, and you could learn from him.'

Col sat back in his chair and relaxed. Jas got the impression that a weight had been lifted from him, something had reached a conclusion, and Col was relieved about it.

'OK, ask your question Jas.'

'Why is that man in the picture so important to you? Surely it's just another pickup, like the others.'

'Not really. He's very clever and has successfully dodged capture for some time now. It's easy enough to pick up a 'loner' and have him disappear, but this chap is one step ahead of that. He surrounds himself with family, friends, and is well integrated into his local community, so that if we just picked him up, awkward questions would be asked.'

'I'll leave it to Jac to work out the final details, but I suspect he will arrange a suitable accident for our quarry, such that the body will appear to have been destroyed.'

Col blanked out all the screens but one, and then turned to look directly at Jas.

'In answer to your next question, yes, our work is nearly done here. Soon a team made up of the locals will be put together, and they will be trained up to monitor their own world. We can always be called in to handle any difficulties they can't deal with, but usually by this stage they can look after themselves quite well.

'When we arrived, the people here had already put together a system for dealing with general crime which we have rarely come across before. The criminals were allocated points for their crimes and put to hard labour to work them off doing all the jobs that no one else wanted to do, until their debt to the community was paid off. Any attempt to escape or dodge the system was rewarded by an irrevocable death sentence.

'It might appear a little harsh, but it drove home the point that no one was going to tolerate that kind of bad behaviour, and it wasn't long then before crime in just about any form was as popular as a Silurian Slime worm on the breakfast table.'

'When we enlightened them to the fact that killing the miscreants wasn't the most efficient way of handling the situation, they jumped at our answer to the problem. Hence the 'Seekers' and 'Keepers'. Making crime unprofitable was only half the answer, and not really all that efficient. We then introduced the verbal processes which corrected the criminal intent which some people seemed to have, and that only left the really evil ones, which we seek out and deal with.'

Slowly the look of comprehension began to dawn on Jas's face, indicating that he was absorbing data and slotting it in with that which he already knew, so Col continued apace with 'I've no doubt that one day we will come up with a method of dealing with the really evil ones, by mentally removing from their minds that which causes the troubles, but it's a bit more tricky than you might imagine, so until such time, we just ship 'em off to where they can't do too much harm. As I've said before, we work on the principle of 'the greatest good for the greatest number', and if that means a few malcontents have to suffer a little, then so be it, it's their option.'

Interrupted by a small green light which began to flicker its message urgently on the side of the main console, Col said 'We're needed in the Recreation room by the look of it, so let's go along and see what's happened.' The automatic recording devices with their sensors were switched on, and the pair left the room to its own devices, which in fact were almost as good as a human operator, but not quite.

As they entered the room they were confronted by a teenage youth firmly held by two of the local team, still wriggling and squirming against his restraint, and with a look of thunder on his face.

'What have we here?' was Col's first remark.

'Found him outside the main block, dragging a large box of something and trying to place it up against the wall of the building. When we asked him what he was doing, he made a dash for it, so we thought we'd better bring him in and find out what he intended to do with the box.'

'You can't touch me, I'm a junior and protected by the infancy laws.' he squealed, kicking the leg of one of his captors, who promptly cuffed him around the head, bring tears to his eyes.

Col looked him up and down unemotionally before saying,

'Let's get two things straight in your nasty little mind. One, the so called infancy laws don't apply to you, you're too old, and secondly, as far as the outside world is concerned, once you're in here, you've ceased to exist.

'You have no protection in law, except our law, and we make that up as we go along. We can do anything we like to you and no one will ever know. There will be no trace of you left, if we so wish. So toe the line, and stop making such a fuss. If you've nothing to hide, then you don't need to worry, but if you have...'

He let the sentence hang in mid air for maximum effect, but it didn't work, and all he got for his trouble was a deepening scowl and a large blob of spittle, which fortunately for the boy, missed its mark.

'Anybody looked in the box yet?' asked Col.

One of the team produced a metallic looking cylinder with a four pronged plug device on one end.

'He was trying to do something to this, so I took it off him, and then we had our little chase. I haven't checked the box yet, as it looks as if this is a timer of some kind, so what's in the box is dormant, I hope.'

'OK, one of you go look at the box, but be careful. We'll see if we can find out what's going on from our little friend here.' said Col, turning and smiling at the boy.

As one of the team let go of the boy to check the box, Col moved in to place him in a restraint, and got a sharp kick in the ankle for his trouble.

Jas was amazed at the speed with which Col reacted. As the boy's foot contacted him, Col's other foot flashed out in a sweeping curve and the youth was flat on his back, the breath knocked out of him. In almost the same instant, Col's foot was firmly planted on the boy's throat, making his breathing a rasping struggle, while his eyes began to bulge and his face turned red, and then a dirty blue.

'If you want to play, that's fine by me, but you can't win, so behave yourself or we'll drop you down the waste disposal unit.'

As the youth went limp and passed into unconsciousness, Col grabbed him by the hair, dragging him to his feet and said, 'Put him in the chair, we'll give him a little time to think things over, and then we'll see where he's at.'

Jas was still standing there with his mouth open at the speed of events, when Col turned to him saying

'Never start something you can't finish, and be quick and decisive about it. It's no good messing about and being kind and sympathetic with types like that. Go in quick and hard, you can't afford not to.'

The body was carted off to the interrogation room, brought to, and given the 'one week' treatment. One by one, the team assembled for the evening meal, and after it was finished, and the general chatting had diminished somewhat, Col looked up from a small data pad on the table, with a satisfied look on his face.

'Well, unless I'm very much mistaken, we've just got the last of our targets, with the exception of the one who threw himself under the transport the other day.

'Tomorrow we'll check out his profile, and if it's what I think it is, we can all take a break for a while and let things simmer down. Once the local team has been trained and are up and running, we can all move on to our next location.

'The locals should be able to spot the one lone target left, but it will be a few years before he surfaces again, I would think.'

Everyone looked pleased at Col's announcement, as this heralded pastures new, and Jas would be with them from the start, he hoped. He certainly felt like one of the team now.

The rest of the evening passed pleasantly for all, as spirits were high at the prospect of a new challenge. As one of the team told Jas, 'You never know just what you'll get, 'till you get there, and it's rarely what you expect.'

Next day, most of the group went about whatever it was they were scheduled to do, while Col, Jas, and one other went into the interrogation room. The youth looked a little more demure than before, the 'week' must have made him rethink his options, which he must have realized were few and far between.

'Sorry, we almost forgot you in all the excitement. We didn't bother to open the box, just sent it back to the address we found in your coat pocket, with that cylinder thing pushed into its slot so that it didn't get lost. It made a funny clicking noise when we pushed it in, but then all was silent, so I suppose it's all right.'

The youth went an even paler shade of white than before Col spoke, so they knew they'd struck a nerve somewhere.

'You lousy bastards, you'll kill them all when they open it.' the youth croaked out from a sore and very dry throat.

'Oh dear,' said Col, 'we only sent your possessions back to where they came from, we thought you would want us to do that, as you won't be needing them any more. Did they contain something nasty then?' The look of hatred on the youth's face only intensified.

'Right, it's time to talk. We can do this the easy way, or the hard way, it makes no difference to us, but it certainly will to you.'

'Why not leave him another week or two, we have that little job to do down on the coast, and I've been looking forward to that.' said Jas, thinking a little nonchalance might add to the pressure.

'That's a good idea.' said Col, turning towards the door, and that had the desired effect.

'All right, what do you want to know?'

'Not much really, we have all the data we really need from the mind scan, we just need to confirm one or two points to make it legal, from our point of view, that is.' Col added, almost as an afterthought.

Deep down, Jas felt just a little bit sorry for the youth, as he stood little chance against the ever increasing high pressure onslaught.

The three of them tore into his now confused mind, dredging out all the information they wanted with quick fire leading questions, often rephrased to check that the answers given were contiguous to those already received.

By midmorning, they had extracted all the information they needed, including how the youth had found them in the first place, what his intentions were and who else was involved.

'The cunning little devil must have realized there was a team like us operating in the area, due to some leakage in his memory from his last life experiences, and had been looking out for us for some time. I'd better pass this concept up the line, as I don't recall it ever happening before.' Col's fingers flickered across the touch pads in a series of lighting fast moves, and the information was dispatched onwards to the Dark Ship's data banks for future use.

Col showed Jas which pad to touch at the back of the chair, and the youth slumped forward, unconscious.

'OK, pack him up for dispatch, and let's get on with the work for the day, Jac should be here soon.' were Col's parting words as he left the room. The comatose body of the youth was unceremoniously dumped into the transporting box, and the lid secured.

'You're getting good at the questioning bit.' Jas's companion said, as they pushed the box into a hole in the wall which had opened to receive the container, closing over again immediately.

'You seem to have a natural bent for it.' he added with a chuckle, as they left for the Rec. room.

'What will happen to the box?' Jas asked, almost running to catch up with his companion.

'Oh, that's taken care of by someone else, he'll be sent to the Keepers who will decide what to do with him. We only have to catch 'em, they dispatch 'em.' he added with a grin. As they entered the Rec. room, there was a new face to greet them, along with Col.

'This is Jac, our supercharged field operative.' waving Jas towards the newcomer. A jovial round featured man of athletic build stepped forward with a wide grin on his face and one hand held out.

They touched palms, as was customary at a first introduction, and then all sat down at the table. Jac waited until he had their undivided attention, and then commenced with

'I understand you will be accompanying me on a pick up. 'Ginger' is a slippery customer to say the least of it, so you'll have to be on your toes all the time. He's surrounded himself with a lot of people who know him well and owe him some allegiance, and will therefore protect him if he's threatened. That should give you some food for thought as to how we can extract him from his surroundings with the least amount of trouble, and make it look as natural as possible.'

'I'm sure Jas will come up with some ideas before you arrive at the pickup point, anyway, we've got to get him one way or another.' Col said, checking his data pad for details which might be of use to the pickup team.

'One thing which seems to run through the last three lifetime profiles, according to the old records, is that he's totally hooked on power, controlling people that is, and that could well be used to our advantage. That's if we can find a way of interesting him in expanding his operation to include a trap of our own.'

Ideas were batted back and forth for the rest of the morning, but nothing conclusive was arrived at, as they all agreed that circumstances could have changed by the time they arrived, and would no doubt, have to be reassessed then. As the meeting broke up, Jas hesitated before leaving the table, and this was instantly picked up by Col.

'What's your question then?'

'Well, several times I've heard mention of the 'mind scan' when in the interrogation room, but I've seen no evidence of it. When do you do it, and how?' A grin spread among the faces of the rest of team.

'Come on Jas, surely you've cottoned on to that by now. There is no mind scan, we're not that technically advanced, although one day we may be.'

'The recipient of our attentions doesn't know this, so they usually think we know it all and they have nothing to lose by talking. Those who are just plain stubborn usually get another 'week' in the room, and that often loosens things up a bit.'

'And what about the box the youth was trying to place against the wall of the building, did you really send it back to where you said?' asked Jas.

'No, we didn't. We took it somewhere safe and used a robot scanner to check its contents, which turned out to be a crude home-made explosive. The metallic cylinder was a timing device, which when set and locked into the box would make it 'live' after a set period. Anyone trying to open the box, or remove the timer, would be somewhat disenchanted with the ensuing result.

'We made the explosive safe by neutralizing it, and then burnt it off. We didn't tell him that, as we could use a little misinformation to shift his tone level, so making it a little easier to get him talking.

'You have to use every bit of leverage you can find on some of these cases.'

The group broke up, and Jac asked Jas to collect a few of his personal things together, as they may be away for a few days.

'I think you'll find this an interesting little expedition, Jas. The target is a tough nut to crack, so I'll fill you in with all the details we have on him as we travel, and then you can see if you can come up with any ideas on how to handle the situation.'

Three:
The Pick-Up

LEAVING THE SURVEY Station at midday, the pair headed for the local monorail boarding point, Jac securing a couple of seats in the observation car so that Jas could see some of the stunning scenery they would pass through.

The monorail had been the invention of the inhabitants of the planet, but modified using technology brought in from the Confederation. This was deemed acceptable by the Data Transfer Unit, as it was considered an improvement as opposed to the introduction of a new idea.

It was quick, comfortable, and virtually silent, except for the rush of the air as the bullet shaped vehicle cleaved the air in its headlong dash to the next boarding point.

Suspended from above, and without actual physical contact with the rail due to the magnetic cushion the vehicle rode on, there was only air friction to hinder its progress, and streamlining reduced that to a minimum, as the countryside flashed by.

Part of the journey was through a desert area, and after the novelty of this had passed for Jas, Jac began to enlighten his companion about the target.

'What's the problem with the target?' asked Jas.

'Let's get the terminology correct first,' said Jac. 'a problem is whether to do something or not, a difficulty is how to do it. There's no doubt about what we want to do, the difficulty is how we are going to achieve it. The target makes sure he's never alone.

'There's always a small group of his buddies around him, or he's shouting his mouth off at some well attended meeting or other. A fatal 'accident' would seem the best solution, as long as we can get the body out in one piece, and reasonably unharmed.'

'It would have to look as if the body was totally destroyed in the accident, so that we can take it. So if you have any bright ideas, let's have 'em.' The desert gave way to a sand and rock strewn area where nothing grew, and all was dark grey and black.

'There's something odd about this terrain, almost unpleasant, apart from its colour, that is.' Jas said, not quite getting his feelings into the correct words.

'If you look over there, you'll see why.' Jac pointed out, indicating an area of rock which looked as if it had been molten at some time in its history.

'That's what happens when atomics are used by aberrant people, they ruin their world for a long time to come. Fortunately atomic fission is now banned, so they've developed fusion to supply their power needs.'

'Why they didn't begin with fusion beats me, as it's relatively clean and just about as renewable as you can get.'

The speeding monorail suddenly swung away from its straight course, and approached a mountain range.

The rail seemed to end at the rock face, but as they drew nearer, a tunnel became evident, and they swept into its inky blackness with a hissing whoosh as the air ahead of them was compressed and tried to escape around the sides of the vehicle.

Although the inside of the monorail was well lit, there was no detail of the tunnel walls as they raced by. Jas queried this, and was told that the passengers seemed to feel better if they couldn't see the walls speeding past, so the windows became 'one-way' for the period they were in the tunnel. Jas had to agree they had a point.

Suddenly the monorail began slowing down, and Jas looked at Jac with a worried expression on his face.

'Fear not, we are stopping at the terminal in the very heart of the mountain. It's for the research centre they have built in a depression in the middle of the range, I would assume for its security potential. An interesting place, you should go there if you have a chance, although clearance isn't all that easy to get.'

They had stopped for what seemed like only a few seconds, before the monorail accelerated up to full speed again, pressing them hard back into their seats. After a while, there was a slight change in air pressure, and the windows slowly became transparent again, giving a view of thick forest vegetation, which almost encompassed the rail system in a dappled green tunnel.

'That's a neat trick.' said Jas.

'Yes, isn't it. It saves having to screw up one's eyes with the sudden change of light level. Take a close look out of the window, focusing your eyes about two or three metres away. See that fine mesh? It sets up some sort of energy field and prevents any growth from encroaching into the path of the vehicle and that goes for wildlife too, but you can still see the scenery.'

The forest gave way to open plains, and then huge areas of cultivation before coming to the outskirts of the next town.

Either there was no one to get on or off, or the monorail didn't stop here anyway, for it sped on through, the buildings becoming a blur as it cut through the outskirts of the built-up area, and headed on out to the rolling countryside beyond.

Vast grain fields spread out across the horizon, pale brown and gold in the late afternoon sun, setting a gentle and tranquil scene, far removed from the forthcoming job in hand for the two travellers on the monorail.

Another band of desert separated the far south of the land mass from the main body of the continent, isolating it almost like an island. The sandy desert gave way to a rugged area of rocky peaks and pinnacles, with deep ravines dividing the ridges of rock into many separate groups, making travel on foot almost impossible.

'Without the rail system, how did the southern tip of the country every get into trade with the rest of it?' asked Jas, 'unless it was by sea.'

'Makes you wonder,' replied Jac, 'but more to the point, how did they get the rail system built in the first place, I wouldn't like to have been on that job.'

The light was just beginning to fade a little as the monorail swept round a slight bend to avoid a particularly large ridge, and out into the open green of the country again.

As they drew into the terminal, dusk had settled in for the close of day, and the city turned its lights on in a welcoming gesture, little knowing of the events which were to come. The monorail sighed to a halt, and settled down onto its main supports with a series of dull clunks as the elevating magnetic fields were turned off for the night.

'Let's go and meet the rest of the team,' said Jac, heading for the exit port, 'we're a close knit bunch, but easy to get on with.'

As the pair left the terminal building, a small mobile drew up beside them, and a door slid open.

'Ah, our transport has arrived,' waving Jas towards the vehicle, 'I'd like you to meet Kranzsliknos, or Kranz for short. This is Jas, who is to join us for our next little operation.' As the driver turned, Jas smiled and nodded his head politely, as he climbed into the rear seat behind the man at the controls.

The mobile surged forward and blended in with the other early evening travellers, switching lanes and weaving in and out of the teeming traffic like a demented beetle on a high.

Suddenly, the vehicle careered to one side and shot down a slope and into a well lit tunnel.

'This will bring us out into the suburb where we have a small residence, and from there we do our survey work,' said Jac, 'along with other little projects which are put our way. Good idea this subway system they have here, it enables one to travel very efficiently from the outskirts of the town to the central area, without having to do battle with a lot of other traffic, which probably isn't going in our direction anyway.'

They sped on, the traffic thinning out as spurs bled some of the other mobiles off into other areas. By the time they had reached the open air again, night had fully fallen, and the sky was bright with a dusting of sparkling stars.

A few moments later, and the mobile drew up before an imposing looking building with a sign on its front announcing 'The National Survey Institute', in large black and gold letters on a dark purple background.

'That looks very smart.' said Jas, as the vehicle slowly drove between two high hedges of dark green shrubs and promptly dropped like a stone into an underground room with no warning.

'Sorry about that,' called Kranz, as he slid out of the side door of the vehicle, 'I received a warning blip on the console, so took the emergency entrance.' Seconds later he confirmed it was a false warning, 'the alarm tells us if we are being followed or approached by some unauthorized person or persons, but all's well, probably an insect crawled into the outside sensor box, and triggered the warning.'

The three of them made their way over to a blank part of the wall, Jac pressed a dirty mark on it, a section slid back, and they were into the lower area of the main building.

A small lift whisked them up to the ground floor, and as they left it, Jas noticed it too was disguised as a piece of the wall panelling, and would be passed by unnoticed by the uninitiated. Observing Jas's smile at the hidden lift, Jac said, 'Can't be too careful, you know.' with a grin.

Entering the main room of the building, where meals and leisure time were spent, Jas was introduced to the other four who made up the full team. An evening meal was taken, and then the serious business of the day began.

'Right,' said Jac, 'lets see what we know about our target, and go over the possibilities of capture.' Everyone but Jas had data pads, and these were in constant use throughout the meeting, feeding information from a central data bank.

'The target is for definite capture,' Jac continued, 'as all his past profiles tie up, without exception. Another team nearly got him in his last lifetime, but he eluded them, choosing death to capture, so we will have to be very careful this time.

'He is very rarely seen without an escort of some kind, it usually being a big man with dark grey hair, and built like a mining truck. Him we don't want, as it will only complicate matters.' Here Jac paused, looking from one to another of the team in turn, inviting additional information or suggestions.

'We have an audio copy of his voice,' said one of the team, 'and Hass is quite a good mimic. Perhaps with a little facial padding and makeup, together with a ginger wig, he could impersonate him for a short while, as we take the original into custody?'

'Good idea. We'll have to get just the two of them on their own for that, so where and when would that be possible?' asked Jac.

The ensuing silence dragged on for ever, or so it seemed to Jas. At last, almost in desperation, he came up with an idea, 'Could they be followed to see if there is a repetitive pattern to their movement which would include a period where the two of them are together, such as when the target relaxes or something?'

'That's a good idea,' said Jac, looking up from his data pad, 'right, we'll take it in shifts to see if there's a window of opportunity. If we find one that's repetitive and predictable, we'll work out a method of capture and substitution based on that data. Hass, perfect your voice impersonation, find a wig, and get the facial make up ready. We may need it in a hurry, so make it a priority.' He paused for a moment, mentally going through the action, and then added, 'Oh, and check his clothing details, we may need several different sets to suit the occasion. Things are looking up, we may have a viable operation yet.'

Eight days later, the full team was called to a meeting to discuss the information gathered so far on the target.

'OK, let's see what we've got.' said Jac, looking around the table.

One of the team, with a very satisfied look on his face said, 'I think we've just found what we're looking for.

'Every two or three days the target goes for a contemplative walk along the cliff edge just south of the town, at least, that's what we assume he's doing. His bodyguard is always with him, but on these occasions he is trailing behind by fifty metres or so, but never quite out of sight of the target.'

'Prior to their arrival at the cliff, the target calls in at a small refreshment bar in a vehicle park, goes in, uses the toilet facility at the rear of the building, and picks up a pie to eat later on his walk. He doesn't pay for it, so we think he's known there. The walk takes about half an hour in duration, whereupon they both return to the mobile and drive off, normally returning to their headquarters.'

'That sounds like a promising option,' said Jac, 'anyone like to expand on that?'

'If we can get access to the rear of the building, we could do the switch in the toilet area' said Jas, 'The only unknown part of the operation is when the target returns to the mobile. Does he give instructions to the driver to go to the cliff walk area, or is this assumed to be the next action the driver normally takes?'

'Right, we'll check that out using long range optics,' Jac interrupted, 'carry on Jas, what's next?'

'According to the local records, the ocean is not a very nice place to swim in, in fact no one does. There's a fair selection of predatory sea creatures which would make short work of anyone entering the water, so that could be used as our means of 'losing the body' after the switch. One suggestion I would like to make is this, we do the switch in the food bar, Hass taking the place of the target from that point on.' Hass didn't look too overjoyed at the proposal.

'He will go out to the mobile, and if necessary give instructions to drive to the cliff area. He will then leave the vehicle after telling the bodyguard to stay inside. Hass will then proceed to the cliff edge, and getting as far away as he can from the vehicle. So far it has always been parked in about the same spot, so we should be able to choose the place where the 'accident' will take place.'

'We can prepare a section of cliff so that it will collapse on command, and as Hass goes over the edge he can pick up a prepared rope, and so get safely down to water level. A boat will pick him up, and should make it around the promontory and out of sight before the guard can get there.'

Jas paused to see what the others thought of the idea, and was surprised to see that they were all looking at him intently, waiting for the next revelation.

'So far, so good,' said Jac, 'we have our accident, the body would obviously be destroyed by the sea creatures, leaving no remains, and we would have our target safely tucked away by then. What happens if the guard insists on accompanying the target on the cliff walk? We will have to have that covered somehow.'

They all looked at Jas to see what other bright ideas he may have on the subject. One of the team mentioned something which Jas didn't even know existed.

'We have two stun units, and if the worst comes to the worst, we could stun the bodyguard as he leaves the vehicle just long enough for Hass to reach the cliff edge. But then we have the possibility that the guard could have his memory recalled if he knew how, and then suspicions would be raised among the brighter members of the group.' The look of query on Jas's face prompted Jac to explain.

'Stun units are not known here, and are therefore only used in extreme circumstances. They beam out a pulse of sonic energy which, depending on the setting of the unit, will hammer the nerve endings, so rendering the target unconscious, or if set higher, will paralyse the nervous system to the point where it is inoperative, and the target will have no heart beat for a while. This usually means death for the target, so we are very careful how we use it.'

'If the guard stays in the mobile,' said Hass, 'and I make it to the cliff edge, as soon as I'm out of sight, he is going to come running, so the descent will have to be a quick one, as will the waiting boat.

'To add a little authenticity to the event, would it be possible to delay the mobile when he goes for help, so that we could spatter a little of the target's blood on the rocks at the bottom of the cliff, just in case there's an enquiry?

'We could take a small donation when we bag him in the food bar, and then rush it to the person in the boat before he goes around the peninsular to the drop zone.'

'That's a nice touch,' said Jac, with a grin, 'I like that, I like that very much. The timing of this operation will have to be absolutely spot on for it to work, but it should be a lot of fun.'

Jas was surprised that it should be considered as fun, but then realized that they had probably been doing this kind of thing for a long time.

'OK, I think we have enough to go on now. Everyone get their bits and pieces ready, check out any other little details you think might be important, and we'll keep observation on the target for a few more days to check out if a verbal command is given to the driver to go from the food bar to the cliffs.' All heads nodded in silent agreement.

'I think this should work quite well, but do realize, we only have one bite at the pie, so let's get it right.' Jac added.

With that, the meeting broke up, and Jac took Jas to one side. 'You are learning fast, young man, and could be a very useful adjunct to our future operations, but I think you may be destined for higher things somehow. Pity, I'd be very pleased to have you as a permanent member of the team.' Jas didn't say anything, as he didn't quite know what to say.

Several days passed, and the team members practised their individual parts as best they could without the actual surroundings in which the operation would take place. Hass's ginger wig and makeup surpassed their wildest dreams, and he said he was tempted to hold a meeting of his own, just to see if he could get away with it.

Although this caused a lot of merriment among the team members, Jac gave a very firm no to the idea as there was too much at stake.

The grin on his face as he said it indicated that he was really sorry, and would no doubt have enjoyed the spectacle immensely. They had chosen the point on the cliff edge where the slip would occur, and primed the edge ready for the accident.

A practice run at abseiling down the cliff to a waiting boat was carefully timed, as was the boat journey to the promontory, so that they would know how much time they had to complete the operation before the guard showed up.

The final confirmation that the target didn't speak to the driver after leaving the food bar, was all that was needed to make the operation viable, and they got that two days later, much to everyone's relief.

There was a final briefing, with everyone going over their part and checking their timings, and then it was just a matter of waiting for the signal from Jas, who was trying to anticipate when the target would next go for his walk.

After two days without the ginger haired man showing up at the cliff, Jas thought the next day would be a good possibility, and set things in motion for the capture.

Jac and Jas would shadow the target in a mobile, being as discreet as possible by changing over to three different models placed strategically along the expected route.

Hass, complete with makeup and another disguise on top, would be with his companion behind the food bar, having trouble with their mobile, and armed with a 'knockout shot' and a suitable transport box for the target.

Another member of the team would be in a small high powered boat, waiting behind the promontory for the signal to pick up Hass, while another, armed with a stun unit, would be masquerading as an artist near the target's normal stopping place, in case anything went wrong.

Everyone had a small communication unit complete with scrambling device, so that they could keep in touch, and not be overheard.

'What I don't understand,' said Jas, as they patiently waited just within visual range of the target's housing complex, 'is why he would go for these walks along the cliff. He doesn't seem to meet anyone or pick anything up, he just walks, and somehow that doesn't seem to fit in with his character.'

'I know,' replied Jac, 'I've been thinking about that too, but from the observations we've made, that's all he does. I hope that's all he does, or we may have some difficulty in making a clean capture.'

Time dragged for the pair, and a feeling of desperation was beginning to take its toll on both men when the target appeared along with his guard, and they entered the mobile and drove off.

'We have a party.' Jas said into his communicator, and they set off, keeping a discreet distance behind the target as it wove in among the other traffic on the busy highway.

Instead of following the expected route, the target's mobile headed north for the town centre, stopping outside one of the long blocks of trading buildings, and the ginger haired man left the mobile and went into one of the units.

'We've lost one of our exchange vehicles because of the different route he's taken.' said Jac. 'I don't like the feel of this, there's something going on we don't know about.'

Eventually, the target came out of the building with a large package cradled in his arms, dumped it into the rear compartment of the mobile, and then got in himself. The vehicle moved off, and the watchers followed, allowing two other vehicles to get between them and the target to try and hide their presence.

'He's heading in the right direction at long last, so we may be in for the exchange part of the operation.' Jas commented, as they dropped down into one of the main exit tunnels to lead them out of the town centre.

'If that package was full of pies, he won't be calling in at the food bar.' added Jas, not realizing in time that his hopefully witty remark might contain an element of truth.

Jac gave him a withering glance instead of the expected amused grin, and they drove on in silence. The line of mobiles left the exit tunnel, and the road split up into three main highways, the target taking the one leading to the food bar area and subsequently the cliff top leisure park.

'We're coming up to the second swap of vehicles, Jas, so make it snappy.' They took a small spur road and pulled in behind a factory complex, changed vehicles, and were off again to join the main road. A heavy transporter got in their way, and it was some time before they could safely overtake it, and catch up with the target mobile as the food bar hove into view.

'Our guest is arriving.' Jac breathed into the communicator, as if he thought the target might overhear him. They pulled in behind a clump of dark green shrubs, well away from the little food bar, but with the quarry in full sight.

A man got out of the vehicle and went into the building. From where they were, they could see Hass's mobile tucked away behind the bar, but of the two occupants there was no sign.

'They must be inside, ready to do the swap.' said Jas, feeling that saying anything would help to break the unbearable tension. Jac said nothing in return, as he scanned the building with the long range optics.

'He's been in there twice as long as normal.' Jac hissed to himself, when a ginger headed man came flying out of the doorway of the food bar, tripped, and nearly fell. Recovering his balance and a little of his dignity, the man walked purposefully towards the mobile, wrenched the door open and climbed in.

The vehicle took off at once, heading for the cliff area and the waiting artist, who by now had done a very reasonable rendition of the seascape, acquired a couple of admirers of his painting, and was desperately trying to get rid of them in case his services were needed.

Picking up the communicator, Jac spoke softly into it, 'Take up your fishing position please.' and put it down again, trying to disguise the slight tremble in his hand.

The target's mobile stopped in more or less the same position as it usually did, and the ginger headed man got out, followed by the guard. They assumed it was Haas, but had no way of knowing for sure, as his disguise had been so good. An apparent argument ensued, with much waving of angry arms and other gesticulations, before the target, or was it Hass, moved off towards the cliff edge.

Jas could feel the hot salty sweat trickling down his forehead and into his eyes, causing them to sting and blur his vision.

The man at the cliff edge had stopped, and was looking out to sea, while a disgruntled guard strolled around the mobile, kicking at any loose stones which were unfortunate enough to be within his reach.

The artist's admirers had now wandered off, carefully holding the still wet painting as if it was a passport to the promised land, and talking. The man at the cliff edge shrugged his shoulders, turned, and began his walk along the twisting path leading to the prepared area of the accident.

'Krindlings' gasped Jac, 'This is too much, we don't know for sure if it is Hass, and if it isn't, then what do we do?'

The question was rhetorical, but Jas did his best to answer it. 'If the man returns to the vehicle, it won't be Hass, so stun them both, push the guard over the cliff, and take the target back with us to base.'

'You blood thirsty little ... but you're right, it's the only option left, but that's if there's no one else around at the time.' said Jac.

The guard had now turned back to the mobile, and was in the process of getting in, when the target suddenly disappeared from view. Jac slammed the drive unit into full power and the vehicle surged forward.

'I'm going to drive up just behind the guard's vehicle, we'll get out and start a fight. That should take the guard's attention off things for a moment, and give the others a chance to get out of sight.' They slid to a stop a few metres behind and to one side of the guard's mobile, and the guard spun around to see what all the fuss was about.

Jac and Jas began shouting and waving their arms at each other, eventually exchanging a few blows, while the guard looked on undecided whether he should interfere, or leave well alone and enjoy the entertainment.

'OK, that's enough for now, let's make up and get out of here.' said Jac, picking himself up from a particularly vicious leg throw delivered by Jas.

'They should be out of sight by now,' Jac added, 'and we don't want to be around when our friend finds his master's missing.'

A well acted pretence of reconciliation, a quick dust down, and they were both back in the mobile and heading back towards the food bar and out of the leisure park, Jas wiping a bloody nose, and Jac rubbing his leg.

The artist was still painting, having acquired another admirer.

The little mobile hummed along the highway, eventually turning off onto the orbital road which would lead them back to their base.

Neither occupants said very much, as the result of the operation was not certain, and a fair degree of tension still persisted.

Upon arrival, they were greeted by a grinning Hass with traces of makeup still on his face.

'I'm getting too old for this kind of caper,' he said, 'although, I must admit it went off without a hitch.' He paused, looking the pair up and down. 'What ever happened to you two?' Jac grimaced.

'Your end might have been trouble free, but we had our hearts in our mouths half the time, not knowing if it really was you at the cliff top. We then had to stage a diversion to distract the guard as you disappeared over the cliff, and the artist got himself an audience and wouldn't have been able to use the stunner if we had needed it. I trust you've got him?'

'Oh yes, and tucked away in his little box, sleeping like a new born.' Hass was certainly pleased with himself.

'OK,' said Jac, 'we'll get some food, wait for the rest to arrive, and then do a debrief.' With that, they all split up, going their separate ways to do what ever it was that each deemed necessary, to meet again an hour later in the main room.

'Well, we've done it. Well done every one,' said Jac, opening the conversation.

'Right Hass, how did your end go?'

'We arrived at the food bar, parked around the back as agreed, and had a little 'trouble' with the power unit of the vehicle. Unfortunately, one of the dinners came out back, and offered to help. Of course, he turned out to be a mobile technician and found the wire we'd pulled off in double quick time, and then couldn't understand why we still hung around.

'Nann slammed the lid of the power unit down a bit too hard, the blast of air escaping from the compartment blew my disguise hood back, and the technician saw my full makeup. Obviously he knew the target well, or had certainly heard of him, for he gave me a very polite nod of the head, followed by another one, and then disappeared into the building like a scared kelchip. We just sauntered around, trying to look occupied, and waited until we got your signal, whereupon we went into the facility and hid in one of the cubicles. Using a small piece of mirror, I was able to view the rest of the facility through the partly open door of the cubical, and one of the bar customers came in, did what he had to, but then hung around for a while.

'Then the target came in, went up to the other man, and gave him a small package, the other man then left. As the target approached the urinating bowl, we slipped out and gave him the shot.'

'Nann whisked him out the back way and into the mobile and back here. I went into the bar, went up to the counter and gave the bar attendant a long hard look. He seemed scared, and promptly wrapped up one of the biggest pies and gave it to me, bobbing his head up and down as if he was trying to shake it off.

'Having acquired the obligatory pie, I made for the main exit door, and as I opened it, the bar attendant rushed forward, thrusting a big package into my hands.

'I was caught off balance, and made a very ungraceful exit to the parking area. I then threw the package into the back compartment of the vehicle, told the driver to go, and we did.

'We arrived at the cliff area and I got out, telling the driver to stay put, but he began to argue and got out also. I got very angry, he began to sulk, but at least stayed with the mobile.

'Pausing at the cliff edge to make sure the driver was still with the vehicle, I then made my way along the cliff path until I reached the marked section, looked over the edge and saw the rope. With a quick glance back I could see that the driver was about to enter the vehicle, so I jumped over the edge, grabbed the rope, and slid down to the waiting boat, scraping my knuckles on the rocky surface in the process.

'When I pulled the release cord to free the rope, it triggered the cliff fall, and we nearly got flattened as a large section of the cliff descended in our direction. If it hadn't been for Brak's quick action, we'd have been a crushed and drowned.

'As we rounded the promontory, something large and hungry tried to eat the rear end of the boat, smashing the power unit, and probably breaking its teeth in the process,'

There was an audible sigh as they all sat back in their chairs, not realizing the degree of tension which had built up during the recounting of events, and then Jac turned to Krel. 'And how did our artistic friend fare?'

'Well, I got to the site a little earlier than expected, set up my materials, did a few simple sketches, and realized what a beautiful setting it was. I applied some colour, and soon had a reasonable representation of the scene. I had no idea I was so good at it.

'Just before the target arrived, I acquired two admirers who wanted to purchase the painting, and as they wouldn't go away, I asked an astronomical price for it. The man handed over a fist full of credits without thinking twice about it, and they left.

'I saw what I assumed to be Hass go to the cliff edge and disappear over. Then there was the ruckus put up by Jac and Jas, which was very realistic and entertaining, and as they left in a cloud of dust, I acquired another admirer of my artistic work.

'I was able to see the demented guard rushing up and down the cliff edge, looking for his master, and nearly going over himself. He then left at great speed, going for help, I assumed.

'My new admirer also wanted to buy my partly finished painting, so I finished it, and asked twice the price of the first one just for the fun of it, as I really wanted to keep it. He paid up without a whimper, and I then came home.

'I think I might take early retirement, you know, as I can make just as much without the stress.'

This last comment brought a small nervous laugh as the tension eased still further from the gathering, and then it was Jac's turn.

He told the tale as it had happened, trying to keep a straight face as the funny side of events became apparent, and they all finished up with tears running down their faces and quite exhausted.

'And that concludes another successful operation. Tomorrow Jas and Hass can escort the target back to our main unit, and they can see if there are any loose ends for us to clear up. Pity you can't stay with us Jas, but I've had orders to send you back, so it looks as if someone has something in mind for you.'

Jac produced a bottle of some rare liquid from which they all imbibed copiously, retelling the day's events over and over again, complete with some doubtful embellishments here and there, but by bed time, no one cared.

Next morning, Jas said his goodbyes to the team, regretting the fact that he couldn't stay a little longer as he had found them to be a most congenial and light-hearted group, which more than somewhat belied the seriousness of the work they were engaged in.

The box of 'survey results' was loaded into a mobile, and Jas and Hass drove off to the local transport terminal to begin their journey back to the main base. On the way, Hass went over many of the exploits he had been engaged in over the last few years, and how they had filtered out most of the troublesome citizens, restoring stability and order into the community. This only whetted Jas's appetite for more of the same, and he was keen to report in, and get the next project underway.

Arriving back at the main base, Col greeted them like old friends, and that evening the story had to be told again in all its finest details, as only bare outlines of the event had filtered through to them.

Next morning, the interrogation of the ginger headed man began. At first he seemed to co-operate, until they realized that he was telling them no more than what they already knew, so Col gave him the 'week' treatment, while they assessed the data they had collected from the team down south.

As the main base team had nearly completed their mission, with the exception of the man who had killed himself, and who may or may not show up in his next lifetime, the atmosphere was a little more relaxed.

They had captured the really tough target, and it was now only a matter of getting him to reveal his contacts and the network he had constructed, so that it could be dismantled and the people involved in it cleaned up, as Col put it.

All those involved in 'Ginger's' intrigue would be given the chance to find out why they supported such a disruptive principle, for, as Col had pointed out, often people are not consciously aware of the reasons for some of the things they do, but when they do discover the reason, they usually change their minds.

That evening, after their meal, Col took Jas aside to explain a few things to him, as he put it. First he went through the usual procedure for debriefing a target, applying mental pressure by way of the 'week' treatment which only worked because the victim was convinced that it was about a week.

Jas wanted to know how this was done, and was told it was brought about by a little gadget from the Dark Ship, and the base had no idea how it worked, just that it did.

After extracting all the data they could to correct troubles in the area of capture, the target was sent off in a deep sleep to the Keepers, who had the means for deeper probing.

If they considered the target was beyond all redemption, then it was given some sort of treatment which held it indefinitely in deep sleep, until a Dark Ship was in the vicinity, and could collect the unwanted item.

What happened then was only speculation, but they thought it would be sent somewhere from which it couldn't return to its native world, and could only do harm to those around it, who were of a similar nature.

Jas thought it was a crude sort of justice, in a way, but was beginning to get some reality as to why anyone would want to change a perfectly good system, let alone wreck it.

'All this, and much more will be explained when you next visit the Dark Ship.' said Col.

'You are here to gain a little experience of the actual physical work done, so that you have something tangible to build the later theory on. It's a well tried and proven practice, believe you me.'

Next morning, Col and Jas visited the interrogation room to see if the target was in a more co-operative mood, and got a mouthful of abuse and a couple of new swear words for Jas to add to his vocabulary. He really did look as if he had been left to his own devices for a week, the skin was considerably paler and drawn, and his eyes had shrunk back into his head.

'Apart from your previous comments, do you wish to tell us what we need to know to clean up the mess you've left behind?' Col was being very polite, but Jas could sense that his patience was not going to last much longer, and wouldn't like to be on the receiving end when it finally gave out and he really put the pressure on.

'Go tell your mother she was mated to a Kalpiccer, and you were the best result that nature could come up with.'

Although the target's reply didn't seem too offensive to Jas, he realized that in the target's eyes, it was just about the highest pinnacle of verbal insult it was possible to make, and as the intent was there, he waited for Col to take suitable action.

At that moment the communicator pinged, and Col picked it up, listening intently to the voice on the other end.

'That sounds great, we've been looking forward to that for ages. Thanks, we'll be with you as soon as possible.'

Col's face quickly changed from that of a stern and angry man to one of an excited adolescent, and turning to Jas said,

'We've all been invited for a couple of week's vacation up in the mountains, I went there once, a long time ago, and it was fantastic. Come on, get your things together, the transport will be here in about half an hour.'

'But what about...' began Jas

'Oh forget it, if he's still alive when we get back we'll start taking him apart limb by limb, that should loosen his tongue.' and with that Col turned on his heel and left the room.

Jas turned towards the target, shrugged his shoulders, and left also, slamming the door hard behind him.

'That should do the trick.' said Col, when they had returned to the recreation room.

'You mean, the vacation was all a...' began Jas.

'Yes, of course, sorry about that. If it fooled you, it should have some effect on our friend in there. I'll set the equipment up for two 'weeks', which for us is two days, and we should get a result this time.'

'Gentle but firm.' muttered Jas, as he sat down. Col did a little grin to himself, the new lad was learning, and he wondered how long it would be before Jas came up with some novel ideas of his own.

Later that afternoon a stranger arrived, and Col disappeared for several hours, to return to the recreation room just as the rest of the team were preparing to turn in for the night.

'Tomorrow we start to wind down the operation, we'll spend the next two weeks training up the local team to take our places, and Hass will be coming up from the south to join Jas who will then escort the target to the Keepers.

'Well done men, we've been very highly recommended for our work here, and it would seem that we've earned ourselves a considerable amount of leave into the bargain.'

A rousing chorus of cheers rang through the room, and Jas couldn't help feeling he was now really part of the team, but then realized it wouldn't be for long.

The following day a small group of the native population joined them, and the training began. Jas wasn't involved in the actual instruction of the new team, but joined in where he felt he could be of use. The locals were certainly a bright group, and once the basic principles of the operation had been explained to them, they showed an enthusiasm for the work which surprised him.

Two days later after leaving 'Ginger' to his own devices, Col and Jas returned to the interrogation room, breezing in and talking as if they were the only ones there.

'I expect it's dead by now,' said Col, not even looking at the hunched up figure in the chair, 'we've no further use for it, so stuff it into the disintegrator, and then flush it down the sewer from whence it came.'

A groan came from the direction of the chair, as parched lips tried to form words in a desperate attempt to show life still persisted. Jas moved over towards the crumpled figure.

'I think it's still alive.'

'Shove it in just the same' came back from Col, bent over the instrument panel. There was a gasp and a rattling sound, as the man struggled hard to draw breath.

'What do'u wana know?' the captive had great difficulty in forming the words.

'We don't really, we have all the names but one, and we can no doubt get that easily enough from the others.' Jas said nonchalantly.

Again the dry rattle of breath, as it was desperately sucked into a parched and restricted throat, to be followed by a long list of names, and the positions they held.

'What's it bleating about now.' asked Col, looking up from the controls.

'Seems like a list of the people he used to know down south, but we've got 'em already.' said Jas, showing as little interest as possible.

'Can't help wondering why he did it in the first place though.' he added, as an after thought.

'You lot wo'ent un'erstand, an I wo'nt tell you.' With that Jas reached around the chair, touched the pad, and the figure slumped forward in deep coma.

'That's all we'll get from him, I think. At least we've got the names to go on now, so we'll let the Keepers find the rest of it.' Col said as he left the control desk.

'The new team can get some practice in loading the transport box, and we can go take a well earned rest. Except for you that is, you'll be taking it to the Keepers, along with Hass.'

They threw a bit of a party for Jas that evening, the new team joining in as if they had been there all along. It was quite a bash, but somehow Jas didn't get the usual buzz from it he would have expected.

There was a touch of sadness next day as Jas said farewell to the rest of the people he had got to know so well, and together with Hass, he set off with their box of 'surveys' to the nearby transport terminal.

A short journey on the local monorail brought them to the high speed system, which linked all the major cities throughout the elongated continent.

Although it was very efficient, there was little joy in travelling on the system, as the scenery flashed by so quickly, and quite a considerable amount of the journey was spent underground in tunnels bored through the mountain ranges.

By late afternoon they had arrived at one of the terminals which was linked to a district monorail, and although this was a little slower, there was still little to see, as the light was beginning to fail.

The end of the line was reached, and as they left the terminal, a long dark mobile slid up beside them. The box was manhandled into the yawning goods section at the rear, they both piled in with the driver, and the last stage of their journey began.

Soon they had left the little town behind, with it's neat rows of multi coloured buildings and bright lights and were now racing out into open countryside, not that much of it could be seen except for that lit up by the brilliant forward lights of the speeding vehicle as total darkness had now closed in.

This was the worst part of the journey for Jas, as he wasn't used to travelling at such speeds without being able to see where he was going, and sought solace in the fact that the driver seemed to be competent at his job, and had probably travelled this route many times.

Four:
The Keepers

Two HOURS LATER they arrived at what they assumed to be the entrance to the complex. The mobile had stopped on a ledge of rock overhanging an inky blackness, with a sheer rock face behind extending up for as far as they could see in the wash of light form the vehicle. A stern faced man appeared out of nowhere, introduced himself as Kranz and ushered them in through what seemed like a well disguised doorway.

A short distance down a rocky passageway their guide opened a door into a small room and asked them to wait a moment as a light meal would be provided. By the time it had arrived they were ready for anything edible, but not for the head spinning beverage which came with it. As soon as they had finished the stern faced Kranz suggested that they retire, to be fresh for the following day.

They were shown into a room with adjacent toilet facilities, which it was intended for them to share, and the door closed behind them with a pronounced clunk.

'Can't say I'm really ready for bed yet.' said Jas, looking around the bare and rather plain room.

'Don't think we were given much option, somehow.' replied Hass, sitting on the edge of his bed, his face in his hands.

'You all right?' asked Jas, concern in is voice.

'Yes, just thinking what a hard cold place this is compared to our little number back down the line. I suppose it'll seem a little better in the bright light of day, but I doubt it.'

They tended to their toiletry needs, got into their beds, exchanged a few jokes and other pleasantries, and fell fast asleep. They were a little more tired than either had suspected. Or was it the drink? In the early hours of the morning, two men in white uniforms came into the room, and stripped back the covers on the sleeping pair.

Both bodies were examined minutely, and seemingly satisfied with what they found, Hass and Jas were unceremoniously turned over onto their respective faces.

A curved metallic instrument of some kind was placed on the nape of their necks, touch pads were touched and readings noted. A few grunts and monosyllables broke the otherwise total silence of the operation.

After a few minutes the operators of the equipment seemed satisfied with the results of their security check, for the covers were put back on the recumbent pair and the operators left. Both were sleeping like the new born, totally oblivious as to what had happened.

The pair were awoken early next morning by the sound of the window coverings being drawn back automatically, it was only a slight sound, but they were both snap wide awake before the cycle had been completed. Hass slipped from his bed and went over to the window.

'You've got to see this to believe it.' he called, but before the syllables were finished, Jas was by his side, mouth open in astonishment.

Below them the ground fell away in a sheer drop of some thousands of metres, the plain below just discernible but shrouded in swirling tendrils of the early morning mists, snaking their way up and down the valleys.

Ahead they could see a range of majestic black mountains, and another range behind that until the far horizon was just an indistinct blur, tinged with the pink of a rising sun.

A few of the larger and nearer stars still scintillated overhead, as if reluctant to give up the night and holding on until the sun would burst through the distant haze in its full glory. It seemed like another planet, and for a moment they both wondered just where they were.

'What I don't understand,' said Jas, 'is where's the country we travelled through yesterday? We have the mountains ahead, and a solid rock face behind us, at least, I think we do.' he added, hesitantly. Having dressed, and packed away their things, Hass opened the door and was greeted by the taciturn Kranz who had appeared as if by magic.

'Please follow me, and meet the others.' he said in a dull flat monotone. They followed the enigmatic Kranz down the corridor and into a very small room which turned out to be a lift.

The floor fell away beneath them, and Jas and Hass looked at each other in disbelief as their respective stomachs tried to reach up to their mouths. Kranz must have seen the look of discomfort on their faces, saying as he opened the door at the bottom of the long shaft

'Sorry, I used the wrong speed for you.' and with that strode off at a pace which made them trot in order to keep up with him.

The trio hurried along the main corridor with its many side branches and innumerable doors, until Kranz stopped in mid stride with no warning opposite a doorway much like all the others, Jas and Hass almost stumbling over him with the sudden change of pace.

'Here you will meet the others of the team.' Kranz said, his tone of voice implying that the others were different to him in some way. The door swung open, seemingly of its own accord, and Jas and Hass entered the room beyond. The door swung silently shut behind the pair, and locked itself with a very definite click.

The room could be best described as being basic and functional, without being too unkind to those responsible for its decor, or lack of same.

A long table occupied the centre space, with a spattering of chairs around its periphery. More chairs were lined up along one of the walls, above which were several viewing screens of different sizes, all angled towards the centre of the room.

'A couple of pictures on the walls wouldn't have gone amiss,' said Jas, 'or even a bunch of flowers in a pot.' he added, trying to lighten the otherwise rather austere atmosphere of the chamber. Hass merely nodded his head in reply, his attention obviously taken up by something else.

Before Jas could add any further remarks, a portion of the wall slid back and two smartly dressed men strode purposefully into the room.

'Greetings gentlemen, I trust you slept well and feel refreshed after your long journey?' They both nodded in unison, too surprised by the sudden appearance of the pair to give a verbal answer.

'Good, I am Muttlish, generally called Mutty, and head of operations here. This handsome looking creature is my second in command, and goes by the name of Duffring because we can't pronounce his native name without undergoing major surgery on our vocal cords first.' The ice had been broken by the light-hearted introductions, Jas and Hass visibly relaxing and feeling more at ease than they had done for some time.

'Both of you will be here for a while to learn a few tricks of the trade, but Jas will then be moving on to pastures new.

'So who is who?' asked Mutty with an open and friendly smile on his face. Hass introduced himself, stating his former position with the Seeker unit and then brought Jas into the conversation, outlining the progress he had made in the short period since he had been with the Seekers.

'Your skills have preceded you, and we are very pleased to have you with us for a while, as a fresh viewpoint on a situation is always welcome.' Mutty indicated the seats at one side of the table and said 'Please be seated, we have a lot to talk about, and we may as well be comfortable while we're at it.'

As they sat down, Jas and Hass were surprised to find the seats adjusted themselves height wise so that the weight was taken off their legs for just the right amount to be comfortable and the base of the seat moulded itself to fit their rear ends perfectly.

'Good aren't they, we have only just received these latest models and we still find them a little amusing.' Mutty added, as he took his place at the table.

'As you must know by now, this is a Keeper unit, and although it is officially designated as a research station, some research actually does go on here, but not the kind the outside world expects.' He looked around to see if the newcomers were in doubt as to the validity of his statement, and seeing nothing to cause him to doubt their understanding of the situation, proceeded.

'The majority of the trouble makers on this world are handled quite well by one of the teams the like of which you have just left. Sometimes you get a really hard nut to crack, and they are sent here for the final breaking, as it were. We have the means to strip the very soul of a troublemaker to shreds if need be, but it usually doesn't come to that. We can extract all we need to know, and leave the person still in one piece, although a little shaken sometimes.'

Mutty paused to let the two newcomers absorb the full content of his short speech, and seeing no sign of surprise on their faces, carried on.

'It is not always a pleasant job, but someone has to do it for the sake of the rest of the system, and you tend to get immune to the more unpleasant side of it after a while. All you have to remember is that a few may well suffer a little for the greater good of a great many, and in my book, that is quite acceptable.' Again he paused, and Jas raised his head a little.

'You wish to say something Jas?'

'Well, er, yes, if I may.'

'Go ahead young man, you are free to say anything you wish, there is no restraint whatsoever on what you may say, or ideas you may wish to express.' Mutty sat back in his chair, which immediately readjusted itself to his newly acquired position, and waited.

'I am fully aware of the harm that a malcontent can do to society, and I totally support the principle behind the Seekers work, but I am a little concerned about the fact that a person's 'rights' are no longer taken into account in the work that we do. A little coercion to get the information we need to clear up the mess some people leave behind them is quite acceptable, and some of the tricks we use seem to do no permanent harm to the recipient, but from what I have gathered about the work done here, the pressures and techniques and resulting state of the person being interviewed, goes against all that I have considered to be the basic rights of an individual.'

Jas anxiously looked around the table to see if he had said a little too much, but no one had changed their facial expressions or looked as if they were about to say anything, so he carried on.

'I don't know, it's something I feel deep down inside me, something I don't quite feel is right somehow.'

'Maybe I have failed to understand something, but I am quite willing to have it explained to me so that I can accept without question the work I have to do.' Jas sat back, wondering if he had said too much, and blown his chances of ever being a full member of the Keeper's team.

For the first time, Duffring, the deputy head of operations, spoke in a deep and powerful melodious voice, the kind which commands full attention and respect to those who were honoured enough to be in his presence.

'I hear what you have said, and fully understand what you are trying to express, and in an ideal world I would agree with you one hundred percent. Unfortunately, a perfect world doesn't exist, at least not in this galaxy, as far as I know. We do our best to try and reach that state, but there is always some little anomaly we miss or can't resolve. Remember the basic principle upon which we work. The greatest good for the greatest number. That means, if a few individuals have to suffer for the benefit of the rest, then they suffer, there is little doubt about that. But they do have a choice.

'They don't have to create chaos and mayhem, no one is making them do it, or even trying to persuade them to do it. It is their own choice. If their actions look as if they will destabilize an otherwise stable situation, or cause a lot of suffering and harm to the general populace, then they are removed and any upset in the area is cleaned up as best as we can.

'If this means using a little force here and there, then I think it is fully justified.' Duffring paused to allow his words to sink in, and then continued.

'It is very rare that an individual is so damaged that they can't live a normal life thereafter, albeit far removed from the area in which they caused the trouble in the first place.'

'They are, as I am sure you know by now, sent off to join others of like inclinations, so that they can play their little games of destruction and mayhem among others of their kind. I think that is about as fair as we can make it in an imperfect world. You see, we consider that if you decide to upset the status quo for others, and thereby make their lives a misery, then you have lost any 'rights' you may have had, and what happens to you is brought on by your own actions.'

The other three nodded in silent agreement, and Jas couldn't fault the well put argument.

'I agree entirely with what you have said, but there is still something niggling away at the back of my mind,' said Jas, 'but no doubt it will resolve itself in time.'

'Yes, it usually does.' replied Duffring. 'Many relative newcomers to this unit have gone through the same mental tussle with their well meaning ideals, but they get resolved in time, as do all things.' Again the solemn nod of heads.

There was a barely audible sound as a panel slid back at the end of the room, and the sombre figure of Kranz was revealed. 'Do you wish me to proceed with the new visitor?' he said in a flat monotone to no one in particular. Duffring looked around towards the opening in the wall and the cimmerian figure.

'Not just at the moment Kranz, I would like our new friends to witness the procedure, so we will postpone the interrogation for a while, and I'll contact you when we are ready.' The panel slid back into place, and the four of them were left alone again.

Duffring looked up and smiled at Jas. 'We may as well fill you in with the rest of the story, as you will only guess the sequence of events anyway, and it's best you get it right first time.

Jas found his attention and eyes locked onto Duffring's, almost as if he had been hypnotized. There was the instinctive urge to look away, but he couldn't, and put it down to the inclination to politely pay attention to the speaker, but deep down he doubted if that was all there was to it.

Duffring turned to Mutty,

'Carry on,' Mutty said in answer to the unasked question, 'you're explaining things as well as anyone can.'

'Thank you.' replied Duffring, more in acknowledgement of the instruction than gratitude for the implied compliment.

'The Seeker teams do a very good job of sorting out the trouble makers which they locate, extracting most of the information needed to clear up any mess which has been caused by their actions. Sometimes the miscreant is a little tougher than the Seekers have the wherewithal to handle, and so the unfortunate is passed on to us for processing, so to speak.

'We extract the necessary information, using whatever methods we need to, passing the data back down the line to the Seekers who then do the necessary corrections in the local environment. The miscreant is then held here, usually in a state of stasis, or suspended animation, until we can dispatch him, and it's usually a 'him', on to the next Dark Ship to visit us. We usually refer to them as the 'Sweepers', for that is what they do, sweeping up the dross of the Confederation.'

At this point Mutty joined in the conversation, filling in the next sequence of events.

'When we have collected several of the local villains, obtained all necessary data from them in order to correct the troubles they have caused, we get in touch with the Sweeper ship, and they give us their schedule of contact.'

'If it is several weeks away we put them into 'deep sleep' or stasis, and then ship them up when the Dark Ship is next in the vicinity.'

'As you probably know, or have reasoned out by now, most of the intelligent life in the known universe, or at least that part of it we have had contact with, is of biped form. They sport bodies like ours, two arms, two legs, a trunk and a head. Albeit, some are short and stocky, some tall and thin, and all possible variants in between. Skin colour varies according to the climate and other considerations, mainly chemical. To us, some are ugly, approaching hideous, while others are beautiful in the extreme. But do not be fooled by looks, they can be very deceptive indeed. Take my colleague here.' Mutty turned and waved a hand at Duffring.

'You would think he was a gentle quiet type, without a scrap of hardness. Just wait until you see him in action. We don't have him on the team for his good looks, I assure you.'

Mutty leaned back in his chair to see how the two newcomers were taking the revelations, and relaxed visibly at the lack of surprise on their faces. He did something to the edge of the table and a section in the centre opened up and a tray of drinking vessels and a decanter of beautiful crystal rose up.

'Time for a little liquid refreshment, its dry work, all this talking.' Mutty poured out a generous portion of a sparkling amber liquid into each vessel, and then passed them around to the other three.

Jas was surprised as he took the first sip. It seemed to flash around his mouth of its own accord, tickling his taste buds as it went, the flavours changing from moment to moment, reminding him of all the delicious drinks he had tasted.

Then he remembered, he had sampled this concoction once before, on board the Dark Ship when he was first recruited by the man with the steel grey eyes.

Mutty was watching Jas for some reaction to the beverage, and poorly concealed his disappointment when there was so little reaction to the amber liquid.

'You must have tried this refreshment before.' Mutty offered, looking straight at Jas.

'Well yes, I have, when I was first recruited and onboard the Dark Ship.'

'You've actually been onboard a Dark Ship? An astonished Mutty expounded. 'You must be something rather special then. I don't mean to imply anything by that remark, except that someone somewhere has singled you out for some specific purpose and we had better do a rather good job of training you to accept whatever it is they have in mind for you.'

A new look of respect came over the faces of the other three as each assessed the import of the statement from Jas.

'Well, having got over that little surprise, let me continue.' Mutty was somewhat put off his stride by the revelation, but tried not to show it, and failed.

'The Dark Ships travel great distances in their work, and as you may know, the Confederation covers a vast section of space now, with many different races of people on many very different planets. Some worlds sport several different races, each belonging to their own land masses, and some have even mixed the races up, cross breeding among themselves. The possible variations of the human form from one extreme to the other is indeed multitudinous, and that has in the past caused problems for the Dark Ships when it came to finding homes for their 'guests.'

'They solved the problem by holding the mixture in stasis until they could locate a planet which was either devoid of human life, and was suitable for colonizing, or finding one that already had a species sufficiently similar to some of their charges that they could be added to the existing race without causing too many raised eyebrows.'

Mutty paused to refresh his dry throat, or perhaps he just liked the amber liquid, and this was a good excuse to indulge in another draught.

'The exact details of how the 'guests' are delivered, or even convinced that they belong to their new homes has not been revealed to me, as it is not pertinent to the work we do here. No doubt, it will all be explained to you at some later date.'

Jas had difficulty in hiding a feeling of self importance as the full impact of just where he may finish up dawned.

He realized that there was a long way to go yet, and there could well be many a slip on the way. He would have to work very diligently indeed if he was to make it through to the ultimate position of power on one of the Dark Ships.

'Well, gentlemen, that about sums up the necessary data for the time being, we had better get along and join Kranz and his 'guest' or he will be getting impatient.'

With that, the meeting was over and they all left the austere room and filed out into the corridor.

Jas was about to ask just how big the complex was, when he saw a detailed map of the passageways on a metal plate let into the wall. He managed to suppress an audible gasp, but the look of surprise on his face was noticed by Duffring, who volunteered,

'It's quite a large set-up by any standards, although we don't use all of it at the moment.'

The party walked on for a while and then paused at a large panel set in the wall. Someone must have activated something unseen to the newcomers, for the panel slid back and they all stepped into what Jas assumed to be a lift.

He was right, but this time it didn't give them the gut wrenching feeling they had experienced when escorted by Kranz.

How far they had dropped, or for that matter went up, Jas had no way of knowing, as there was no sense of motion which he could detect, and suddenly the panel slid back and they were out into a wide corridor which stretched out into the distance for as far as the eye could see in both directions.

'Not long now gentlemen.' said Duffring with his beautiful smile, and Jas wondered just what sort of person Duffring really was.

Mutty suddenly disappeared from sight around a corner and then they were looking down onto a small room from a glass-like aperture set in its ceiling.

The ginger headed man was sitting in a chair-like contraption, although Jas suspected it was a little more than a chair in reality.

Kranz was slowly walking around the equipment units in the room, adjusting a dial here, a knob there, and generally looking as if he knew exactly what he was doing, which he probably did.

The general air of competence was beginning to unnerve 'Ginger', and Jas could see his mouth working overtime as a continuous stream of verbals issued forth. To begin with, Kranz totally ignored the outburst, but after a while as he passed 'Ginger' his foot flickered out in a lightning fast movement to contact 'Ginger's' leg, causing his mouth to open in a soundless scream of abject pain.

'Ginger's' scream must have been ear-splitting by the way his mouth opened and with the contortions on his face, but because of the intervening transparent ceiling between them, not a sound was heard.

'Ginger' issued forth with another stream of abuse as the pain subsided, but stopped in mid blast as Kranz turned to look him full in the eyes.   At long last he realized that he would get nowhere by antagonizing his keeper, and resorted to a glum sullen silence instead.

Kranz continued to adjust the controls of the various pieces of equipment until he had a row of green lights along the top of one of the panels, and this seemed to be the signal he had been waiting for, as he left the control panel and sat down opposite the now somewhat subdued 'Ginger' who returned his impassive stare with a scowl.

'Let's go down and join Kranz to see what he can extract from our friend.' and with that Mutty touched the wall beside him and another panel opened to reveal a small chamber into which they all crowded. A few seconds later they were at the entrance of the 'enquiry' room and were greeted by the now expected stream of abuse from 'Ginger'.

Although 'Ginger' was in no visible way restrained in his chair, there was something preventing him from leaving it, but Jas couldn't see just what it was. The stream of invectives from 'Ginger' was finally silenced by another sharp foot tap from Kranz, who had now left his seat and delivered the glancing blow on his way to one of the control consuls where he was joined by Mutty.

'There are only a few details we need to know before we can release you, so it would be in your interest to co-operate fully so that we can get this whole sorry mess cleaned up and we can all go home'.

Mutty's offer was greeted by the now familiar blast of objurgations from the man in the chair, which in turn caused Mutty to show the first sign of impatience Jas had yet seen in him.

'OK Kranz, he's all yours, just get what we need to know.' Mutty said, his tone of voice hardening to the degree that a cold shiver went down Jas's back.

Now he would see at first hand just what the Keeper team was capable of, and he wasn't too sure he really wanted to.

Kranz swung a small panel attached to a long arm out from the wall and positioned it in front of 'Ginger', who promptly passed several insulting comments on the apparatus and the parentage of the person who had dared to move it into his space.

'He never gives up.' Jas commented to no one in particular. 'Small wonder you had a problem with him.' Mutty added, 'But we should be able to get what we want, with a bit of persuasion.'

Kranz drew up a small chair and sat down in front of the now silent 'Ginger', who had run out of insults and was no doubt trying to think up some new ones to impress his audience with at an opportune moment in the near future.

The questioning began, but only brought forth a solid string of expletives, some of which Jas hadn't heard before and he was about to ask for an explanation of one of them when Kranz decided that enough was enough, and a little encouragement was needed to help things along, and touched a button on the control panel.

'Ginger' stopped in mid word, his mouth locked half open as he was forming the next insult and beads of perspiration formed on his forehead which quickly joined up and began to run down his face.

His eyes protruded like bulging organ stops and threatened to burst while a dry rattle of tortured breath tried to escape a constriction in his throat, powered by a pair of lungs desperate for more oxygen. 'Ginger's' face went dark red, and then a dirty purple shade before all the colour drained from it completely, and he sagged in stature as much as the imprisoning chair would allow.

'What is actually happening?' asked Jas, almost afraid of the answer. Mutty's face was thoughtful as he answered Jas,

'Kranz's little gadget is sending waves of inductive energy into 'Ginger's' body such that all the major nerves are being triggered at once. The effect of this is that all the major muscles are either locked immovably or pulling against each other, depending on what Kranz is doing with the controls.

'The pain level on the receiving end of that kind of treatment is absolutely excruciating, a bit like a bad attack of the cramps, but all over, and much stronger. How the hell he can take it beats me, as it could well kill him if we aren't careful.'

Half an hour later, and they still hadn't extracted the necessary data from the intractable 'Ginger', and patience was visibly running a little short.

'We have one more trick up our sleeves,' said Mutty 'and it looks as if we shall have to use it, although I am somewhat reluctant to do so.'

'What is it?' asked Hass, who up until now had been virtually silent.

'It is a last resort, something we very rarely use because it isn't really sanctioned. Fortunately you will not be allowed to witness the event, not so much because it doesn't officially exist, but because of the inherent danger of being in the vicinity while it is taking place.'

Mutty gave a resigned shrug of his shoulders, as though giving in to the inevitable.

'I had better explain the whole thing to you as you will need to know sometime, and it is probably better that you have the data and the result of such an action in one time period so that if you should ever have to use it, you will know the possible consequences and what is involved.'

Turning around, he said, 'OK Kranz, you have done your best, I think we will have to leave it to Duffring to finish the job.'

Kranz promptly folded the control panel on its long arm back into the wall, switched off the other units, and left the room, showing no emotion at all, which surprised Jas as he expected some sign of disappointment at least.

'Kranz took it very well, I thought.' Jas offered, hoping to elicit some reason for Kranz's enigmatic attitude.

'He doesn't show much does he? And we're not sure if he really feels much either, but he is very good at what he does, so we don't question it too much.' replied Mutty, his arms outstretched, indicating that they should leave the room also.

As they piled into the lift and went back up to the main corridor, Mutty said, 'We'll retire to my office, and I'll explain what is going to happen to our uncooperative friend down there.' Hass and Jas exchanged glances, and the look on Hass's face made Jas wonder if he really wanted to know.

Once in the main corridor, Mutty placed his hand on what seemed to be just an ordinary part of the wall, and a section slid back to reveal a tube-like enclosure containing six seats.

'In we go gentlemen.' said Mutty, and no sooner had they taken up their seats when the panel slid shut and the device accelerated off down the tunnel.

There were several surges up and down, which Jas thought would be consistent with a change of level, but didn't like to question it at the moment as it seemed too petty considering the import of what was about to happen.

The transport device suddenly stopped, and the wall section obligingly opened to let the travellers out and into a room overlooking the distant mountain ranges.

'Please make yourselves comfortable while I arrange some refreshments.' and with that Mutty seemed to melt into what appeared to be the solid wall.

Hass and Jas exchanged astonished glances at this latest surprise, but then their attention was taken up by the sumptuous surrounding of the Chief Executives Office.

There were soft comfortable looking chairs, ornate carved pieces of exquisite furniture from many cultures and a series of pictures on the wooden panelled walls of far away places, only one of which could have been of this planet.

The pictures were in true three dimensional projection, just as if the viewer were looking out of a window onto the scene itself.

Having taken in the opulence of the office and admired the decor, two pairs of eyes were now firmly focused on the point where Mutty had disappeared, and were awaiting his return.

Suddenly Mutty reappeared as if by magic with a tray in his hands, and seeing the pair staring in his direction, let out a little laugh.

'Just one of my little foibles gentlemen, I have a little room behind this wall where I can prepare the odd refreshment should I desire to, and the doorway is covered by a projection of the surrounding wall to finish the illusion of the office being a complete room in it's own right.'

'I think it sometimes helps to keep one human if one can do some little thing for one's self, instead of relying totally on the mechanized systems to supply all one's needs.'

With that Mutty spread out the contents of the tray on a nearby table, and invited his guests to avail themselves of food and drink.

'Right gentlemen, let us get down to the basics of what is happening somewhere down below us at this moment. Duffring will get the information we require, make no mistake of that, but if we lose our 'guest' at the same time, we will be back where we started, but more to the damn point, so will he.'

'Duffring has a particular skill, which as far as I know, only exists on one world and then only a very few of its inhabitants poses this unique ability.

'He is able to look into another persons mind, sift through that persons pictures, alter them to suit his needs, and put them back in, causing the recipient to experience the contents of those altered pictures. Now that may not sound very terrifying, but let me explain how it works, and what the end result can be.'

Mutty paused to take another drink, slowly sipping the beverage as if to delay any further explanation. There must have been some doubt in his mind as to whether he should divulge what he knew, but then he must have made his mind up, for putting down the drinking vessel with a firm and definite gesture on the table, he continued,

'I would like both of you to add together two three figure numbers in your heads, OK? You have an answer?' But before either of them could say anything, Mutty said 'The answers are not important, the method by which you arrived at them is.'

'When adding them up, you must have actually seen the numbers in your mind, even if only very fleetingly, but you saw them. Right?'

They both chorused 'Yes.' together.

'Good,' said Mutty, 'that is the point I am trying to make, as simple as it is. When you think, you do so in pictures. It is the only way to think, it can't be done any other way.

'Now bear in mind that you usually only have access to pictures of this lifetime, but older pictures, and how you felt in them from the main time track going back through aeons of time are accessible when you know how, and Duffring does know how.'

Mutty looked from Hass to Jas and back again to see if the point was understood by both, and seeing no sign of confusion on their faces, pressed on with his explanation in great haste, almost as though if he took his time, he wouldn't be able to complete the story for some reason.

'Your mental image pictures, whether you are aware of it or not, contain all your feelings, emotions, and sensations, and that includes terror, complete with pain and any real or imagined threat to do with that incident.

'Just imagine if someone were able to dig around in your mind and drag up an incident where you experienced extreme pain and terror, and finally lost your body under the utmost duress, and then was able to add a few extra bits to the incident to make it even more awful, and shoved that mental image package back into your mind and made you rerun it again and again. To you, the rerun of the pictures would be just as real as they were when first created, complete with all the feelings.'

The look on the faces of his two listeners must have satisfied him that the point was well made, and understood.

Mutty relaxed back in his well upholstered chair, as did the other two after a while, and awaited the inevitable questions that would follow. There was a long pause before anyone said anything, and Mutty took advantage of the respite to take another long pull at his drink, as if it would somehow wash away the flavour of what he had just spoken of.

Hass began to tremble slightly, his eyes were out of focus and beads of perspiration broke out on his forehead. Jas reached out to touch his arm, but Mutty beat him to it, restraining the comforting gesture and said, 'No, you must let him come through it, he must reach the end of what ever he is into, otherwise the incident will stick and we will have a very sick Hass on our hands'.

They waited for what seemed an age, but in reality was only a few seconds, before Hass shook himself, his face now ashen grey.

'I see what you mean. I dug up an old incident I had a vague recollection of, and dug a little deeper, and now wish I hadn't. This is something which is not to be fooled around with, I can assure you,' Mutty was deadly serious now, and continued, 'after a lot of persuasion, I got Duffring to give me a little taste of what a recipient could expect, as I wanted to get some reality on the matter. I was still shaking two days later, and that was only a little taster of what could have been dug up and run, according to Duffring.'

'Looks like 'Ginger' is in for a rough time then.' Jas said cheerfully, trying to bring back a lighter side to the conversation.

'That's if he comes through it in one piece.' added Mutty, with a tinge of doubt in his voice. 'We should hear from Duffring soon, it doesn't usually take him long to get results'.

They had to wait a little longer than they had expected. Duffring eventually came into the room and sat down, the weariness clearly showing on his face. He sat there, staring into space for a moment, the handsome smile missing completely, replaced by a long drawn look of concern.

They instinctively left him to make the first move, thus allowing him to reorientate himself into present time and out of what ever he had been in. At last he raised his head and spoke.

'Well, that was a close thing. We almost lost him. His heart burst, or to be a little more accurate, it split with the colossal rise in blood pressure.

'Fortunately Kranz had anticipated the likelihood of such a happening, and was standing by with synthetic blood and a bypass machine. We only just managed to connect him up to it in time. Kranz is operating on him now to sew the split back together. There must have been a weakness there, and it was missed when we examined him earlier.

'It looks as if he'll make it though, he's a pretty tough customer, both mentally and physically.' And with that Duffring eased himself back into his chair and visibly relaxed a little.

'Did you get what we needed from him?' asked Mutty, his tone of voice indicating a fear of a negative answer.

'Yes, we did.' Duffring replied. 'You were right to suspect that someone else was behind his operations, and the operations of some others we have picked up in the past. It's a little complicated, and the main subject is off world, but I think I know where we can find him. It would seem that some joker looks out for possible recruits, like 'Ginger', and then somehow gets 'em stirred up by taking them back track to a point where they felt very hard done by.'

'To the memory of the incident, he, and I think it's a he, then adds a little of his own ideas, as I do when putting the pressure on a case, but using a different method, as far as I can tell. The clever bit is he then somehow covers up the memory of the replaced 'incident', so that the recipient has no recall of it ever happening, leaving a trigger point or maybe just a phrase or keyword exposed, which is the restimulation point in later life.'

'So there could be many years between the time our targets are set-up as it were, and the point in time when they go into action.' Mutty added, more as a comment than a question.

'Yes, and that makes it more difficult to track back to the originator of the troubles.' Duffring had recovered his old composure by now, and the gentle firmness which had returned to his voice added a calming effect to the whole proceedings.

'I will try and bring 'Ginger' back to his senses, if he recovers, but I doubt if we have the technology sufficiently advanced as yet to undercut the original implant the 'Joker' put in, in which case he'll have to be shipped out along with the others. I would like to think we will be able to rescue these poor souls one day, but until then we'll just have to stick to the system we have in place at present.'

At this point Jas asked a question,

'See if I've got it right, there are two main types of people who are causing the troubles, those who have been primed with an altered memory, as per 'Ginger', and those who, like the 'Joker' who do it out of pure evil intention. Some of the primed ones can be made to see what has happened, and can be rehabilitated, while the other category which includes the 'Joker' are beyond our present technology. These others have to be deported to another world to stop them causing more trouble in an otherwise orderly society.'

'Yes, that's about the size of it,' replied Mutty, 'but there a few subtle points which need to be explained a little further. Some of the data will only be released to you when you join the Dark Ships, which I'm sure you are destined for, but I can tell you a little more of what we know.'

'Basically, just about everyone knows instinctively right from wrong, even at a very early age. It seems to be something born in us, if you will pardon the expression. A wrong act can be something which we do which we know is harmful not only to others, but to one's self. Also it can be an omission of something we should do.'

'You see some one about to have an accident due to a wrong decision or poor observation of the facts, you could step in and prevent it, but you don't. That is just as wrong, the degree of the wrongness depending on the severity of the end result.'

Mutty looked at Jas and Hass to see if they were following his train of thought, and seeing a look of comprehension on their faces, continued,

'We have another category, a person does several wrongs, and realizing it, has to try and get these wrongs accepted by those around them. One way to do that is to try to get others to do wrong as well, the idea behind the principle is that if others are doing the same, then 'my' act can't be so bad, after all.

'It may sound crazy, but it is an observable fact, although it doesn't happen quite so much now that we have stabilized this planet's population.'

Duffring raised his head, signalling he wished to add to the conversation.

'Greed, avarice, jealousy and the general feeling that one could obtain things for which one has not contributed anything in exchange, or theft to put a name to it, are, or I should say, were, one of the main driving forces for bad acts here at one time.

'As we stabilized the situation, people began to look towards those who didn't commit wrong doings as their examples, and so things got better. This left us with the real 'baddies', the like of which you have both had dealings with, and their numbers are almost down to zero now. Very soon we will be able to hand over the 'keep the planet clean' policy to the native inhabitants, many of which are being trained for the job. We then move on to the next planet which requests our services, and there are quite a few of them as the confederation expands ever outwards.'

Jas looked around at the other three, to make sure no one else wanted to speak, and said, 'I don't see how you can dump a load of people onto another planet and expect them to just melt into the local population and be accepted without questions being asked by both parties. For my part, I'd kick up one hell of a fuss if it happened to me, so how do they do it?'

Mutty leaned forward and replied, 'We are not privy to that information as it is not needed in the work we do. It will no doubt, be revealed to you when you need to know.'

The panel at the end of the room had slid silently open and they felt rather than saw the presence of Kranz standing there. Mutty twisted around towards him and said, 'What news, will he make it?'

'Our guest is alive and stabilized, a full physical recovery is expected within two weeks at the outside. There is little more that I can do for him.'

'As for his mental state, I would request Duffring to access that as it is a little outside my abilities after what he has been through.' The panel slid to and Kranz was gone from view.

'Now that's someone I'd like to ask a few questions about' offered Hass, but before he could expound on his request, Mutty butted in with, 'we would all like to ask some question about our friend Kranz. So far we have very little in the way of answers, no matter who we've asked. He says very little, the people who sent him just gave us the run-around when they were approached, so we have given up on the idea.'

'He is very good at what he does, and so we have just accepted him on that basis. Whether he is truly a human being, we don't know for sure. We can't even find out where he came from originally. He never seems to sleep as we do, and I've never seen him eat anything unless we invite him to, and then we don't know if it goes into a stomach or straight into a disposal bag. As far as I know he has no sense of humour, which seems to be a human trait, but then some humans don't have one either.' said Mutty brightly, grinning.

'Well gentlemen, I think we had better break this meeting up as it has served its purpose of getting us out of the way while Duffring did his work and filled in a few gaps in our new member's knowledge of the unit and what we're all about. Let's go down and see how 'Ginger' is getting on, and then we can take a look at some of the rest of the complex.'

They all trooped out into the corridor and into the transport device, retracing their steps to the interrogation room, and then down two levels to where the somewhat battered 'Ginger' was laid out in a transparent capsule, pipes and wires adorning him like an untidy plumbing system that someone had abandoned out of sheer frustration.

'Well, the old sod looks peaceful enough now, at any rate.' said Hass, his tone of voice intimating that he didn't have very much in the way of sympathy towards the unfortunate Ginger.

A long vivid scar ran the full length of his chest, out of which three tubes sprouted along with several different coloured wires, a machine somewhere behind a screen made soft and low breathing sounds while an only just audible burbling sound indicated that his body's fluids were being attended to by something mechanical rather than being under his own control.

'There is little we can do for him now, so we'll just have to wait and see if he pulls through as Kranz said he would and then Duffring can work his magic on him, but I have my doubts about that being successful somehow. He will probably have to join the rest of our merry band of voyagers.'

They left the now placid Ginger to the tender care of the machines and went down several more levels to come out into a large tunnel with bare rock hewn walls.

The light level was low compared to what they had been accustomed to above, and it took a little while before their eyes got used to the general gloomy nature of the place.

As their eyes adjusted, the details of the surroundings became more apparent.

The tunnel was far larger than needed for the passage of a group of human beings, and although the floor was quite smooth, the walls were crudely cut from the living rock, no attempt having been made to dress the stone or make it look in any way aesthetic or pleasing to the eye.

Mutty walked over to a recess in the tunnel wall which immediately came ablaze in a hard white light to reveal a long cylindrical mobile.

'OK gentlemen, hop aboard and we'll show our new recruits some of the instore samples we have on offer.' Mutty was now in a rather jocular mood after the rather taciturn attitude he had adopted back in his office.

The mobile made little sound as it sped down the seemingly never ending tunnel, side branches flashing by so fast their details were hard to discern. At long last the journey was over, and the four left the mobile behind as they entered a small chamber in the tunnel wall.

A series of coloured square plates adorned the far wall of the recess, and Mutty walked over to them, his hands flickering from one to another until there was a soft sigh, and the wall slid up into the rock above and they were through into a vast chamber which was even more gloomy than the tunnel they had just left.

'We'll only go a little way in, as it is much the same for its entire length.' Mutty had walked a few metres into the vast cavern and stopped. There was a sharp click, and the place was flooded with a soft pink light. Before them was a vast array of transparent cylinders, arranged row upon row, and stretching off into the far distance.

Some of the cylinders closest to them had a pale violet glow surrounding them, which seemed to flicker and move of its own accord, but was only just visible to the eye.

'This is where 'Ginger' will finish up for a while, unless I'm very much mistaken.' said Hass, an ill concealed touch of pleasure in his voice.

'Yes, he probably will.' replied Mutty.

'Let me explain a little of what you see before you. The cylinders are the deep sleep modules in which the 'guests' are held until we have the signal from a Dark Ship to get 'em ready for dispatch.'

'The apparatus looks after all their bodily needs, their metabolism being slowed down so that it only just ticks over. They are confused by the energy field which surrounds each capsule, and so are not aware of the passing time, or anything else for that matter. It's about as humane as we can get with our present technology.

'This way a complete human being, consisting of body, mind and being itself, can be held in suspended animation for as long as we wish, within reason that is. Between us and the capsules, you may notice a rather thick screen of transparent material.

'This is to protect us from the effects of the energy field you see surrounding the capsules. You would drop like a stone if you got just one flicker of that around you.'

Jas walked forward, coming up hard against the screen as he did so and let out a very ungentlemanly expletive in the process.

'I should have warned you, not everyone can see the screen in this light, so it comes as a bit of a surprise to some.' There was a hint of mischievous delight in Mutty's voice, and then he carried on in a more serious tone with his dissertation on the complex.

'The energy field is kept on while the capsules are transported up to the Ship and while they are onboard thereafter, this implies that the whole operation is done by mechanicals.

'The capsules are lifted down from the ledges and placed on a special transporter which comes from the Ship, so we don't see any more of the operation from this point on.

'There is little more to see here, so we may as well return and I'll tell you what your duties are for the next few days, after which you will be expected to take full control of your own work, only reporting to me with the results.'

'This place is so huge, so where are the rest of the personnel?' asked Hass, 'we have only seen you and Kranz, and a few others so far.'

'That's because we are the only staff left here now, apart from two other technicians. Before you two came, there was only Kranz, myself and three others, one of which has moved on up the chain, to be replaced by Hass.'

'Jas will be moving on by the look of things, when he has learnt what he needs to know of our operations, and then we will be reduced to five again. It is enough for the work left here now, but at one time, this was a very busy place, being the holding station for this planet and the other two worlds of this solar system.'

'But that was a very long time ago. I would suggest that we take an evening meal now and relax a little, tomorrow is going to be a busy day for us all. Please follow me to the recreation room, where we eat and generally take things easy when there is little else to do, which is getting to be more frequent these days.'

The party returned the way they had come, and it was only sometime later when Hass and Jas were discussing what they had seen that they realized the colossal size and complexity of the holding station, and the amount of work which must have gone on in days past.

The whole place was running down now, its useful days almost at a close, although the physical structure would no doubt remain.

The present personnel would be replaced by a few well trained native operatives until the job of clearing the planet of types like Ginger had been completed, and then it would be just a matter of keeping an eye on things to hold the world in a sane and stable state.

When the group reached the recreation room, the other two operatives where already there, and although introductions were made they were not a talkative pair and tended to keep to themselves. The meal passed with polite conversation flowing between, and then the group broke up, the other two going their separate ways leaving Jas, Mutty and Hass looking at each other, all conversation spent.

Jas asked for directions to go outside the complex and take in the evening air, as he put it.

'Why do you want to do that?' asked Mutty, a look of surprise on his face.

'To take in the magnificent view and the smell of fresh air.' replied Jas, suddenly realizing that he may well have insulted the complex for not providing it.

'It's just something I like to do before retiring for the night.' he added lamely. Mutty smiled,

'You are most welcome to do so. Just follow the signs marked 'Fresh Air' and you will wind up at either the air conditioning plant or the ledge just below us.' This raised a laugh from the otherwise silent pair, who were obviously enjoying some in joke to do with the station.

'Sorry about that Jas, just my funny sense of humour. Just take the lift outside the recreation room and drop four levels, exit the lift and follow the wide passage straight ahead of you.'

'There is a security screening device which will allow you to go out and return when you place you hand on the plate by the doorway. Enjoy your outing, you are right, it is quite a sight out there, but I suppose we are used to it by now.'

Jas felt a little tinge of annoyance at being made the butt of a joke he didn't understand, but the feeling soon evaporated when they emerged on the ledge outside the complex.

Below them was a sheer drop of many thousands of metres to a long and twisting valley. Fingers of mist were already swirling along its long and torturous course and spreading up the lesser side vales, while the first of the larger stars beginning to twinkle high above them.

Ahead, the mountains seemed to go on for ever, fading into the distance where they met the sinking sun in a blaze of red and yellow light.

Hass turned around to look back at the complex, and was astonished to see no sign of the windows he knew to exist, in fact no sign of any man made interference to the mountain face except the exit they had just come out of, and that could be easily missed unless one was looking for it.

'To say this place is well camouflaged is a bit like saying that space is quite large.' retorted Hass.

'Without a very good map and a homing beacon, you'd never find this ledge, let along the complex. So I wonder why they went to such great lengths to keep it so secret?'

'Don't know.' replied Jas,

'Unless they feared attack from some group opposed to the regime they were trying to impose on the people, but it would take a mightily well equipped force to make any impression on this place, that's if they could find it in the first place, and I expect they have a defensive system anyway, although I've seen no sign of it so far.'

'What we keep forgetting,' Hass added, 'is that this place was built a very long time ago, and we don't know the conditions which prevailed at that time. Maybe things were considerably more uncertain then and there was a faction which opposed us, so this kind of fortification was necessary until things stabilized somewhat. Perhaps Mutty will tell us, if we ask him.'

They lingered on the ledge for some time, admiring the rugged scenery and the changing colours as the light faded, throwing the distant mountains into deep shadow until the whole area was merged into one dark mass, with little detail left to observe. High above them, something long and sleek, clothed in steel grey fur to match the surrounding rocks, looked down hungrily on the pair, but fortunately for them could see no way down to the ledge.

They had some difficulty in finding the well concealed entrance to the complex, and the security plate proved even more elusive. In the end, chance took a hand as Hass slapped the wall in frustration, and the doorway opened up.

After a lengthy discussion of the day's events, sleep came easily, and was barely disturbed by a deep rumble as something came down out of space and entered the mountain above them.

Next morning as they were getting dressed, there was a soft sigh and a 'ping' of annunciation as a panel in the wall opened and two trays of food appeared as if by magic.

'I wonder how they get their timing right without actually spying on us.' asked Jas, not really expecting an answer.

'Makes you think, doesn't it. I wonder if the food is the real stuff or synthetic. Can't tell really, anyway it tastes good.' said Hass tucking in as if it was his last meal for a long time.

They had just finished eating, when Kranz materialized out of nowhere and announced that they were required down in the interrogation room as soon as possible, and as he didn't move, they assumed that meant right away.

Down the corridor they went, into the lift, both having to hold on tight to their early morning meals as Kranz sent the lift plummeting down several levels.

'He does it on purpose.' Jas muttered as they left the lift, and they both later agreed there was a slight trace of a grin on the normally stone like face of the mysterious Kranz.

Mutty greeted them as they entered the interrogation room, and with a sweep of his arm indicated the latest arrival to be given the honour of occupying the dreaded chair.

It was human insofar that it had all the necessary appendages required by the human form, but apart from some very scanty clothing, was covered in fine dark brown hair.

The head was far from refined, having a primitive look about it, and the hands were hard and callused from doing some tough manual work.

'From the data we have collected over the ages plus that which came with our friend here, it looks as if we have a recurring problem on the third planet from the sun. There are two main groups of people there, members of our guest's tribe and a more sophisticated lot, both of which seem to get along quite well with each other, despite their physical differences. They trade with each other, and mix quite well, although there is no cross breeding that we can ascertain.' Mutty turned his head towards Hass and said as an aside, 'Which is hardly surprising.'

'Again, from the data acquired, it looks as if someone is stirring up a religious cult from time to time, and it catches on like wildfire for a short period.

'No great harm in that, except this one promulgates the concept of everyone shares out all that they possess. Everything gets redistributed out evenly, so that those who have made a bit of progress are stripped of all they have gained, and those who have done little, gain a lot. On the face of it, there is little harm in this, as long as it is confined to small consenting groups.

'But it isn't, and it's getting in the way of the general commercial progress of the planet, to a degree that is causing a great deal of instability.

'There is now a counter group setting itself up with the idea of trying to control the others and stop the spread of the cult. Trouble is, they are not having a lot of success, and are now resorting to arms.

'If we don't put a stop to this soon, there will be a wholesale war, and that will put them back several generations. We'll see what we can get from this chap, and then I would like you two plus Duffring to go and see just what is going on, and put a stop to it.

'As the same pattern seems to reoccur time and time again, and over vast periods of time with hardly a variation in the basic principles, it looks as if it could be some sort of outside interference, although we have not been able to trace it. The only other explanation I can think of is that there is something on the planet which triggers off the cult from time to time, but what that can be is beyond any ideas I have. This should be an interesting one for you gentlemen, and I almost wish I were coming with you.'

Jas and Hass looked at each other and then at Duffring.

'Where the hell do we start?' asked Hass, of no one in particular.

'At the beginning.' replied the calming voice of Duffring as he moved smoothly over to a readout console, his fingers flying over the touch keys.

'It looks as if this cult starts up every thirty to forty years, usually ending in a general punchup between the opposing factions, and then the whole thing calms down to just a few isolated groups and then dies out. It is the regularity of the reoccurrence that is puzzling though.'

'Let's see what we can extract from our friend, and then formulate a plan based on the whole of the data.' Hass said, and then realized he may have spoken out of turn.

Mutty strode over to the nearby readout console, and said, 'OK Jas, you're in charge of this one. Get Kranz to extract all he can, use Duffring if you have any obvious gaps in the data, and assimilate the whole lot with the stored data on the old records here.' He looked at the panel and then continued, 'Come up with an action plan, and we'll discuss it over our evening meal.' With that Mutty left the room, leaving a perplexed looking Jas standing on his own and with the others looking at him for instructions.

Taking a deep breath, He turned towards Kranz and said, 'Right, you do your thing, and try not to kill him in the process, then report back to me when you have all the data you think might be relevant.'

'Duffring, would you like to check back through the records and see if there is any particular area on the planet where the cult seems to originate from, and if there is, then get as much detail of the terrain in that area as possible.

'Look out for any buildings which might have been there for a long period of time and have a special significance to the locals. Hass and I will act as co-ordinators of the data, trying to find a pattern which runs through the whole series of events.' He felt pleased with himself, not a bad start he thought.

By midday, the poor creature in the chair had offered up all he could remember that was relevant to the questions asked, and volunteered several ideas of his own, being totally overwhelmed by so much science and gadgetry. Duffring had done a good job of laying out the sequence of reoccurring incidents of the 'share it all' cult.

He had managed to locate several major areas where it had taken hold particularly strongly. Pinpointing where it originated from was proving a little more difficult, but there was a suggestion of 'Gurus' coming in out of the wilderness, having seen the 'light' and determined that all should bathe in its glory.

What caused most surprise was the speed with which the cult spread, and the willingness of so many to apparently lose so much during the periodic share out.

The Pundits didn't seem to gain much from the spread of the cult, or so it seemed, unless there was something else going on which the team hadn't as yet discovered.

By the end of the day, the 'guest' had seen the error of his ways and beliefs, and was quite happy to return home and spread the good news that the cult was not such a good idea for the many reasons he had had explained to him.

The only danger was that he might get a little over zealous and join the other lot and take up a cudgel. It was eventually deemed that it was safe for him to be returned, but the memory of his stay in the mountain would have to be wiped clean. A job for Duffring.

Come evening, all the data which seemed relevant to the case was collated and placed before Mutty, who between mouthfuls of food and slurps of liquid, grew more and more excited.

'It looks as if you boys have cracked it.' he said, a half eaten piece of food stopping on it's way up to his mouth while the words tumbled out.

'The main origin of the gurus seems to be a barren range of hills set in the middle of the main continent. Even allowing for the diverse paths they have taken, it looks as if they all came from roughly the same area.'

'I suppose we shall have to visit the place then.' Hass sounded a little reluctant at the thought, but knew it was inevitable really if they were to solve the mystery of the reoccurrences.

'Yes, I think that's the only way we shall solve the mystery once and for all.   If we can find the actual cause of what inspires the Gurus to go forth and upset the status quo, then we should be able to do something about it.' Mutty replied.

It was finally decided that the team comprising Hass, Jas and Duffring should leave next evening for the third world from the sun, and then contact the local team to see if they had managed to gather any more information about the cult.

Overland transport should be available locally, and it would then just be a matter of visiting the area they had singled out to see what they could find.

Most of the information they thought they might need was sifted out from the huge pile of data they had gathered, and condensed down to a more manageable form. Maps of the area of interest were acquired from the main archives and duplicated in case they might help in locating any strange anomalies which could lead to the cult's starting place.

Although there was little of fine detail on them, they at least could be used as guides to get the team into the local area and from then on it would be a case of look and learn as you go.

Jas wanted to know how they would get there, and Hass told him that they had their own local shuttles which could operate well within the distance required.

They would leave in the evening so as not to draw too much attention to the operation, and the landing would coincide with nightfall at their destination point, at least according to Duffring's calculations.

According to Mutty, there was an old seeker station set in the desert area just north of one of the little towns which had been troubled by the new cult, and although it hadn't been used very much of late, the old man who ran it was well versed in local folklore and should be able to help.

Hass went back to the old records to see if he could find anything else on the matter of cults which suddenly sprang up and to make sure they hadn't missed any vital bits of information in their first search.

He didn't find anything much to speak of except an old report of 'untold riches' to be found if you followed the signs, but the tale didn't relate directly to the cult data, so it was put aside as 'possibly of interest' as most cultures had something similar in their makeup.

Jas went over the data they had extracted from the little hairy man to see if there were any obvious gaps in the flow of what he said, but could find nothing of significance. They had milked the poor man dry of anything related to the cult and if they had pushed it any further, he would have had to resort to making up what he thought they wanted to hear.

Kranz was all for putting a little more pressure on their 'guest', but Mutty explained that he didn't think there was any more to be gained from the man as he seemed to have volunteered the information quite willingly.

Kranz showed his displeasure at not being able to exercise his not inconsiderable skills by pulling a long face and vacating the room without a word.

'You know,' said Mutty, 'I think he's getting to be more human by the day!'

The evening meal took a lot longer than usual, as the eating process kept being interspersed with theories and ideas put forward by everyone in turn.

Discussions of what they would do and what they might find went on well into the late evening, most of which was sheer speculation, as they really had very little to go on, apart from what they had gleaned from the hairy little man in the chair.

According to him, a guru had come out of the desert doing all sorts of magical tricks to attract attention, and then proceeded to sell the idea of fair shares for all. To those who had little because they had made no effort to acquire anything very much, the idea seemed a dream come true, and these then formed the hard-core of the band of savants who would then tour the countryside, spreading the good word.

The little hairy man had been recruited in the second phase of the operation, and was therefore as close as anyone to an actual instigator of the cult this time around. If they could track down the person who had recruited him, then they stood a chance of finding out what had triggered off his interest in the whole set-up, or at least that was the theory.

By the time they had exhausted all possibilities, it was late into the night, and Hass and Jas had great difficulty in settling down to sleep, as new variations of what they might do kept cropping up in their minds.

Eventually they got to sleep, but within minutes, or so it seemed, dawn was upon them, and reluctantly they prised themselves out of their beds and prepared to greet the day as best they could.

Their bleary eyes prompted a few choice remarks from Mutty, who couldn't pass up a chance to make a joke, while Duffring just smiled at them, and that was even worse as he looked as cool as ever, and probably hadn't missed a single wink of sleep.

By early evening all was ready for their departure, and Mutty led the way down several levels to a main tunnel complete with its transport machine.

The mobile sped off into the darkness with it's cargo of travellers, who were a little perturbed as there was no lighting in the tunnel, and this only magnified the apparent speed they were doing. There were several lurching changes of direction before they were thrown forward in their seats as the mobile lost speed rapidly and slithered to a halt.

'Duffring will be your pilot, as he has done this journey many times in the past, and is really very good at it.'

Turning to Hass, Jas said, 'Why is he making a point of that when he knows we are not trained for flight and Duffring is the only person who could fly the damn thing anyway? Is he trying to reassure us knowing that Duffring isn't a proper pilot, but is quite good at it anyway?'

Before Hass could answer, they were hustled into the long sleek craft, the box containing the 'hairy one' being already strapped down in place, and the hatch closed behind them.

Hass and Jas exchanged looks, sat back and slammed the safety harness clasps home simultaneously. What they didn't expect was that the shuttle promptly turned through ninety degrees into the vertical position and accelerated upwards, pushing them back into their seats and distorting their faces beyond recognition, not that it mattered one jot as their eyes were pressed back into their sockets and their vision was too distorted to be of any use anyway.

The most unnerving thing was that there was very little sound apart from a deep swishing noise as the air was being forced up ahead of the ever accelerating craft. Suddenly the pressure eased off and they were out in free air, or was it space?

They were enclosed in a jet blackness neither had known for some time, as there was nothing to be seen from the forward viewing position at all.

The next moment the forward view bay was full of bright and twinkling stars, brilliant diamonds of pure light blazed out to them and a voice with a smile in it said, 'Sorry about that, I forgot to put the internal low level lights on when we took off. Bet you wondered where you were for a moment.'

They would have forgiven Duffring if it hadn't been for the smile in the voice. Jas and Hass looked at each other, and without saying a word, both knew that one day they would even the score.

The stars slowly wheeled across the viewing screen as the craft, still under a somewhat reduced acceleration, sped on towards its goal.

'We're on automatics now, and there is little to do until we reach the outer atmosphere of the planet, so we may as well go over the opening stages of our approach to the guru our friend told us about, that's if we can find him among all the other acolytes.'

Duffring had casually left his control seat and joined the others as if this was an everyday happening, like taking a meal or some other mundane action.

By the time they had reached the orbit of the third planet in from the sun, they had refined their approach to what they thought would be the ultimate in tact, and were feeling very pleased with themselves.

Hass asked where the third planet was exactly, and Duffring explained that there was little to see of it as it was on the opposite side of its orbit with regard to them, and would only show up as a bright star.

'One thing I don't quite understand,' Jas said 'is why do we have to keep undercover, as it were? The inhabitants of all three planets must know what we are doing on their worlds, surely?'

'Well, yes and no.' Duffring looked a little uneasy. 'It's to do with the way things were set up a very long time ago. When the Confederation begins to trade with a new world, we wait until we are approached by them, enquiring how we seem to be such a stable outfit.

'Bit by bit, we tell them how we achieved the stability in our people, and it's not long after that that we usually get the request for help. It was found that the fewer who knew about what was going on in the beginning, the better the system worked, until, of course it really got underway, and then when it became general knowledge, everyone pitched in to help as the benefits to all became apparent.

'The exact working of the system differs from world to world, but that is the basic method used. Where we are going, only the top brass know what is happening, as the main body of the two races seem to be a little slow on the uptake, as it were.'

'But surely, if everyone was told what was going on, it would speed up the whole operation.' Jas commented.

'One might think so, but look at it from another angle. You would warn all those who's sole purpose it is to cause disruption of one sort or another that they were on the hunted list to be removed from the system, and then they would keep out of sight and make the clean up so much more difficult.'

'No, I think it works quite well as we have it now. Maybe in the future, we will find another method, but we'll stick to that which we know works well, for the time being.'

Duffring was looking more and more uncomfortable as he talked on, so Jas reasoned that there was something Duffring was not saying, or was reluctant to disclose to them.

'How are we going to get our little friend in the box to track down the guru who got him started on his crusade?' Hass asked.

'That shouldn't be too difficult if we are careful. He will remember nothing of his capture or journey to our world. He will wake up with all memories of the event well covered up, and will probably think he has had a little memory loss or something.

'Persuading the guru to co-operate might be a different story, but I have the clearance to use any means in my power to get the job done, and quickly. Locating the guru will be the most difficult part of the job, as we have to rely on our friend to recognize him in the first place, after that it should be fairly easy.'

With that, Duffring went forward again, presumably to make a course correction, or just to get out of answering a question he didn't want to answer for the time being.

Jas had a little difficulty moving around smoothly in the virtual lack of gravity, while Hass had obviously been out in space many times before as his dexterity in manoeuvring about the shuttle proved, leaving Jas feeling a little inadequate in that department.

A sudden slight lurch to one side indicated that a course correction had been achieved either by Duffring or the automatics, and Duffring came back into the main compartment to advise them that a landing was not far away and that they should make sure they were strapped in securely.

Another sideways movement caused the two passengers to hastily take their seats and apply their restraining straps.

'It might be a little bit bumpy coming in to land.' Duffring's voice floated back to them from the pilot's position, accompanied by a faint whistling noise as the shuttle cut into the planet's atmosphere.

There were several shuddering shocks and violent sideways movements, before the craft steadied in its downward plunge to the surface below. The noise built up to an ear piercing scream and then they were rotated through one hundred and eighty degrees as the craft positioned itself for the actual landing.

There was one final thump and then silence, apart from the odd creak of cooling metal and the rustle of Duffring's holding straps being thrown off.

'Come along gentlemen, we've landed. Let's get our little friend out and back to normality so that we can set up the meeting for tomorrow.'

'Doesn't waste a lot of time, this Duffring chap, does he? Jas quietly commented to Hass as they disentangled themselves from the security harness.

Somehow the craft had landed within a building or been very quickly manoeuvred into one, for there was no sign of the sky above, and they were surrounded by very solid looking walls of rock.

As the exit door of the craft hissed open and lowered, they were greeted by an elderly man dressed in a long white cloak and a strange looking hat on his head.

'Welcome, my friends.' He said, and turning to Duffring adding, 'New members of the team?

'Yes.' replied Duffring, with his broadest smile. 'I'd like to introduce you both to my friend Kim, who apart from a little help from two natives of the planet, runs this little outfit all on his own.'

The elderly man bowed low, sweeping both arms out sideways, palms uppermost, so Jas and Hass not knowing what else to do, began to do likewise but an anticipating hand from Duffring restrained them from completing the movement.

'I'll explain later.' Duffring quietly hissed, and pushed the pair forward towards an opening in the wall ahead.

'Sorry about the rather rough ride down, but the shuttle is of a rather old type, it's still quite efficient but probably not the type you are used to.'

Duffring glanced over his shoulder to see the old man unloading the transporting box with the hairy one in it onto the shuttle's loading ramp, and pushed Jas and Hass into the hole in the wall and the passage beyond.

'The old man has been here so long he has taken on board some of the local customs, and made them his own, or so it would seem. As this is his place, and he is senior to you, he makes the first move.'

'The bow means that you are welcome to his house and all he possesses, while the outstretched arms shows that he carries no weapons and will therefore do you no harm.'

'You are supposed to accept his offer with a very slight bob of your head, any more than that, and he will have to make another gesture of even greater significance, and that would be embarrassing for him, as apart from grovelling flat on his face, there is little else he can do.'

Duffring had stopped as he reached the end of the passage, and turning said, 'Crowd together gentlemen, and we'll go up to the surface.' He touched something on the wall, and the floor area on which they were standing rose rapidly though a little shakily upwards into the shaft above.

'We have landed on the outskirts of the main inhabitable land mass, to the north it's just desert and rolling hills of rock and scrubland. I'm not too sure about the building we are about to enter, but I think it was here long before any of us came along.'

The old man has made it into a sort of temple of learning, giving the natives a helping hand with their technology, but only just ahead of what they could have worked out for themselves'.

'We have to be careful not to give too much help. A local race must advance at its own pace for stability, so care is needed in helping them.'

The platform juddered to a halt, and they stepped out into a brightly lit room, furnished with a few simple pieces of furniture, chairs, and a long table down the middle.

From the window they could see the rolling hills mentioned by Duffring, a barren landscape stretching out to the horizon terminating in a range of snow capped mountains.

'The old boy will be with us in a moment, he's probably getting his helpers to unload the equipment I brought with us and the box containing our little friend.

'Kim won't be actually helping us on this expedition, we'll just be using his place as a base to work from.' Duffring had seated himself in one of the chairs, and indicated that the others should do likewise.

Jas opened his mouth to ask a question, but before he could form the first word the lift platform in the corner of the room rattled it's way up to floor level and disgorged Kim, his two helpers, two boxes of Duffring's equipment and the box containing the hairy one.

Kim released the clasps on the box, and the limp form of the hairy one was gently placed in a chair.

Duffring moved behind the sleeping form, removing the ornate metallic head band from around its head, and quickly slipping it behind his back. As the incumbent's eyes opened, Kim moved towards him, doing the bow with outstretched arms and saying,

'You must have had a mystical experience, and passed out, but you are all right now, and among friends. Here drink this, and you will feel much better.' offering the hairy one a container of liquid, which was enthusiastically consumed in double quick time.

The hairy one was only too pleased to co-operate fully with regard to the questions asked about the new cult, and thought he had found some new converts by the interest shown by all present.

They managed to find out the approximate area where the guru was operating when the hairy one was picked up initially, and resolved to try picking up the trail at that point.

Next day the party set out, Kim seeing them off as Hass, Jas, Duffring and the hairy one climbed aboard one of the local mobiles, and headed off to the nearest small town.

It was an old model, and rattled and creaked as it made its way over the rough ground.

Looking back, Jas saw the tumbled ruins which comprised the home of Kim and his helpers, and smiled to himself at the thoroughness of the organization, no one would ever dream of the actual use the site was being put to, even if it had been suggested to them.

Upon reaching the little enclave of buildings, the hairy one was dispatched to try and find the guru, returning some time later to say that the wise one had moved on to the next town with a small entourage of keen followers, eager to spread the good news further afield.

'Well, if that's the good news, I don't think I want to hear the bad version.' said Duffring quietly, as they left the township, 'the place is in utter and total chaos, from what I can see of it.'

They had to spend the night in the cramped confines of the mobile, although the vehicle did have good lights, it was deemed too risky to continue the journey along the rough tracks in the pitch black of night, as the track was hardly discernible from the rest of the terrain in places.

By the late morning of the following day, the next group of buildings hove into sight. This was a much bigger complex of structures than the previous one they had visited, and many more people were milling around. Something had disturbed them, and a lot of shouting and waving of arms was going on.

'I don't like the look of this,' said Hass, 'it's not exactly a happy place, by the look of it.' His comment only extracted a grunt from Duffring, who swung the vehicle around in a circle, and headed back out to the fringe of the complex.

'Let's have a chat with the natives, and see what's going on.' he finally said.

They stopped the vehicle outside a ramshackle building, outside of which stood a very old man leaning on a stave and with a disgruntled look on his face.

The hairy one was dispatched to make enquiries, and returned later to inform them that the old man could recall the last time the 'good news' had come this way, and the ensuing disruptions it had caused.

Some of the older folk had tried to raise this point at the meeting held in the town square, and had been run out by the enthusiastic youngsters, who could see no further than the rather snub noses on their faces.

The hairy one looked a little disappointed at the revelations of the old man with the stave, but brightened up when it was decided to go back into town, and join in the meeting.

The site of the meeting was easy to find because of the noise generated by the enthusiastic crowd of followers.

There must have been a few dissenters left among them, for every now and again, a great shout of derision went up and a few elderly members of the meeting left, looking very worried and dejected.

'Lets move in and try and locate the guru.' said Jas, but the restraining hand of Hass stopped him short.

'Better stay on the periphery for a while until it calms down a bit, then we can move in and perhaps get an audience in person with him.'

The meeting went on for some time, the crowd milling about and growing in number as more people were attracted by the commotion. It was about mid afternoon before groups began to disperse, and the guru was left with the hard-core of his followers around him.

'Now's the time to move in.' said Duffring, moving forward and followed a little hesitatingly by the others.

Duffring's stature and very presence soon commanded the attention of the acolytes and he was shepherded into the inner circle and up to the guru, while the others stayed on the outskirts of the little crowd, trying to look excited about the new era of oneness that was about to dawn upon them.

'I have a meeting with the guru later this evening.' said Duffring, when he returned to the group. 'It's not going to be easy to get him on his own, but we'll have to do it somehow as he isn't saying very much about the origins of the cult at the moment, and that's what we need to know.'

They retired back to the mobile, had a quick meal from the provisions they had brought with them, and then tried to work out a means of getting the guru away from his little group of cohorts.

Duffring explained that he thought he might need to apply a little 'mind power' to extract the necessary data, and they would have to be ready for a quick get away if things went wrong, which caused a look of concern among the others.

The hairy one had been allowed to rejoin the other acolytes, as he seemed to be none the wiser about the true purpose of the team and would only be an encumbrance if he still remained with the group.

Time, as always in such circumstances, dragged, and the team began to get a bit edgy, except for Duffring, who if he did feel uneasy, certainly didn't show it.

As dusk began to close in, a grey clad youth approached them, and said that the guru would be pleased to see the leader of their group for a short while, and Duffring was escorted away leaving the other three in a state of doubt and apprehension.

It was pitch dark when they saw a cluster of lights moving towards them, and a tired looking Duffring flopped down on the edge of the mobile entrance hatch with a look of concern on his face. The light bearers left after many gesticulations, arm waving and happy smiles, the ensuing silence was almost solid.

'Well gentlemen, we have a tricky one on our hands, it seems that the guru is always accompanied by his closest acolytes, but he did let slip that he goes out into the waste lands to commune with something or other every now and again, so all we can do is keep watch and nab him if and when he does.'

'We'll have to be ready to move quickly and firmly, whisk him away and do what we have to, returning him hopefully in an undamaged state so as not to arouse too much suspicion of what we are up to. We'll move the vehicle between their encampment and the barren lands beyond, and hopefully if he does go for a little jaunt into the wilderness...'

They moved the vehicle as unobtrusively as possible to the point where they thought it would be best placed for their clandestine operation, and waited. For three days.

On the fourth evening, a lone robed figure could be seen walking out towards the distant low hills, and Duffring and Jas followed at what they considered to be a safe distance.

Instructions had been left for Hass to follow in the mobile some minutes later, but to keep well back and flash the lights if anyone else from the town followed the party.

Hass waited for what he thought was about the right time, started up the power unit, and gently eased the mobile into its traction mode. It made little noise at low speed, but he didn't dare go any faster as the lights couldn't be used for fear of attracting attention, and as it was almost dark it was getting harder to see where he was going.

As fear began to turn into sheer panic because Hass couldn't be sure if he was on the right track, two figures with another slumped between them loomed out of the darkness.

'Quick, get him inside and let's get the hell out of here.' Duffring was in no mood for gentility, and a rather limp guru was bundled unto the vehicle, the main lights switched on, and they were off into the foothills as fast as it was deemed safe to go, Hass complaining that the noise of the vehicle alone would bring the rest of the township out looking.

With the main headlights swung as low as they would go, so as to only illuminate the immediate ground before them, they rattled on into the darkness, the odd large stone throwing the vehicle one way or another until Hass had had enough, and called out,

'Cut the damn speed, no one is going to catch up with us now. Anyway, we'd see 'em coming a mile away as they would have to use lights as well. I've got more bruises than a Quailian punch bag.'

The vehicle reduced speed and before long it was considered that they had gone far enough to be safe from interference from any one who had any notions of trying to follow them.

'Now begins the tricky bit.' said Duffring. 'Strap him into one of the seats and I'll bring him round. We don't want him fully conscious, just awake enough for the questions to register and hopefully get some answers.'

Using just one of the interior low level lights, the others stood well back in the shadows and watched as Duffring began his quest.

Fishing about in one of the equipment boxes he had brought with him, Duffring extracted a small metallic looking headband, and placed it upon the guru's head. A slight adjustment of the knobs and buttons on it brought the response he had been looking for, as the guru's eyes half opened.

The questioning was long and boring, with each question being repeated but in a rephrased sense, so that comparisons could be made between answers to even out any anomalies or evasions put up by the guru. Jas and Hass had long since left the vehicle and were sitting outside on the ground when Duffring came out.

'May I ask you to wear these headbands and take a long walk over that way, I'm going to have to use a little pressure to get the final data we need, and you may well be effected by what I'm going to do.'

'He'll be all right, afterwards, I mean?' asked Jas, none too keen to have the township after their blood if a battered guru was returned to them.

'Yes, I haven't lost an interrogatee yet, although some are a little confused afterwards.' Duffring retorted with a chuckle in his voice.

As they put their headbands on and stumbled off into the rock strewn darkness, Hass said 'I don't think that was a genuine funny remark, I think Duffring really has a tough case on his hands, and he'll stop at nothing to get results. That could leave us in a rather nasty position, unless we can spirit the remains of the guru away should we need to.' Jas said nothing, but thought about the possible consequences for a while.

The pair had been sitting on a rocky outcrop for some time when the vehicle lights flashed once in the far distance, and they made their way back to see if Duffring had been successful or dropped them all into a situation of jeopardy.

When they entered the vehicle they could see an exhausted Duffring sitting slumped in one of the seats and the guru still strapped in another. His forehead was bathed in sweat, some of which had trickled down to dampen the collar of his robe, while a thin trickle of blood ran from one nostril and curved down to intersect his lips, and having filled the small gap there, ran on down to join his sweaty collar.

'Are you all right, Duffring?' asked an anxious Jas.

'Yes, I'm fine, or I will be in a moment or two - Is the guru still breathing?'

'Yes, or at least his chest is still moving, although he looks even more battered than you do.' replied Jas.

'I'm not surprised,' added Hass, 'he was on the receiving end, poor sod. Anyway, did you get all the data we need?'

'Yes, but you won't believe it, or at least you may have difficulty in making sense of it. Let's get things stabilized again and our friend here returned to his people, and I'll go through what I've found out so far.'

The unfortunate guru was cleaned up, although they couldn't do a lot with the collar of his cloak, except sponge a little of the blood stain out of it.

Duffring recovered very quickly and was his usual smiling self as they finished tidying up the recipient of his labours, and they then set off for the little township to return their borrowed guru.

Getting into the outskirts of the town was no problem, and by the lack of activity, the guru hadn't been missed by anyone, as yet. But what to do with him? This they hadn't thought out, so the mobile was stopped just short of the first buildings, and parked in the shadow of one of the larger blocks.

'We can't just bundle him out to stagger around on his own,' was Jas's concern, 'he'll need some reason for being somewhere else to that which he remembers from earlier this evening, also an explanation for the bloodstained collar of his cloak.'

'We could take him back to where we picked him up, and make it look like an accident, that's if Duffring can add a little to his memory to that effect.' Hass said.

'Yes, I can do that, it will only take a few minutes, and it's a very good idea. In fact it's the only idea we have at the moment which seems feasible. Good work Hass.'

They turned the mobile around and headed back the way they had come, looking for the spot where they picked up the unfortunate guru.

'I doubt if we can find the exact spot where we found him, but I don't suppose it will matter much as long as we are somewhere in the general area.' Hass was driving the vehicle with the lights slung low again, and straining his eyes to pick up the faint track.

Some while later after much grumbling and muttering, he let out a yell, 'Hey, this is where you two left the mobile and went on foot, I recognize the rock formation over there where I waited. You must have picked him up somewhere ahead.'

'OK, this will do.' said Duffring, and Hass cut the power to the drive unit.

'We have one small problem, and that is to make it look as if he tripped over something and banged his head. I can give him a memory of that, but making it look convincing is going to be difficult.' Duffring looked at the other two for ideas, and Jas came to the rescue with,

'How about we whack his foot with a stone to give it a nice bruise and do likewise to his nose, which has already bled, and let some of the blood trickle onto a convenient lump of rock?'

'I see our genteel young apprentice is learning the wicked ways of the world at long last,' commented Duffring, 'but joking aside, that's a good idea, and we may well get away with it. OK, this spot will do, give his foot the treatment, then make his nose bleed over that block of stone, and then lay him down as if he had landed on it, nose first.'

There were no volunteers for the foot bashing, so Jas was left with the job as it was his idea in the first place.

The body was laid out in what they thought to be a realistic pose, and they all stood back in the subdued light of the head lamps to survey their handiwork.

'Looks pretty good to me,' said Duffring, 'anyway, he'll wake up with a bit of a head and so will not be too concerned with the authenticity of the scene, I would suspect.'

'Right, you two put the headbands on again and take the mobile down the track a short distance, I'll give our friend his memory of a fall, and join you in a moment. I have already blocked out his memory of the interrogation.'

Hass and Jas didn't have to wait for long before a panting Duffring jumped into the vehicle and said, 'Right gentlemen, let's get out of here in case the whole thing blows up in our faces.' and with that they moved off into the darkness, skirting the little town ahead, and set course for Kim's retreat in the foothills.

They took it in turns to drive, so easing the not inconsiderable eye strain caused by the rough and faint track, but as dawn broke, the tension eased, and the inevitable question was asked by Hass.

'You haven't told us what you found out from the guru yet.' Duffring didn't reply for a while, and when he did it wasn't with his usual jocular tone.

'Who or whatever gave our friend the treatment, did a very good job of it. All I could get was a somewhat scrambled series of pictures of a rocky scene, a tunnel and a cave-like structure. He seemed to be drawn to the area, entered the tunnel and was then in the presence of a shrine-like construction. It spoke to him, as far as I can make out, and then there is a blank in the pictures.'

'The next thing I picked up was the first meeting held in a little town, and the spreading of the new cult ideas.'

'Doesn't give us much to go on, does it?' from Hass, who was now driving the vehicle.

'A little more than you think.' replied Duffring.

'Consider the time over which this cult thing has been going on. It can't be a living entity behind it as I don't know of anything which could live so long, so therefore it must be mechanical, or something approaching that kind of thing.'

'It would have to be in an area either well guarded from the casual observer or wanderer, so some means of deterring people from finding it must be in operation. So we will have to look for some place which has a taboo on it, or an area where no one wants to go because of some fear.'

'The other odd thing is the thirty to forty year reoccurrence of the cult. According to the records, it is quite regular, and that smacks of something more akin to a machine than a living entity.'

'But who would want to set up something like that in the first place?' asked Jas. 'It doesn't make much sense to me. There's no gain for anyone, especially for those who set it up, as it was so long ago.'

'That's all part of the mystery.' replied Duffring, who had now brightened up somewhat, and seemed to be enjoying the discussion.

Ideas were bandied back and forth for the rest of the journey back to Kim's place, and they finished up with more theories than answers, but were in a cheerful mood as they drove into the compound at long last.

After some food and a good night's rest, the pressure of finding the guru over and with Duffring's jovial quips interspersed in the conversation, the team felt more like their old selves once again, despite the disappointment of not locating the site of the cult's starting point.

This did not resolve the fact that they were faced with the almost impossible task of finding the 'indoctrination site' where the gurus were converted to do the will of whatever it was that did the indoctrination, but at least they felt better about it, and not quite so overwhelmed.

Kim brought out all the maps of the area which had been painstakingly made over his period of time at the station, but they found nothing which led them to believe that they had found the 'site' as there was little in the way of concise detail which they could recognize as a likely place to search.

They would have to find another method of locating the site, but so far, ideas on that were a little thin on the ground.

The next day Jas had an idea.

'How about if we send Kim's two local helpers out to the surrounding towns, and see if they can pick up any rumours of areas that are avoided by the locals, or places which have a history of being haunted or something like that?'

'Good idea, Jas.' said Duffring,

'What do you think of that Kim?'

'Best idea yet, in fact it's the only workable idea we've come up with, well done young man.' replied Kim, turning to Jas with a benign smile.

The two helpers were briefed on what to look out for, and warned not to make it too obvious to those they were interviewing. It would take several days, no doubt, so the rest of the team spent the time stocking the mobile with supplies and any equipment they thought they might need in their quest, going over the maps once again in case anything had been missed, and generally taking it easy. A busy time lay ahead.

Kim's two helpers returned four days later, with good and bad news.

The guru had returned to his people, and seemed none the worse for his experience, but of tales of forbidden lands, there was little to go on. There were several suggestions on an area fifty kilometres north of the station which no one liked to go to, mainly because there was nothing much there except bare rock and sand, but of any 'hauntings', there was no sign or mention.

One person interviewed spoke of a voice which called to him, telling him of untold riches if he were to go to a certain cave in the hills, but as this person was of a very simple nature, and seemed to be stoned out of his mind most of the time on a local brew, the helpers tended to discount his story.

'It doesn't give us much more to go on.' said Duffring, disappointment clearly showing in his voice and face.

'I suppose we could check out the area north of here and see if there is anything which might give us a clue.'

The local drunk who had offered the story of the 'untold riches' didn't indicate where the place was, so they had no reference for the location to tie in with any other bits of information they had obtained.

'We can't possibly cover the whole planet, and the only indication of anything unusual so far is the area just north of us, so let's go see what's there. The only alternative is to stay here, bemoaning our lack of progress, and generally making ourselves miserable.' Jas was going to take control at long last.

'OK, that seems about the best suggestion so far, let's do it. We'll set out tomorrow morning so that we get there in daylight and have a general scout around before it gets too dark. Next day we'll quarter the area and give it a good search.' Duffring at least sounded a bit more enthusiastic again.

Five:
The Pillars

THEY SPENT THE evening in Kim's private room, regaled by stories of the old days when he was a young apprentice, and of the strange happening which occurred from time to time, mainly when the planets seemed to line up, and that was every forty to fifty years, as far as they could tell.

It was Jas who spotted the possibility of the planets 'line up' tying up with the occurrence of the new cult, but there was little more in the way of facts to convince the rest of the team.

Jas, Hass and Duffring set out next day for the foothills, armed with copies of Kim's maps and every bit of data which they had managed to collect, which didn't amount to very much, once the obvious local folk law have been filtered out of the stories they had collected.

The initial part of the journey went smoothly enough, the track being well worn as it was a connecting link to the next town, but when they reached about one third of the way in what they thought was the correct direction, the going became considerably rougher, and great care was needed in order to keep the vehicle from being tipped over on some of the more stone strewn stretches they had to traverse.

It was a tired and bruised party which eventually reached the first steep incline up into the hills beyond the plain, and decided to make camp here for the rest of the day, as the going ahead looked very rough indeed.

During the night, they all had bad dreams, bordering on nightmares, and didn't feel as rested as they would have liked, but the excitement of what they might find spurred them on.

Breakfast was over by the time the sun broke the horizon, and they packed away their belongings, and then cleared the site of any sign that they had been there.

There was little or no track to follow now, it was just a matter of trying to steer the mobile along the least stone strewn part of the ever steepening rise up into the hilly land ahead.

A few sad looking wizened bushes struggled to grow on an almost barren soil which the wind had deposited between the larger rocks, and apart from a dark green creeper like plant, there was little other vegetation to be seen.

'Small wonder no one is keen to come here.' Jas said, swinging the mobile around a particularly large rock, and then promptly slammed on the brakes, sending the other two flying along the walkway between the seats. Having regained a small degree of composure, Duffring exclaimed,

'You could've given us a little warning, young man.' rubbing a bruised leg.

'Sorry about that, but look ahead.'

Before them stood a tall column of stone completely blocking their path, not a rock as such, but a pillar constructed of large pieces of rock, and very carefully put together.

'Now that is the work of man, by the look of it.' remarked Hass, who hadn't contributed much to the conversation for sometime. 'Let's have a close look at it.'

They left the vehicle, and as Jas was about to touch the column, Duffring reached out and knocked his hand away.

'Wait, you don't now anything about it, and it may not be what it seems. It's too prominent for my liking, and obviously been put here for a purpose.'

They skirted around the stone column, but it was just the same from which ever angle they looked at it. Duffring withdrew a small metallic tubular device from a pocket and applied it to one eye.

'What on earth is that.' asked Hass.

'Oh, it's a very old fashioned viewing enhancer.' replied Duffring, twiddling the ring at the end off the tube.

'As I thought, this column isn't quite what it purports to be. The stone at the top looks like all the others, but it's not. It is far too symmetrical for my liking, and there are signs of it having been shaped by something other than nature. Bring the mobile up a bit closer, and I'll climb up to get a better view of that top stone.'

Jas moved the mobile up as close to the column as possible and then Duffring scrambled up onto the top of the vehicle, walking along to the end nearest the column with an air of purpose.

'There's a small pointer carved into the top of the stone, and it indicates that direction' he pointed up the slope with an arm.

'Get a map out and try and find our position on it, then I'll give you a more accurate direction which we can enter on the map. I think it may well lead us onto something.'

A map was found which had a vague resemblance to the area in which they were, and Duffring having got the others to confirm that it was orientated correctly, indicated the exact direction the arrow on the top stone denoted.

'Now, we'll have to be careful about this, but one of us will have to touch the column to see if it responds in the way I think it will. So who's going to do it?

Jas moved forward, raising his hand.

'Stop.' called Duffring, 'I want you to only touch it briefly, just a glancing stroke, and then stand well back and notice anything you consider out of the ordinary that happens.'

Jas suddenly looked a bit nervous, but having committed himself, felt he couldn't withdraw his offer to touch the column.

Duffring and Hass stood well back from the stone pillar, while Jas reached forward and gave it a glancing smack with his hand, immediately stepping backwards, as if it would bite back.

There was very faint 'pinging' sound, and Jas staggered on his feet, as if something had given him a gentle push, putting him off balance.

'What happened Jas?' asked Duffring.

'Not quite sure, something seemed to pass through me, like a wave of energy and I felt very disorientated for a moment. I'm all right now, the feeling has gone completely. Odd that, can't say I liked it though.'

'I wouldn't mind betting that if you had kept contact with the column, you would have got an even bigger surprise.' said Hass, not wanting to be left out of the conversation.

'I think the column is a guiding beacon, perhaps leading on to the next one, and then on to what ever the constructors intended someone to find.' Duffring said, 'and if you had kept in touch with it, you may well have got some sort of compulsion to follow the direction indicated, as many others have, it would seem.

'We can follow the direction now that we have it on the map, but without the control of who or whatever put it here in the first place, which puts us one step ahead, or at least I hope it does.' Duffring added a little doubtfully.

'Right, let's follow up the trail and see where it leads us, anyone want to take bets it's another column?' There were no takers of Jas's offer.

The mobile rumbled and shuddered it's way up the slope, the occupants holding on as best they could to whatever came to hand, and were relieved when they reached the upper level, which proved to be a little less stony.

Several kilometres later another stone column hove into sight, and they approached it a little warily, just in case it reacted in some unexpected way. No one was taking any chances at the moment.

Duffring got out his image intensifier and confirmed his theory that there was indeed a pointer on the top of this column too. The direction was marked down on the map, and they swung the vehicle around onto the new route.

'Before we go tanking off, let's see if this one also has an effect on us.' Duffring looked at Jas and smiled,

'Hmmm ... all right, I don't suppose it will do any permanent damage to me.' he said, with little conviction in his voice.

Jas walked up to the column and gave it a slap as before, but this time he didn't stagger.

'Didn't feel anything this time,' he said, 'but I did get the idea of something nice if we go on ahead, something I have always wanted, but I don't know what.'

'Looks as if we are on the right trail after all, any bets as to what we'll find next?' still Jas got no takers.

A third column came into view after another hour's bumpy ride, but only elicited a rather bored proclamation from Hass 'Here we go again.'

This stone pillar also indicated a direction, up into the higher hills region, and they wondered if they could get the mobile up there.

'We'll have to, as we can't lug all the equipment up, who knows how far it will be to the next pillar or what ever is at the end of the trail.' Hass was not known for his athletic abilities, and wasn't keen to improve on those that existed by carrying heavy weights up a mountainside, so he volunteered to take over the driving.

Several times, as they wound their way up the hillside, they had to get out and manhandle some of the larger stones and rocks out of the way of the mobile, but eventually they reached the next plateau and Duffring called for a rest from the buffeting and exertion of the climb.

Ahead of them was a huge cliff face, completely barring any further progress.

'As we can't go any further, it looks as if we have arrived at the place intended by the 'whatever', so after a bite to eat, let's get looking for anything out of the ordinary.'

Jas was feeling more confident now that he had contributed to the expedition by bravely touching the stone columns when no one else wanted to.

They sat around the mobile on some convenient stones, none of which 'pinged' or gave them any odd feelings, and took an early evening meal as the sun began it's slow drop over the rocky horizon above them.

Jas had walked over to the cliff face after the meal break, while leaving the others just sitting there, resting after the arduous journey up the hillside.

The cliff was made of a different kind of stone to the surrounding ground, almost as if it had been thrust up from deep within the hillside, to stand as a sentinel for all to see. Walking to one end of the cliff Jas soon realized that there was no way around it, and the way up was barred to anyone, even on foot. A quick check on the other end confirmed their earlier conclusion that this was indeed the end of the trail, if trail it was.

'I think we had better leave the exploring to the hard light of day.' a rather tired Duffring said. 'We can't afford to make any mistakes at this point, and who knows what this place is supposed to be.'

'There may be nothing to find, or the timing is wrong to trigger off whatever is supposed to happen, but I for one, want all my senses about me when we start poking around. It smacks of something rather alien, somehow.'

It was agreed by all that a good night's sleep was required to restore their full faculties, which next day would be put to the full test by this strange place. Surprisingly, sleep came easily, with few dreams to speak of, although Hass said he thought he could hear voices as he was drifting off.

The sun heaved itself over the distant horizon, but by then the team had eaten, attended to their ablutions and were ready for whatever the day might hold for them.

'We had better start at one end of the cliff, and inspect it very closely for anything unusual, as there is nothing else of interest on the plateau itself.' Jas was taking command again, and the others seemed quite happy with his decision.

They worked their way along from the far end where the cliff went up vertically to meet the sky, and with a sheer drop down to the next plateau at its edge.

The plateau itself was half moon shaped, with the widest part where the mobile had clambered up the day before.

Although it was obvious in retrospect, they found what they were looking for almost opposite the point where they had arrived earlier. Somehow in the gloom of the previous evening, or maybe it was the way the light refracted off the rock face, the opening in the cliff only became obvious when they were actually upon it.

'Careful gentlemen,' called Duffring, 'let's check it over before we go in'. The opening was rather deeper than it looked from the outside, being about two metres in section, giving just enough headroom to stand up in, not that anyone was too keen to enter it.'

'I'm going to get a light beam to see what's at the end of the opening, as I can't focus my eyes on it.' Duffring called back as he went to the mobile. Quickly returning he turned on the light generator in his hand and played the beam into the cave's opening.

'There appears to be a solid block of stone of a different kind to the rest of the entrance, and it only shows up as different in artificial light, so we're not meant to see the difference, so that's why I couldn't focus on it.'

He slowly edged into the opening a short way.

'I don't suppose a wandering local would have a light generator.' added Hass, his voice taking on a hollow sound.

'One thought has crossed my mind, though,' Jas broke in, 'and that is it might be booby trapped in some way. Who ever put it here, wouldn't want just anyone to come barging in, so there must be some deterrent to keep out the 'unchosen' ones, so to speak, and that could well include us.'

'Our little lad is doing well in the thinking department.' Duffring quietly said to Hass, who nodded in agreement.

Jas picked up a large stone, and standing well back, threw it into the opening. It just rattled along the rocky ground and hit the solid wall at the back of the cave, and lay there.

'I think it would need something warm blooded to trigger off whatever is to be triggered off,' Duffring commented, 'and I don't think we should be it.'

'So how are we going to get into the place, if place there is at the end of the tunnel? Hass was showing a small degree of impatience in his voice.

'The only safe way in is to cut a parallel tunnel to bypass the door, that's if it's a door in the first place, and then go in at right angles to meet up with the tunnel beyond, so bypassing any gimmicks to do with the door.'

'How the hell are we going to cut into solid rock like that?' exclaimed an astonished Hass.

'I have a small laser cutter in the mobile, it shouldn't take too long to get in.' and with that Duffring almost ran to the vehicle to retrieve the necessary cutting equipment.

Setting up a small portable screen a few metres away from the cliff face, he pushed the tripod mounted laser through a hole in the screen and advised the other two to stand well to one side and not look at the machine or the cliff face, because of laser light bounce.

'How will that cut a hole big enough for us to get in?' asked Jas, not used to such equipment.

'It has a very tightly focused beam of considerable intensity, and is pulsed. It will cause the rock surface to expand rapidly and then flake off in quite large pieces, rather than a cutting action. It won't take long, believe me.'

Duffring fiddled with the controls, and then nearly tripped over the power cable which snaked back to the mobile. This unintentional error eased the mounting tension, and then Duffring made a final adjustment to the instrument, and pressed the button.

A nearly invisible staccato series of light pulses flickered out from the machine, and the rock surface gave way to the far superior force directed at it, coming away in a series of large flakes, to fall in a heap beside the cave opening.

When a large pile of rock fragments had piled up, and were hindering the progress of further cutting, Duffring asked the other two to get some implements from the mobile and clear away the debris.

Glad of something to do, Hass and Jas joined in willingly, making the odd joke about labouring for a living, while those of superior intelligence looked on.

Once the stone flakes were cleared, the laser got to work again and soon a deep opening had been made besides the cave entrance.

By midday, Duffring was actually inside the new opening, and had begun to direct the laser towards the side wall of the tunnel he had cut, his progress impressing Jas and Hass greatly.

Late afternoon saw the actual breakthrough into the tunnel beyond the stone door in the cave, and the cutting equipment was withdrawn and returned to the mobile.

'Tempted as I am to go in, I think we will do as we did yesterday, and take a rest before we enter the cliff. Tomorrow will be soon enough.' Duffring, as usual was right, and the others agreed.

'It should be safe enough to go in, as any detection system would have been triggered by the door being forced, and we have now bypassed the door and it's system, if it existed.'

'But caution must be our watchword, there is no one to help us out if we hit trouble, and who knows what's in there.'

The evening meal was gulped down rather than eaten in the excitement of the preceding events, and Jas suffered an upset stomach, and the consequent dreams which go with it, or was it something else causing the strange pictures?

However, next morning saw them all looking chirpy and ready for what could well be the most dangerous part of their mission.

By now all three had portable light emitters, and the beams sparkled off the shattered rock surface as Duffring and the others gingerly entered the new entrance he had cut into the cliff face.

'Seems all right so far.' he called back, his voice echoing with an odd hollow quality about it.

'I am now in the actual tunnel behind the door, and there is some odd looking mechanism tucked away in one corner which doesn't look as if it has anything to do with a door opening. It may be the deterrent we thought might be there, so don't touch it.'

Jas was next into the tunnel, followed by Hass eagerly close on his heels. When they were all in the original passageway made by the 'whoever', it was decided that only one should go in any distance, and then check out the area very carefully before the others joined him.

Volunteers for the leadership of the party were not offered by Duffring or Hass, not so much out of cowardliness, but because they wanted to play their part in getting Jas to take the initiative where possible, as long as the danger was not too great.

Duffring took a small cylindrical object from his belt and handed it to Jas.

'What's this?'

'It's a water vapour generator, very simple really. Just a container with a little water in it and a small ultrasonic unit underneath it. A power pack supplies the energy when you press the button on the side, vaporising the water and driving it out in a little jet. A small amount of di-ethyl chlorozene and a pinch of chloro-tri-bolamine added to the water causes the vapour to fluoresce and give out a light we can see when exposed to infra red or ultra violet light.'

'Most detection systems I've come across use invisible light where ever possible, and this little gadget will advise us of their presence.'

Taking the canister, Jas stepped forward and took a few faltering steps down the tunnel, looking to each side as he did so and pressing the vaporising button.

The light played on something at the tunnel end, but they were too far away to see any details. Metre by metre, the party crept along the passageway, making sure there were no surprises on the way, until Jas was in visual range of the tunnel end.

'It could be another door.' Jas called back to the others, 'I'll get a little closer to make sure.' Hardly had the words left his mouth when the tunnel around the suspected door began to glow in a pale violet light, and all three beat a hasty retreat back down the passage.

'I think it was triggered by our presence.' Duffring called from the rear of the party.

'Go back and see if it comes on again, and then check the area around it with the vapour can. If there is a detector beam, it should show up.'

Very carefully Jas moved forward, and at a critical point the violet glow lit up the new doorway clearly for all to see.

Jas activated the vapour can, and a small puff of water vapour rose up to the roof of the passage, illuminating twin beams of purple light cutting across the width of the passage.

'There's your trigger point.' said Duffring, a satisfied look on his face.

Once all three had gathered a couple of metres from the door, they both looked to Jas to make the next move and go forward to see if he could open it.

As he took a step towards it, the doorway shimmered and disappeared. They were looking into a large hall or room, the walls of which were hard to define as they seemed to shimmer and dissolve in a continuous swirling movement of light pulses, only to reform slightly differently in the next second.

'What the hell is this?' a startled Jas retorted.

They all stood there fascinated by the display of the continuous reforming structure of the room, no one wanting to enter such an unpredictable area but knowing some one had to.

'OK, I'll go in.' said Jas, but with little enthusiasm in his voice.

'Let's attach a length of cord to you first, just in case you lose control of your movements, and whatever it is in there takes over.' and so saying Duffring passed a length of fine rope to Jas who tied it around his waist, passing the other end back to Hass.

'Here goes, then.' Jas stepped into the doorway, and was engulfed in the swirling patterns of light.

The other two could see him clearly as he walked a few paces into the room, but the indefinable walls stayed the same, pulsing and twisting about with a life of their own.

Jas looked at a scene he could hardly believe. Ahead of him stretched the garden of his home with the rolling hills gently undulating into the distance.

In front of him was his swing, hanging from the fruit tree in the middle of the lawn. He remembered his father making the swing for his seventh birthday, and he couldn't wait to get on it and swing himself up into the lower branches of the tree.

He stepped forward again to reach for the swing seat, and was suddenly jerked out of his trance-like state by a tug on the cord.

The gentle pull on the cord guided Jas back into the passage, where an anxious Hass gave him a couple of light slaps around the face to make sure he was out of the trance.

Jas told the others what he had seen, and the urge to get on the swing as he had done in his early youth.

'We only saw you walk into the room, surrounded by the swirling whatever it is that seems to fill the space in there.

'It's your turn, Hass, tie the cord on, and as you go in I want Jas to follow you a few paces behind with the vapour can. Play it above his head, I've got an idea.' and so saying, Duffring moved to the back of the little party.

To say that Hass was a little reluctant to enter the chamber, is a grammatical kindness, but he did, with Jas a couple of metres behind him, the vapour can sending a thin jet of cloudy vapour over Hass's head.

The water vapour soon lit up a beam of light which followed Hass's progress towards the centre of the room, and Duffring called out for them to return.

'As I thought, whoever enters the room has their movement monitored, and presumably when the right position is reached, something happens. What did you see Hass?' asked Duffring.

'When I was at collage, I obtained the 'Chair of Honour' for a term. It's just about the highest award a student can get, and I remember the tremendous thrill as I sat down in that throne-like chair with the admiration of all the other students flowing around me. I saw the chair, and as far as I was concerned, I was back there, and wanted to sit in the chair again. I can't get over how real it seemed'. Hass seemed too stunned to say any more.

'There's something in the middle of the room, I couldn't see it clearly, but it looks like a seat of some kind with something else surrounding it, like lots of tree branches. I only saw it very briefly, just as Hass turned to return to the passage.' Jas looked as stunned as

Hass had done, and vigorously shook his head as if to clear something intangible away.

'Right. It's my turn, let's have the cord.' and Duffring walked into the indoctrination chamber.

This time Hass followed Duffring into the swirling space, playing the vapour dispenser above Duffring's head to track the light beam which followed his every movement.

Duffring went a little further into the chamber than the others, and turned as if to sit down, when Jas gave the cord a good firm tug which nearly toppled Duffring over.

A constant pull was needed to extract Duffring from whatever it was that held his attention in the chamber, and he returned to the passageway even more dazed than Hass.

'The chair-like thing in the middle of the room showed up quite clearly just as Duffring turned to sit down. They aren't tree branches you saw Jas. They look like tendrils or tubes of some sort, and I wouldn't mind betting that if you sat in that chair, they would wrap around you and hold you there until the equipment had done whatever it is designed to do.' Hass got it all out in one long breath, as if fearful that it might disappear from his memory if he gasped for air midway.

By now, Duffring had regained his senses a little, and although a bit dazed still, confirmed the chair-like link between each of their experiences.

'I think I've worked out the sequence of events deployed by the equipment here. Somehow, the first pillar selects a suitable person for the indoctrination process, and guides him on to the next pillar, eventually winding up at the cave entrance.

'If all criteria are met, the cave opens to admit the unfortunate, and he progresses on down to this doorway, where he is drawn in, and is assailed by pictures from his mind of a moment of great joy or excitement from earlier times.'

'All our incidents involved a chair of some sort, and it looks like a chair-like structure is in the middle of that space in there.'

'The tube-like things you described, but which I didn't see, are I would think, some means of restrainment, and possibly also involved in the actual indoctrination process. Having given the chosen one a new set of ideals, and no doubt covered over all traces of his experience in the chamber, he is returned to the outside world, where he goes forth and does his thing.'

'What do we do about this place?' asked Jas, who was visibly shaken by the implications of what they had found.

'The first thought is to destroy it, but let's think again before we act too hastily.'

'This is a technology somewhat different from ours or anything I have come across so far. We could no doubt learn a lot from it, if we can dismantle it bit by bit, and render it safe. I will report back, and I expect a team will be sent down to do just that.' With that, Duffring sat down on the floor of the passage, and leaned against the wall, deep in thought.

'According to Kim's account of the cult, it has been going on for a very long time, right back into their earliest recorded history, so who or what would want to set up such an elaborate system, and for what ends? I can't see what anyone could gain from this set-up, and gain of some sort is usually the driving force behind most things.' said Hass, who then joined Duffring sitting against the wall.

'Well,' said Jas, 'there is little more to be gained from staying here, and I'm certainly not going to try the chair just now, thanks very much, just in case either of you two though it might be a good idea.'

Duffring chuckled, having now recovered most of his composure.

'No, I don't think it would gain us much to have you trotting around the countryside, spouting forth about equal shares for all, quite apart from the fact that such is just about unobtainable in society.

'I think the best thing is to collapse the roof over the entrance of our new tunnel to discourage any wanderers who might just pass this way, and report back to those who make decisions on such matters.'

With that they gathered up their bits and pieces, and withdrew from the alien complex, Duffring using the laser to bring down the roof of the new entrance they had made as a passing gesture to those who might accidentally follow in their footsteps.

On the return journey, Duffring suggested that they remove the guiding stone from the top of the first pillar, just to make sure no other unfortunate should be lured into committing himself into the new cult.

Going down some of the steeper slopes proved more hazardous than the journey up, and it was a very battered and bruised trio who finally reached the first pillar, the intent to dismantle the pointing stone somewhat depleted, but Jas manoeuvred the vehicle into position, and Duffring climbed up to see what was needed to dislodge the stone.

'I can't get the laser up here and line it up with the stone, so I think the best thing to do is cut the pillar in two a little lower down.'

They set up the shield and laser, directing the beam at the pillar a couple of metres from the base. The stone chips soon flew in all directions, and the top of the pillar toppled over with a mighty thud.

What did cause a gasp of surprise was the core of the pillar, which seemed to be made of some ceramic type of material, with what Duffring described as 'wave guides' down the middle.

'This implies that they are, or were, using microwaves of some sort. Whether it was part of the 'go on to the next pillar' feeling imbued to the person who touched the pillar, or as a link to the next pillar to say someone was on their way, I don't know, but it is a little surprising, to say the least.'

'We could, as I have said before, learn a lot from this technology, if we take it apart carefully.'

The rest of the journey back to Kim's station proved relatively easy to what they had experienced earlier, and they were in a more rested mood as they entered the compound to be greeted by a rather distraught Kim.

'It would seem that the guru you intercepted has flipped his lid, and is alternately for and then against the new cult.

'This has had the effect of splitting the town's folk into two factions, those for and those against the changes. The last I heard was that a series of fights had ensued, and I reported this to my superiors who didn't seem to be very interested at all. Can you do anything?'

'There's not much we can do,' replied Duffring, 'we are only three, and even with your outfit, it only makes six. We would probably cause more trouble than we could handle, and we'd all lose out.'

It will most likely die down once a few of 'em get a bloody nose or two' and with that the subject was closed.

'Trouble is,' Duffring said as an aside to Jas, 'the poor old boy has been here so long now, that he thinks he's one of them.'

Six:
The Ovoid

THAT EVENING THEY told Kim of their experiences and what they had found and done, brought the map of the area up to date, and made copies of all the relevant data for the next team to use.

'How about we go into town to see what is going on?' Jas asked, when there was a lull in the general conversation.

'If that's an order, we'll do it, but I would advise against it really. We don't want to get embroiled in a fracas with the locals if we can help it, and there is little we can do to calm the situation anyway. It'll sort itself out naturally, given a little time.' Duffring replied, trying to sound as neutral as possible.

Jas didn't like the prompt put down, but thought about it for a moment, and then had to agree, the more experienced man was right of course.

Later that night, they began their journey back to the main base on the first world out from the sun, their mission accomplished, or at least it was as far as they were authorized to go. Jas expressed a wish to be on the team that would follow in their footsteps and examine the alien complex, but Duffring doubted very much if it would be permitted.

'It's really a job for the technicians, and you don't need that type of experience for your work, as interesting as it may be. What I'd like to know is who or what put it there in the first place, and what was their motive?

'Also are there any more of these complexes on this world, and do any other worlds have something similar on them, but perhaps of a different nature or principle?'

They discussed their adventures for most of the way back, trying to make more sense of what they had found, but gaining little from it in reality.

Mutty greeted them like old friends, and the story had to be told all over again, not that anyone minded as it sounded so preposterous, the feeling was that in the retelling it might become a little less so.

Mutty collated all the data they had brought with them and dispatched it off to those whose job it was to make the next move, expressing his wish to be in on the action as well, but knowing full well he wouldn't be.

The following day, Duffring and Mutty were in deep conversation, when Mutty took a sideways glance at Jas, nodded his head and walked off.

A little while later, Duffring took Jas aside and said, 'I'd like to show you something. Not many have seen it, or are allowed to see it, but I think you might be interested, and the knowledge may be useful one day.'

They went down several levels into the depths of the mountain, and boarded a mobile the like of which Jas hadn't seen before.

'This is a rather old model and it's been here a very long time, but works quite well. You'd better use the safety harness, as it gets a little bumpy later on.' said Duffring.

The hatch slammed to, and the sudden surge forward took Jas by surprise.

'I didn't say it was slow.' said Duffring with a grin which was beginning to spread across his face as they accelerated down the tunnel at a fearful pace.

There were several violent changes of direction as the vehicle rattled its way along in the subterranean tunnels, finally screeching to a halt in a dimly lit cavern which looked as if it had been an underground quarry or mine at some time in the long distant past, although there was no sign of what had been sought here.

'We go the rest of the way on foot, it's not far, and well worth the visit.' Duffring produced two light generators, and the set off down a roughly hewn dusty tunnel, only just wide and tall enough for them to walk upright.

Jas was just about to make a comment about the distance travelled, when Duffring stopped, Jas bumping into him, and both nearly losing their balance in a tangle of arms and legs.

A series of clicks, and a door opened to let in a brilliant flood of sunlight which hurt their eyes momentarily. As their eyes adjusted themselves to the glare, the scene below came into full focus. Jas let out a gasp of surprise, to be followed by another one.

'I thought it might interest you.' said Duffring, beaming from ear to ear.

Below them was a deep valley, completely enclosed by towering mountains with no visible way in or out.

On the valley floor was an eighty metre pale grey ovoid object, lying glittering in the sunlight.

'We have no idea how long it's been here, or how it got here. It was found by the light reflecting from it on an aerial survey done many, many years ago, and so is mentioned in our earliest records of this region.'

The way down was by a long line of carefully carved steps in the native rock.

'Someone must have put a great deal of importance on it for all this labour.' Jas managed to get out as he clambered down from the dizzying heights of the ledge they had emerged from, to the valley below.

Finally they reached the bottom of the stone steps and walked across the valley floor towards the shimmering grey ovaloid.

'We have had many teams of experts go over this thing with the proverbial fine toothed comb, and they have come up with nothing which makes any sense at all.

'If you look closely you will find there is no sign of a join, joint, or other conventional means of fabrication whatsoever. There isn't a seam, line or mark where sections have been joined together. We just don't know how it is possible to construct such a thing, if construct is the correct word. We can't cut it, dent it, or mark it in any way.

'It shows no sign of wear and somehow keeps itself clean, as there isn't a speck of dust on it anywhere, and that defies all science that we know of.' Duffring paused for breath before carrying on.

'And now for the biggest surprise of all.' Duffring reached into a pouch on his belt and brought out a small metal box with a solitary button on its top.

'After many years of research and fiddling about, some bright spark came up with this. No one knows how it works, it makes no sense if looked at with what we know of electronics, and the constructor said about the same.'

'He was just messing about in a random fashion, when, hey presto, the hatch opened, and we were inside the vessel.'

Duffring placed the little box against the side of the hull and pressed the button. There was the faintest of clicks, but whether it was from the ovoid or the box, they weren't sure.

A large section of the hull slowly swung down to ground level, making a convenient ramp up which they could walk, if either had the nerve to do so.

The opening was nearly six metres across and high, far more than was necessary for mere humans, but as Duffring later pointed out, it may have been the only entrance and was needed this size for freight, as there was no other opening.

'Shall we go in?' Duffring gave an exaggerated bow and Jas hesitatingly put one foot on the ramp.

'It's quite safe, otherwise I wouldn't let you go in.' he added. In the end they both went up the ramp together and into the vast hull.

The size of the passageways and rooms inside the vessel indicated that either the original occupants were considerably larger than the normal run of humans, or they liked a lot of space around them. They went from empty room to empty room, there being nothing in the way of furnishings or equipment that they could see, and somehow the internal space seemed bigger than it should have been.

No seats or tables, cupboards, shelves or anything apart from the bare smooth walls and floor, all made out of the same seamless pale grey material.

'Let's go up to the main controls, at least I think that's what they are.' said Duffring, and marched ahead as if he owned the place.

After what seemed like an endless journey up a long featureless tunnel of self lit pale grey glass, they emerged into a large semicircular room with what could have been a large curved viewing port at its end, except it was opaque.

In front of the viewing port was a long curved bench-like structure, which in effect was just a continuous upsurge from the grey floor, there being no joint lines, just a gentle curve where the bench met the lower level.

There were no controls as such, just a series of shallow depressions along the top of the bench, in two neat rows.

Apart from the bench-like structure, there was nothing else in the room, and as Jas pointed out, 'they must have stood all the while they controlled the ship, and that must have been a bit uncomfortable.'

Duffring then led the way deep down into the bowels of the vessel, where it was thought the main power drive was situated, but they weren't sure if the huge hump-like structure was a power unit or just a lump of the ubiquitous grey material, placed there because someone liked the look of it in that position.

They spent quite a time wandering about the alien vessel, but apart from the odd lump of material which seemed to have grown up from the floor, there were no artefacts whatsoever, just the corridors and featureless rooms, all empty, spotlessly clean, and not a mark of wear to be seen.

As they walked down the ramp, Duffring said, 'We have found no sign of bodies, bones, tools or anything which may have been removed from the vessel, it's as though they cleaned it out completely, polished it up with a magical polish which never tarnished and then just dumped it here, to baffle us for generations to come.'

'If you think the indoctrination chamber we visited was alien, what do you think of this beauty? You will of course have noticed that the technology and construction is completely different from what we found a few days ago, so it looks as if there two lots of visitors around, from different times and places perhaps. It has baffled our best minds, and we are no nearer a solution now than we were at the beginning.'

Jas had leaned up against the hull and was suddenly aware of something.

'I think I can feel something, like a faint vibration, it's there and yet it isn't.'

Duffring was beside him like a flash of light.

'Where?' placing his hand next to Jas's.

'I can't feel a thing, are you sure?

'Yes, Duffring. It's like .... well I don't know what it's like, but I can feel something. Can we go back to the control room for a moment?'

'Sure, follow me.' and they both set off at a run.

Approaching the bench, Jas reached out a hand and gently placed it in one of the depressions.

'There is something there, I can feel it.' His face took on a dreamy look, as if his attention was far away in another place, and then he snapped back to the present.

'I can feel the depression moving under my hand, it's almost alive! It's as if it's trying to contact me, reach out to me, tell me something, it's damn weird, I'll say that.'

'I've been watching your hand and the depression, and nothing moved that I could see, are you sure you're not imagining it Jas?'

'I'm not sure of anything very much any more.' replied an exasperated Jas, 'There is something going on, and I know it is, and that's for certain, but I don't know what.'

'Ah ... I think I've picked up something ... it's the time, the time is not right for what ever it is, sorry, it's gone now, and the feeling or vibration has gone too.'

Disappointed, they both left the alien vessel, and climbed the long line of stone steps to the dizzying height of the ledge where the entrance to the tunnel was.

'Did you notice that the hatch closed after we left, of its own accord, but didn't close the first time we left the vessel? Almost as if it knew we would go back in.'

'Every time we visit the damn thing we wind up with more questions than we started with, except that the hatch has never stayed open like that before. Maybe it recognized something about you.' In reply Jas just shrugged his shoulders, he didn't know either.

They climbed back into the vehicle and headed back to the main base, to be greeted by the inscrutable Kranz who, as usual, appeared out of nowhere, and said, 'Mutty wants' to see you both, there's been a development.'

Mutty was looking a bit pensive when they entered the room.

'You two have certainly opened up a can of worms.' was his greeting. 'The big boys have sent a team of experts to probe around your find, and they don't like what they've come across one bit.'

'I hope they were careful.' said Duffring, remembering the strange hallucinogenic effect of the indoctrination room.

'Oh, I think they were careful all right, they had little opportunity to be otherwise. The team went straight to the plateau which you boys had marked on the map, and as they were going up the slope and neared the top, they were taken ill, one by one.'

'Apparently they were hit by waves of nausea. The nearest anyone got to the cave was the edge of the flat area atop the last hill, the cave just in view, and that was it.'

Jas and Duffring briefly glanced at each other, but said nothing. Each had their own individual thoughts on the matter, but wisely kept quiet for the time being.

Mutty continued, a look of frustration on his face,

'When I say sick, I mean really sick. Some of them had to be rushed back to base for medical care, one only just made it, his internal plumbing twisted out of all recognition and he had to be operated on to straighten it all out again.'

'They've tried every thing, metal insulated suites, naked, behind shields of just about anything you can think of, and then they sent for a remote controlled robot crawler.'

'That got halfway across the plateau, and burnt out its drive unit. What the hell do you think has happened? Did you lot feel ill when you were there?'

'Apprehensive was about the worst we felt.' replied Duffring, looking at the other two

'Can't say I felt ill at any time, did either of you?' The others shook their heads.

'They asked for you three to return to the site, but I said I didn't think you would be able to contribute much more than you have already, and the matter was dropped.'

'If you come up with any bright ideas, please let me know. There's a lot of useful alien technology there for the taking, if we can but get at it.' Mutty added as an after thought.

The meeting broke up, and Duffring quietly indicated that he wanted to speak to Jas and Hass alone, and made his way out of the room and down the lift to the ledge exit which Jas and Hass had visited when they first arrived.

A gentle breeze was blowing up the face of the mountain, and the air had a fresh sparkle to it compared to the pure but clean air within the complex.

'Must say, it's very refreshing out here.' said Jas, wondering what Duffring had in mind, but afraid to ask.

'I've been thinking,' said Duffring, 'the only thing which makes any sense is the fact that we, or I should say I, cut that first pillar in two.'

'Suppose the pillars are linked to each other and to the cave, such that if any part of the complex failed or was interfered with, it would go into protect mode, because that's what I'd do if I had set the system up. Any other ideas gentlemen?'

The other two shrugged their shoulders, it seemed to be the only reasonable explanation so far.

'Do you think it would be worthwhile having someone keep an eye on the place, just in case 'they' return to service the equipment?' asked Jas, wanting to contribute something useful to an otherwise messy situation.

'I doubt it.' Hass was looking worried at the thought of having been involved in a mistake which would now deprive them of a useful technology.

'I have the feeling that set-up is very old, and so far has been self maintaining, the builders have long gone. There is just a slim chance, I suppose, but it's a very long shot.'

'OK, here's what we do.' Duffring interjected. 'I will take responsibility for cutting that first pillar in two, and explain what I think has happened. It's then up to them to decide what else can be done.'

'I don't think we can help much, because there's no way we can repair the 'wave guide' inside the pillar, and that seems to be the key to the whole thing.'

They both agreed with Duffring, and returned to Mutty's room, where Duffring made out his report and passed it over to Mutty for his views on the matter.

'Makes sense to me.' Mutty said. 'I'll send it off, and we'll see what happens.'

They were all a bit subdued that evening, which was not surprising when one considers the loss of a new technology so nearly in their grasp.

Two new 'guests' arrived over the next few days, and Jas was instructed by Kranz as to how the 'persuasion system' worked.

These were not the ordinary run of the mill malcontents, but fairly hard cases which the local Seeker unit had been unable to extract much information from. Kranz looked almost pleased as he led Jas to the interrogation room.

Jas was a quick learner, and coupled with his inbuilt intuition, soon acquired the necessary data to unravel the problems caused by the two interrogatees, which were then sent off to the deep sleep chambers for later dispatch to the Dark Ship when it next called.

Several weeks passed by with Jas refining his technique to a point where Kranz was becoming redundant, and he showed his displeasure at not being needed so much by being even more reticent to engage in conversation, not that he ever volunteered much in the way of chat anyway.

The team working on the indoctrination chamber up in the hills were still making little progress and rumour had it that they were going to give up the project, but leave an electronic sentinel in the area just in case the aliens did come back to see what had happened to their equipment.

Not that anyone really believed that they, who ever they were, would still be interested in it after all this time.

Several times Jas tried to get Duffring to expound on his theories on the ovoid alien craft in the enclosed valley, but his reticence on the matter indicated that he had either lost interest in it, or for some reason unknown to Jas, decided to keep his thoughts on the subject to himself.

Something which Jas had never seen before was snow, and when winter came to this world it was a new diversion to someone who had only experienced a constantly warm climate.

The otherwise austere beauty of the massive mountain ranges surrounding the station were enhanced considerably by the glistening white covering.

Ice began to form from melt water arising from the snow being bathed in the still quite strong sunlight which reached in between the towering peaks, adding to the effect.

Jas was still not very happy with some of the techniques used to interrogate the tougher 'visitors' which occasionally turned up at the Keeper station, and to this end began a little research into how the mind was constructed, aided and abetted by the ever helpful Duffring.

Mutty raised no objection to his efforts, and unbeknown to Jas, had informed those higher up the ladder of command, what was going on.

So it was with some surprise one day, when Jas was requested to attend Mutty in his office, that he should meet up again with the grey man with the steel grey eyes.

'Apart from the general good reports I've heard about you, it seems you have an interest in improving our interrogation techniques, and to some extent have been successful.' looking Jas straight in the eye with an unblinking gaze.

'That is correct, sir.' adding 'sir' for the first time, as he now knew just how high up the command ladder the grey man was, and that demanded a little more respect than usual.

'Would you be kind enough to enlighten me with your theories then?' The grey man settled back in his chair in a manor which was a little more than a polite request to begin.

Jas relaxed a little, for the first time he saw the hint of a smile on the grey man's face.

'I would like to point out that without Duffring's assistance, I would not have got very far with my research, he has been of immense help and encouragement and I would like that noted for the record'.

'It is so noted.' replied the grey man, and still the eyes hadn't blinked.

'Basically what we've found is that the human mind seems to go from lifetime to lifetime, gathering or storing data with each new body taken on.'

The 'being' itself isn't aware of this, except in some rare cases, and so those things recorded in a past life can influence the present one, if they are restimulated, or brought back to life.

'It would seem that at the birth of a new body, when the 'being' takes it on, a mental shutter drops down occluding all past memory, but a command which has been artificially implanted in the mind earlier can be triggered into action and the person thinks it is his own bright idea.'

Here Jas paused for a drink which had been thoughtfully provided by Mutty, who was sitting to one side of the group, and listening intently.

Jas continued to expound on his theory.

'We have found that by locating and examining in detail some of the 'bad acts' of our guests, they tend to take responsibility for them, and generally wish to mend their ways, though not in every case, I hasten to add.

'Having cleaned up a person's mental case to some degree, it is then quite easy to lift the mental shutter, as it were, and take them back in regression to an earlier life, and search for the implanted commands which led to the disruptive behaviour of the present life. We have found that sometimes the commands go back many lifetimes, and are very well concealed from our probing.

'One thing we have yet to find is who, or what, is doing the implanting of these disruptive commands, although they do not exist in every case.

'We have come across some people who are just plain evil, and as yet have not discovered where they get their evil intentions from. The open theory at the moment is that they probably create them themselves, but we have been unable to prove it yet.'

The grey man raised his hand as a signal for Jas to stop.

'Some of what you have told me is known already, but you have opened up a new route into the way the human mind works, and it is with pleasure that I invite you to head up a team to do further work on this subject.

'You will be advised when this will take place at some time in the future, if you should wish to do so, and I hope you will. Without wishing to boost your ego, I am pleased that my earlier estimate of your abilities has proven so accurate.'

Jas sensed that was the end of the meeting, and arose from his chair, inclining his head slightly in the direction of the grey man, and left the room, his head swimming from the possibilities which would now be open to him.

Somehow Duffring must have had some inkling of what was afoot, for he greeted Jas like an old friend who was about to leave his company.

It was several weeks later when Jas received the call to Mutty's office again. When he entered, the rest of the station staff were all there, and Mutty arose to meet him.

'Sadly for us, you are called to higher things it would seem. The instructions for your departure have just arrived, and I thought it would be nice for us to give you a bit of a send off.'

'We have all enjoyed working with you, and will miss your company, which will be our loss and someone else's gain. Jas was beginning to feel a little bit embarrassed, and could feel the colour rising in his cheeks.

Mutty sat down and then it was Duffring's turn to add to the proceeding.

'Mutty has said it all really, but I would just like to add one more thing. You have not only shown extreme diligence in the work which we do, but a degree of compassion which is rare in this occupation. Through your research and no doubt the continuance of same, a lot of people will find their work easier to do, with less stress, and the recipients of our labours will not find the proceedings so traumatic. On their behalf, I thank you.' and he sat down.

Jas was now in a state of emotional overwhelm, and could feel the lump in his throat getting larger along with a pair of moist eyes, but he was not ready for the next surprise. Kranz stood up, walked over to him and taking both of his hands in his said, 'You are the best.' turned, and sat down again. For just one moment Jas saw what he thought was a brightness in Kranz's normally dead eyes.

The drinks came out, along with some exotic food stuffs which Jas hadn't seen before, and by the end of the evening, no one was too sure who was who, let alone who was leaving the station next day.

There was little to pack, apart from his dress uniform and a few odds and ends which he had acquired along the way, so with only one carry bag and a heavy heart, Jas left his room for the last time at the Keeper station.

Kranz appeared out of nowhere, as usual, and took the bag from Jas's hand, and then led the way to the lifts at the end of the corridor.

The rest of the staff were there, waiting, and they all crowded in together, a tight squeeze for all, with Jas's bag held above Kranz's head like a prize trophy.

The floor fell away beneath them, Kranz mumbled an apology, and then they were at a level which Jas had not yet seen.

The tunnel was rough hewn from the solid rock, like the one leading to the enclosed valley, but the vehicle awaiting them was a little different. There was only room for two occupants, and Mutty was the first in followed by a sad looking Jas, who had only just realized how much he would miss all his friends at the station. The hatch closed with a pneumatic hiss, and the acceleration slammed Jas back into his seat, there being hardly time to give a last wave to those left in the tunnel.

The bullet shaped mobile sped along the smooth track with a faint hissing sound for several minutes, and then the deceleration began.

It was only as they slowed down that Jas realized the speed at which they must have been moving, and the huge distance they had travelled.

The mobile left the tunnel to exit into a vast cavern which seemed to have a vent high above open to the sky, but the strange thing was it was a dark sky, with the stars shining.

Jas stopped in his tracks, looking up, and Mutty came to the rescue with an explanation,

'No daylight gets down here as the exit is so high above us, therefore you see the sky as it would be at night. It fooled me the first time I saw this strange phenomenon.'

Mutty explained that Jas would be taken up and into orbit above the planet by the shuttle, and then transferred to another vessel which would take him on to his next destination, without saying where or what that destination was. Perhaps he didn't know himself.

In the centre of the cavern stood a sleek looking craft of a strange dull black colour. The light seemed to be sucked into it rather than reflected from it, and Jas was just about to mention this when Mutty said, 'This is where I leave you to take the next step on what I am sure will be a most extraordinary life. In a way, I wish I were in your shoes, but I'm a little too old for the excitement now, so it is best left to those of lesser years.

'Goodbye, my friend, remember us once in a while, and pay us a visit if you are ever this way again.' and with that he spun on his heel and walked back to the mobile, lest Jas should see the moisture in his eyes.

There was nothing left to do but board the craft, and Jas did so, strapping himself into one of only two seats in the main compartment of the vessel.

As he settled into his seat a force far stronger than the bullet shaped mobile slammed him backwards, the seat turning on its gimbals so that he was facing the direction of travel, and wondering if all this brute force was really necessary.

No sooner had he got used to the acceleration thrust, when it was gone and he was in free fall. His stomach turned over, and he lost all sense of direction.

And then there was gentle pressure at his back again, the forward viewing port opened and his vision was assailed by a vast panoply of stars, slowly wheeling across the heavens before him.

The shuttle cruised on for what seemed like hours when there was gentle bump, and the sense of free fall returned. A sharp hiss told Jas that someone had connected up a transfer duct to the vessel, and he was about to leave this craft for another one. The hatch opened and a cheerful face looked in.

'Good trip? ... Sir.' was added when the pilot saw the insignia on Jas's lapel. 'Yes thanks, although the acceleration was a bit sharp on the way up.' Jas replied.

'A powerful little craft that, I've only been on one once, and it took me by surprise too ... Sir'.

Moving in freefall was something Jas wasn't used to, and he felt that he'd made a right mess of it as he transferred over to the other craft, but the pilot diplomatically showed no sign of amusement at his efforts.

This was a much bigger vessel, and Jas felt a little more comfortable having an actual pilot to handle the craft, although the automatics on the shuttle couldn't be faulted, if one thought about it.

He took the seat indicated to him, and strapped in, the cheerful pilot taking up his position only a few seats ahead of him at the main controls.

A vision screen showed the shuttle slowly drifting away from them, and then it accelerated off into the blackness, soon to be lost from sight.

'OK, sir, here we go.' and with that the thrust back into his seat returned, but a little less vicious this time. The stars wheeled about as the craft lined itself up on some distant target, and then the thrust really came on, and stayed on for some time, the star field movement increasing as the vessel gained speed.

'May I join you, sir?' asked the pilot as he left his controls and walked the few paces towards Jas's seat.

'Yes, of course, nice to have someone to talk to,' Jas added, 'again.' looking at the empty controller's chair.

'Oh, don't worry about that, she's on automatics for a while, I'm only needed in case there's a problem or for docking, which will be much later.'

'I've put the gravity field on as I assume that you're not used to long periods in free fall. It's only partly effective, but will give you some sensation of what's up and down.'

'Most thoughtful of you.' said Jas, warming to the young pilot.

General chat passed between them for a while, and then the pilot went aft to return with a couple of refreshment trays.

'Thought you might like to try some of these.' indicating a fruit Jas had never seen before.

'They are considered a great delicacy by most, and are quite expensive as far as the general public is concerned.'

'Then how come we have them?' asked Jas.

The pilot looked a little awkward, colouring up slightly, 'Well, sir, I suppose the caterers must have known who you were.'

'And just who do you think I am?' asked Jas.

'I don't know, sir, I was told to pick you up, and take very good care of you, no matter what happened. So you must be important to someone higher up. I'm sorry, if I appear impertinent, it is certainly not intended.'

'Oh, that's all right, I just wondered what you'd been told, let's leave it there, and carry on with our conversation.'

The pilot visibly relaxed, and sat down to enjoy the luxury.

They chatted on for some time, exchanging ideas on many subjects, and Jas was somewhat surprised on the overall knowledge of the young pilot. Their discourse was interrupted by a soft 'ping - ping' from up forward.

'Excuse me a moment.' and the pilot went to the controls of the craft, sat down and made some adjustments on the panel before him.

The stars blanked out, and for a brief moment Jas experienced a sickening surge of something which went right through his body, his vision went out of focus and he lost all orientation.

And then the feeling was gone, the star field returned into full view, but was moving across the view port at a much increased rate. The young pilot joined Jas again and explained why they were travelling at an increased rate.

'So the story goes, this Star Drive technique was discovered almost by accident, and as far as I know, no one really understands it fully, but that is only a rumour you understand. Every sun and planetary body has a gravitational field which radiates out for a great distance, and a similar field exists for a complete solar system.

'The easiest way to describe it is to liken it to a pattern of lines, interconnecting everything in space. The drive cuts across these lines rather like a ribbon tracked vehicle grips the ground over which it moves, only with the Star Drive it is energy lines which are being used.

'Somehow the vessel cuts across the lines of force, absorbs and alters them, adds a little of our own power, of which we have plenty, and then uses the resultant energy to drag itself along, although drag is hardly the word to use!'

'What sort of speed can we do?' asked an intrigued Jas.

'I don't know what the limit is, in theory it is infinite, or so I've been told. The faster you go, the greater the lines of force are cut and therefore the more powerful the traction effect. There is a setting beyond which I mustn't go on the controls, and that's all I can tell you really.'

'There's a tale of someone who volunteered to push the system to its limits, and he shot off into the depths of space and was never seen again, hence the limit on the control panel, but it's only a tale.'

'We can only use the drive when we're a certain distance away from a planetary mass, that's why we were only travelling relatively slowly until I engaged the drive just now.'

The pilot paused to take another drink, and hesitatingly reached for another of the exotic fruits.

'So the drive is only used between solar systems and in the depth of space.' Jas making it a statement rather than a question.

Before the pilot could comment further, their attention was taken by a bright dot of light in the view screen which didn't move with the rest of the star field.

'What the hell's that?' asked Jas, realizing that something was keeping pace with them, and as far as he could see, had no right to be there.

The pilot rushed forward, touching several sensor pads in rapid succession on the control board, and then sat back in his chair. The equipment registered the presence of the glowing ball of light and logged the data for future retrieval.

'If you could answer that, you would be famous indeed! These little balls of light have been seen right back into our earliest recorded history. No one knows what they are, where they come from, why they follow us or what their purpose is.

We've never been able to capture one, although many have tried. So far, they have never done us any harm, at least, there is no record of them having done so. They just seem to follow us for a time, and then zoom off into space.'

'Someone, somewhere is interested in us, but so far have made no contact as such. We have checked out all the members of the Confederation to see if any of them are playing a game with us, but they are just as mystified as we are.'

The bright spot of light which had been keeping pace with them sudden veered off to one side, and then disappeared into the distant stars, and they were alone once more.

'Do you have a graphic of this vessel.' asked Jas, curious to see what it looked like.

'Yes sir, I'll bring one up on the screen.' and so saying a picture of what looked like a jumbled bundle of thin sticks with a dark blob in the middle appeared.

'Kridlestones! What an odd looking thing it is.' exclaimed Jas. 'You mean to say that we are encapsulated in that bit in the middle, and the rest of it is the drive unit?'

'Yes sir, she doesn't look very pretty compared to the interplanetary vessels, as they have an atmosphere to contend with and need the streamlining. Out here there is virtually nothing to offer any friction, and so any shape will do.'

Two more course corrections, or what ever it was that the pilot did at such times, and the star field's motion began to slow down, far faster than it had accelerated during the beginning of their journey.

'We shall be at our destination very soon.' said the pilot, 'I sincerely hope you had a good and interesting trip sir.'

'You can say that again' said Jas.

'I sin ....'

'No! I didn't mean it literally.' Jas retorted, with an ill concealed grin.

Ahead there loomed up a dark and forbidding looking mass, growing ever bigger in the viewing port until all motion of the vessel stopped and the docking tunnel clunked into position.

They had arrived, but to what, and where was it relative to where they had started out?

Jas was welcomed aboard by a stern faced man of massive stature, whose head looked as if it had been chiseled out of korlean granite, and a uniform which had been starched and then pressed under a two tonne weight.

Having thanked the pilot for the safe journey and his entertaining conversation, Jas followed behind the solo welcoming committee to exit the docking tunnel into an even more austere room, in the centre of which was a small desk hiding an even smaller clerk.

A feeling of foreboding overcame Jas, this was definitely not the sort of greeting he had been expecting, and the general grim look of the place sent his spirits down into his highly polished boots.

'Book in with all your details here.' indicated the diminutive clerk, 'Leave your bag next to the desk, and follow me.'

Desperately Jas thought of finding some means of returning to the life he had known and enjoyed, the cold inhuman atmosphere of this place was far from his liking.

Disappointment was beginning to turn into anger, an emotion he hadn't experienced for a long time. Kranz was positively friendly compared to this joker, Jas thought.

'Just a moment.' Jas called out in the sternest voice he could muster. The stern man halted in mid stride, and turned to face him. 'You will address me as 'sir', you will stand to attention and look me in the eye when you address me, and you will also prefix any order or request with the word 'please'. A lack of courtesy does not denote efficiency. Is that understood?' He wondered if he had gone too far for a moment.

To say that the stern man was startled, was an understatement. He drew himself up to his full height, thrust his chiselled features as far forward as it was possible to go without over balancing and said 'Yes sir.'

'Well, damn well do it.' was Jas's reply, who was now really getting into the swing of it.

'Please follow me, sir.' came the somewhat grudging request from the stern man, but as he had followed his orders to the letter, Jas felt he couldn't reprimand the man for lack of feeling in his voice, perhaps he had a vocal impediment.

They made their way along a sterile looking corridor, into a lift, and eventually out into a large room which sported several comfortable looking chairs and a long table adorned with mechanical food dispensers.

'This place looks as welcoming as a damn morgue.' Having started on this tack, Jas thought it might be as well to keep the pressure up for a while, for he considered he had little to lose.

'Yes sir.' snapped the gaunt man, spun on his heels and left the room, only just preventing the door from closing with a slam.

Jas wandered over to the food table, his initial desire for a light snack totally evaporating when he saw the dull and lifeless wrappers the food was adorned in.

'Good grief, what a place.'

As he was about to take a seat, another door opened and a pleasant looking man of middle years came in, walked across to Jas and extended a hand in greeting.

'Welcome, young man. Sorry about your initial welcoming party, you certainly gave him a bit of stick though, and deservedly so. He's not usually as gruff as that, I think he must be having a bad day.' Jas immediately felt a flood of relief come over him, perhaps things weren't going to be so bad after all.

'I would have met you myself, but I got a bit tied up for a moment or two, but I did see your arrival on the monitor. What must you think of us?'

It wasn't a question, more of a statement.

'Please take a seat while your details are being sorted out, and then I'll take you to your quarters and introduce you to the team you will be heading up.

'They are a young bunch, most of which have had some experience in your line of interest, but need a leader to help them concentrate on each particular line of work. I'm sure you'll get on very well with them.'

Before long his details arrived in a black folder edged with silver, and the jolly man arose from his seat to receive them, giving them a cursory glance and indicating that Jas should follow him out and into the corridor.

Several levels later, and a good few hundred metres of featureless passageways brought the pair to the suite of rooms which would be Jas's home base for some time to come.

A team of some six bright eyed young men standing in a neat line snapped to attention as they entered the room.

Introductions were made and after the jolly man had left, Jas set about finding out what each of his new team of helpers specialized in.

Things were definitely looking up, and the initial miserable introduction to the station was soon forgotten.

After several months of intensive work, Jas was getting a very good idea of how the human mind worked, and what could be done to repair the damage caused by trauma and interference from others. His team worked well together, and each breakthrough brought them closer to their common cause, the relief of self imposed human suffering.

Jas was just about to begin a lecture to some of the junior members of the station's crew on the structure of the human mind, when the lecture hall door opened, and in walked the grey man from the Dark Ship.

Jas left his position on the podium and went to meet him.

'I happened to be passing nearby, and thought I would call in and see how you were progressing.' said the grey man, although in fact he knew very well.

'Please explain what you are about to do with the crew members' He added.

'We have made many discoveries of late, and one of them is that people can help themselves a lot more than we first thought' said Jas, wondering if perhaps he had overstepped the mark in what he was about to do, and somehow the grey man had got wind of it.

'So far you have told me nothing I didn't know before, so carry on young man, and explain what you are about to do'. The grey man was patient, if nothing else.

'I am about to give a lecture illustrating how the mind is constructed, what we can do about it to increase awareness and communication, and then unravel the trauma areas which can have an effect upon us without us being aware of those effects.'

'That sounds a good idea.' said the grey man, 'I will sit at the back of the hall and listen, maybe I can learn a little something as well.' and with that he almost smiled, turned, and walked to the far end of the hall and sat down on a quickly vacated seat.

Jas returned to the podium and took up his position behind the solid black lectern, which held his notes, took a deep breath, and began.

'As you all know from an earlier talk I gave, we are made up of three basic parts, the body, the mind in which all our memories are stored, and the spirit, the real essence of life, the real you and me, that which is aware of being aware, the being, call it what you will.'

'The body doesn't need much explanation, we've all had a stomach ache or a stubbed toe at some time, and know what a body can do and feel.' A tentative nervous giggle ran through the audience, none were too sure yet if the jokes would be coming in earnest, with the grey man sitting in the background.

'The being itself is a little harder to grasp as a concept. Those of you who have had an 'out of body' experience through sheer fright or during anaesthetic will have some reality on it, the rest of you will have to wait until the processing which is scheduled for later takes place, and then you will have a chance to sample it for yourselves.

'This leaves us with the mind itself, a complex storage system, containing everything you have ever seen, sensed, or experienced. You may well not have easy access to quite a lot of that which has been stored in this lifetime, and further back than that I doubt if many of you can recall very much, if anything.

'Let me give you an example of an irrational behaviour. Anyone afraid of heights could easily walk a ten metre plank supported on two bricks, but if you were to raise the plank up to a metre it would not be so easy. Raise the plank up to ten metres and I doubt the walker would even attempt it. Raise it up to fifty metres and your walker would be long gone, looking for something else to do. But it is still the same plank and just as safe, only the concept of height has changed. So something in the past must have happened to give the walker this fear of heights. If this fear can be erased, the plank can be walked safely at any height.

'And that is the real point, normally you can't get at it, but it can get at you, and you quite naturally think the sensations, pains and impulses are in real time, which to some extent they are because they affect you, but they are restimulated from the past without you realizing it.'

Jas looked around the crowded hall, light had dawned on quite a few faces, but some still looked a little blank and would take a little more convincing.

'In order to clear up this lifetime's upsets, and the fixed ideas which they have brought into being, we have to increase your ability to communicate freely.

'To start with, this means talking to others, and then to yourselves.' A laugh ran through the hall, and Jas knew he had them with him.

'When I say 'talk to yourselves', I mean you will question yourselves in a controlled manner to find out what has happened and what the consequences were, and then you can remove any compulsions attached to the incidents.

'When you have cleaned up this lifetime, you will learn how to go back into an earlier lifetime, and clean that up.

'If we went back one life memory at a time, it would take for ever, so we are working on a method of short circuiting the system to some degree, which means it won't take for ever after all.

'One of the main things we have to find is where and when other ideas have been implanted into our minds, such that we think they are our ideas. Some of these are darn right evil and are designed to cause the maximum trouble for us and others. We needed to find out what put them there.

'The basic spirit of man is good, but evil intentions and the intentions of others modify our actions sometimes, and that is what we have to clean up if we want a sane universe.'

There were several exclamations of agreement from the audience, which he had not often heard before, at least a few of them must have seen the significance of what he had said, and were gaining some reality from it.

'There are two more things of great importance which I wish to bring to your attention, and which will be expanded on in a future lecture.'

An absolute hush had fallen over the assembled audience, the level of interest in the subject matter must have struck home well and truly for most of them, and Jas knew that the processes he wished to run on volunteers from the crew would be well attended, especially when the first results became known.

'The first thing is that the further we go back in time, the more difficult it is to unravel the mysteries we come across, but the research team are making good progress at the moment, and a breakthrough is expected before long.

'It would seem that long before your home planets were populated, we were about in the universe doing what we have always done so well, messing things up!

'Some of the considerations we acquired so long ago are still in force today, and some of them are only held back from affecting our lives because we recognize them as harmful, and that means they are being held back by suppression, and that isn't always good. A new approach is to lift the suppression, and 'run out' the considerations if they no longer hold good.'

There was a startled cry from the audience and a crew member stood up, waving his arms about in a state of agitation. Jas had anticipated the possibility of such an occurrence, as the material he was talking about was likely to restimulate some areas of the time track, and occasionally this led to the person concerned experiencing the earlier incidence to some degree.

Two standby medical orderlies, who had been briefed on what to do, ran forward to take charge of the unfortunate man, and lead him away. Some of the research team would be waiting for him in the processing rooms below.

When the commotion had calmed down, Jas continued,

'The other main point I wish to make, and this is backed up by positive evidence, is that there is life out there, way beyond our galaxy. So far it has only been speculation, along the lines of 'there should be', and 'why not'. We now have proof that there has been, and probably still is.

'We are not alone.'

'I know that the Confederation is a vast organization, covering most of our galaxy, but it is nice to know that other galaxies, although they haven't contacted us yet, are out there, and populated.

'The evidence for this comes from our research, some members of the team being regressed to a point in time when our worlds were uninhabitable because they hadn't finished forming, and they have memories of other vast star clusters which they inhabited. It was from one of these that the layout of our galaxy was seen, and we have now confirmed that it could only have been viewed from that point in space.'

Jas paused to see how the audience were taking it, and observed that it didn't seem to bother them too much.

'And now, perhaps the most important news of all. We have just finished working out the first of the processes to increase your communication levels and so set you on the road to freedom. It is a long road, but will give this galaxy the stability it needs for a very long time into the future, and you will be the original pioneers of the transformation.

'There are a set series of processes which we have mapped out, each one releasing a little more of your abilities thereby enabling you to face up to the next one in the series. From the work we have done so far I can't promise you that it will be easy all the way, but the rewards are immeasurable and surpass anything we have ever envisaged.

'For the first time in our recorded history, we have a means to rid mankind of all the insane actions which we are sometimes prone to, totally erasing them from the mind where they have been stored for aeons of time. At long last, we can be free in the fullest sense of the word. Free to do as we will, but not causing harm to others at the same time.'

'The full limits of this freedom are only speculative at the moment, but it looks as if the sky's the limit, the ultimate state being free as a 'being', and all which that might mean.

'The beauty of the system we have set up is that as you progress, you can repay your debt to the researchers by helping others to gain their freedom. There is an enrolment table at the end of the hall for those who would like to take advantage of this offer. That is all gentlemen, I thank you for your rapt attention.'

The applause was long and thunderous, the crew members standing to a man. Three times Jas came back to the dais to take a well earned bow, and still they wouldn't let him go.

In the end Jas left by a side door to hear cheers added to the hand clapping and stamping feet. Just what had he released on an unsuspecting galaxy?

Could he hope to contain it, and keep the technology pure and true. He would have to, or he would have committed the biggest sin in the universe, and he didn't want the responsibility of that!

Sitting in his own private room, trying to get his thoughts together again, Jas heard a quiet tap on the door. 'Come in, you know it's always open' he said.

The door slowly swung open and the grey man stood there, his face set like stone with no emotion showing at all. He walked slowly into the room and took a seat besides the startled Jas, who in his enthusiasm had forgotten all about the grey visitor at the back of the hall.

'We knew when you were chosen for this work, that you were brighter than average, and your physiological profile was perhaps the best we have ever found, but we didn't envisage just what you would unleash on the peoples of the Confederation.

'You will be given complete autonomy of the system, and this of course, means total responsibility for what happens.

'You must realize that once this data is common knowledge to all and sundry, it will take a tight reign to hold the whole thing together, and keep it pure. I am sure that you also realize that the data could be used for bad as well as the good you intend, so you have made a very stiff rod for your own back.

'We will be behind you all the way, giving support wherever possible, but it is your show, and you must run it.'

The full import of what he had done left Jas shaking, or perhaps it was just the after effects of the lecture, or a mixture of the two.

The grey man hadn't been unfriendly in his dissertation, but perhaps this was not the time or place to show friendliness. He was still feeling uncertain of what to do next, when the grey man gently put a hand on his shoulder, and said, 'You have done well, far surpassing our expectations, and once you have got things running smoothly and can leave them in capable hands for a while, I want you to join us on one of the Dark Ships for a while. The experience on board the ship will drive home the true value of what you have discovered, and will to some extent lessen any feeling of doubt you may have left with regard to the work you are doing.'

Jas relaxed a little, but the feeling of being responsible for running and organizing such a colossal project, eventually expanding into a Confederation wide system to rid mankind of the mental traps of the human mind, still seemed an overwhelmingly daunting task, and he wasn't at all sure that he could cope with it. But then the grey man had promised full support, and that lessened some of the burden.

'Come my friend.' the grey man said, arising from his seat, 'I want you to meet a few people who came with me, and then you should take a short rest, a little relaxation. I will arrange it for you.' and he gently guided Jas towards the door, and the next chapter of a more than exciting life.

The two visitors which the grey man had brought with him caused Jas to hold his breath, inwardly gulp several times and generally reassess his opinion of what a human being could aspire to, if indeed they were human.

Tall, beautiful in the truest sense of the word and with a clearness of face that was almost unbelievable. He could feel the mental freedom of these people, it was almost tangible, something one could reach out to and touch, and be changed for ever.

Jas snapped out of his reverie as the introductions were made.

'Let me explain,' said the grey man. 'Our friends here are in the mental state which you have been researching and trying to achieve for the rest of us. They have it naturally and as far as we know, always have had.

'They don't know how this came about, or what caused it, but we can only assume that it is the true state of man, and we have all fallen far short of it over the enormous amount of time in which we have been populating these worlds.

'They were contacted way out on the fringes of this galaxy some time ago, and then we knew what could be attained, but didn't have the wherewithal to achieve it.

'Hence when we found you, after much searching, I might add, we took a chance and set things up hoping that you would discover those vital clues which were needed to free the rest of us. From what we have seen so far, it looks as if we were right in our choice.'

The two godlike visitors smiled at Jas.

'We wish to help you in any way we can, as your friend here has explained, we find it hard to comprehend a mental state other than that which we are in, but since meeting your people, we realize that much could be done to enable you to enjoy the same state, but we don't know how this could be achieved as we have always been like this.

'Your part in this could no doubt be a kind of bridge, or linking of our two species, at a mental level, finding out what has happened to your people and why it hasn't happened to us.'

Even their voices are different, thought Jas, soft and melodious, yet strong and with great intention.

'We know a little of the work you have been involved with, but as we have never had the need to do the same, we have little in the way of data to offer you, except one thing. We are quite certain that the only way you can reach the state we are in, is to do it yourselves.

'Nothing in the way of information, even if we had it, would alter the mental state of your people, it is something which you have to work out for yourselves, and in so doing, you will gain your freedom.

'This may sound harsh and uncaring on our part, but from what little we have discovered, it is the only way it will work for you.

'We have visited many of your worlds' added the other godlike creature, 'and can envisage the stability which could be brought about using your present technology.

'It is a great achievement of yours and of your people, and we think that co-operating with your research program may well open other avenues of thought, other methods of reaching your goal, and it is our pleasure to so do.'

The meeting went on for some time and Jas's head was in a whirl when it finally broke up, and he returned to his quarters mentally exhausted.

'What the hell have I got myself into.' he said out loud, but deep down he knew he was now committed and there was no way out, except through.

A few days later, and the communication enhancement program was well under way.

Once the potential benefits of this had been realized, it was over subscribed as the gains for each individual became obvious to those who had not tried it.

There was a new brightness among the crew members, art in many forms appeared and the whole atmosphere of the place was uplifted to a considerable degree.

The next stage, as each individual freed up his ability to communicate to his fellows, was the tracking down of the 'bad acts' and taking responsibility for them.

This caused a few hiccups as some came up against hefty deeds which they had committed against themselves, and they would rather have forgotten, but once they had broken through the barrier of confronting the seemingly impossible, and gained the feeling of release which came with it, word got around and they co-operated with renewed enthusiasm.

Jas was hard put to keep up with the demands for the new processes, and realized the danger of being only one step ahead of that demand.

New ideas were tried out on members of his team, refining the methods again and again to make them as foolproof and safe as possible.

All sorts of fail-safe devices and checks were added to the general processes and a careful assessment of each individual's progress and stability was maintained.

The discovery that fixed attitudes and considerations could be changed by the individual, with a little help, brought a new rush of eager participants.

Many of the crew members wanted to join the team, and those thought suitable were trained up in the art of applying the processes, ready to form a new team which would go down to one of the nearby planets in the local system.

Jas realized that if this was successful, the whole thing would take off like the intergalactic ship which had brought him here in the first place, and then control of the whole thing would be out of his hands.

Somehow he would have to construct a self monitoring hierarchy which could take over, releasing him to carry on with the higher level research work which was now becoming increasingly needed.

It wasn't long before another discovery caused a bit of a rethink of what had been accepted for very long time.

It was found that some people seemed to be ill when there was no good medical reason for it, others didn't respond to the standard medical treatment, and some were chronically sick for no apparent reason. What caused the big surprise was that when the illness was addressed by going back down the time track, it cleared up.

Apparently earlier similar illnesses, if they were in some way advantageous to the person in an earlier life, or got that person out of trouble, were recorded in the mind and remained there through time until restimulated in the present life by certain circumstances which were sufficiently similar to the original incidents. The trouble for the recipients of such restimulation, was that the illness in this lifetime didn't have the apparent beneficial effect it had before, and was causing trouble rather than helping.

Some medics felt threatened by this revelation, and tried to oppose it in the beginning, but came to their senses when they saw the results. It also meant that a whole new series of processes had to be constructed to handle the various cases which kept turning up, and that put an extra burden on the research team's resources.

Another spin-off from this discovery was the question that if illness could be caused this way, what else could? And that required another special team to be set up to handle that, and the new processes required to clear up whatever was found. All in all, it was a very busy time indeed.

Eventually Jas built up a structure which was self maintaining with regard to the application of the new technology, and so felt free to concentrate on the higher levels of human attainment, which indicated that they could soar to undreamed of heights in ability and freedom from past actions.

It was while he was putting the finishing touches to one of these processes that he was advised that the grey man wished to see him again.

'I am sorry to interrupt your work yet again, which I have been following very carefully, but I think it is time that you saw for yourself the significance of what you have been doing from a different angle and what it will affect in the future.' The grey man paused to see how Jas reacted to the suggestion.

'It has been decided that you will accompany me on one of our missions, and see what we do first hand. You will then be in a better position to judge how you structure your future work, as it is too important to leave to chance or some other arbitrary.'

'Can you give me a couple of days to tie up a few things here first?' asked Jas.'

'Yes, of course. Also I want you to take that break from your work I suggested some time ago, I think it would be beneficial. I have arranged for you to visit your friends Mutty and Duffring, a few days chatting over old times will do you all good, and then I will come and pick you up for the next stage of your education. Is that acceptable to you?'

'Yes, very much so, I'd like to see them again, I learnt so much there.'

Mutty greeted him like an old friend who had just been rediscovered after thinking he had been lost for ever.

Emotions flowed in a new way, which surprised them both, and the whole thing was repeated when Duffring 'the smiling' returned from a short visit to collect a 'guest' from the next planet.

They spent many hours talking over old times, and while news of the new technology had reached their far flung empire, they knew little of the exact details and felt privileged to get them first hand from Jas.

He gave an impromptu demonstration of the power of the new technology to the station staff by 'unbuttoning' the somewhat twisted mind of one of their more intractable 'guests', much to that person's surprise and possible annoyance, but once he realized what was going on, it was too late, and he suddenly became reasonably co-operative.

Jas had to explain that it was not quite as easy as it looked, as he had had to apply a little trickery initially to get a reasonable degree of co-operation from the 'guest'. For the process to work at maximum efficiency, it needed full and unequivocal co-operation from the beginning and right through to the end, and that sometimes took a bit of achieving.

Time flew by, as it always does when one is enjoying what one is doing, and the grey man came all too quickly.

Seven:
The Sweeper's New Broom

'I HAVE A few charges to pick up, so you had better accompany me from the very beginning so that you get the full picture Jas.' The grey man seemed to be more cordial than before, and tended to treat Jas as more of an equal than a young ships officer, which he still considered himself to be.

The little entourage went down to the deep sleep chambers, and watched from behind the protective transparent screen as the mechanical devices carefully lifted down eleven sleep capsules and their comatose occupants, and then loaded them onto a sledge like transport. This then hurried off into the darkness of a tunnel to the waiting shuttle, to be later transported up to the Dark Ship.

In the company of the grey man, they spent one more evening together, and although he was held in great esteem and awe by the rest of the station staff, as the evening progressed and the drink flowed, they finished up pretty much on the same level.

Next day Jas had to reluctantly say goodbye to his friends all over again, but this time it wasn't quite so emotional, as they knew that another visit wasn't ruled out, and all were looking forward to it.

Only Jas and the grey man took the transport to the waiting shuttle, boarded it, and took off for deep space.

'Where is your ship?' asked Jas, after they had been travelling for some time.

'Just ahead, we'll be there in a matter of minutes.' the grey man replied.

'But I can't see anything, not even on the screens, and according to what I've heard, it is a very large vessel.'

And then Jas remembered, 'Oh yes, I was told about your invisible ship some time ago.' The grey man smiled.

'If you look carefully ahead, you will see a patch of the star field which has no stars in it. They are being blanked out by the ship.'

They had almost docked before Jas could make out the huge bulk of the Dark Ship. It was indeed a menacing looking spectre, 'Small wonder they swanted to keep it out of sight', he thought. The eleven capsules were brought aboard and shipped off to the main storage area, the grey man showing Jas how the system basically worked.

Jas was shown to his new quarters aboard the mighty ship by a junior aide, and later, after he had attended to his ablutions and taken a meal, his presence was requested by the grey man.

Upon entering his private quarters, Jas was surprised to see he had changed from the steely creature he had appeared to be earlier.

'Please sit down and make yourself comfortable Jas, and lets have your questions, of which you no doubt have quite a few.'

'Yes, I do have some.' replied Jas.

'Some!' retorted the grey man, 'I'll bet you have thousands of 'em.' with a chuckle in his voice.

Jas relaxed, it was going to be a good evening, well, he supposed it was evening, as it was towards the end of the working day.

'Before you ask me anything, let me tell you what we do, and how we do it, that should short circuit quite a bit.'

'Right.' said Jas, his awe of the grey man having lessened somewhat.

'We have, as you know, picked up some cargo, and there are several more stops on the way before we go into the next phase of our work.'

'When we have retrieved all that are ready for collection in this sector, they are graded as it were. Let me explain that.' he paused to take a drink from a scintillating goblet of pure crystal.

'A highly trained team categorize them according to stature, skin colour and type, mental state and general structure. Once this has been done, a large database of the planets we use is consulted, and the various groups are assigned to the most appropriate world according to their skin colour and body type.

'The unfortunate 'guests' as you refer to them, are then given a false set of memories, so that they will feel that they belong to wherever we drop them off, and have no recall of being anywhere else. They soon integrate into the general population, and our troubles are over. So far so good?' Jas nodded his head in acknowledgement.

The grey man wanted to make sure that Jas understood everything as he went along.

'Now, as to the worlds which we use. As you know this galaxy is a bit like a vast spinning wheel, densely populated with planets near its centre, and with a few solar systems out on the fringes.

'Habitable worlds on the fringes are the ones we use, they are generally known as the rim worlds, as they are far enough away so that it is most unlikely that the 'depositees can return to the Confederation planets, which is what we want.

'Not to put too fine a word on it, they are in effect, prison worlds. No one ever returns from them, we make sure of that. They are left in a mentally confused state about what to believe with regard to their creation, who created them, what they can achieve, and how they should look upon space travel, just in case they should get around to it.'

'It may sound a little unfair, but we have to give them a little to think about in case they get to thinking about themselves.'

'Surely,' said Jas, 'taking into consideration the state of their minds when we send them to the Keepers, and the fact that you add to their confusion, there must be total turmoil on these worlds, wars, cheating on a vast scale, and general mayhem to mention just a few of the possibilities.'

'Yes, that is so. But it does keep them occupied, and that is part of the imprisonment system. While they are doing that, they won't have much time to unravel themselves and develop a technology sufficiently advanced enough to get back home, as it were.

'Anyway, they would be unable to do what you have done in your research, and that is clean themselves up enough to become good citizens again, so they stay where they are'.

'And if they want to make their own lives a misery, that's up to them, they've done it to others.

'It looks as if all that will change one of these days, if you are as successful in the future with your research as you have been so far, so the whole thing becomes purely academic.

'Perhaps I'm a little too soft.' said Jas,

'Not at all, you are a gentle being, and caring for the welfare of others, that's not being too soft, it's an attribute, not a failing. It's just that up to now, we didn't see any other way of handling the problem.

'So far it has worked very well, it's not as if the deportees are even aware of what has happened, as that would constitute punishment, and we don't hold with that. We do what we do for the general benefit of the great majority, and that's about as fair as we can get at the present.'

'Will these unfortunate people ever be helped to regain some sense of sanity in the future?' asked Jas.

'Yes, of course, but we have other priorities which must be attended to first. I'm afraid they will be on the end of the line, but their time will come eventually, thanks to you'.

Jas felt saddened for those who would be held trapped for many more lifetimes on their designated worlds, but he could see the reality of the problem, and sought solace in the fact they didn't know about their situation and probably thought things were normal.

'I think that's enough of the heavy stuff.' said the grey man. 'Let's talk of happier things. Tell me about your childhood, what were your hobbies and interests?'

By the time Jas had retired to his quarters for sleep, he had to admit that the grey man was human after all, and had a very sharp sense of humour.

They had exchanged stories of their youth, the mishaps and tragedies which in retrospect were amusing, and their general opinions, which over the intervening years had been changed by circumstances as they grew up.

Time aboard the Dark Ship was a continuous thing, there being no day or night, just a series of shifts, broken up into what was considered to be manageable units of time for work, leisure and sleep.

It was during the next shift that Jas was asked to report to one of the lower levels of the ship where the grey man was waiting for him.

'I want you to see the grading process for yourself Jas,' he said, 'it's not really as inhumane as it looks, but it is effective.' The grey man walked briskly down to the end of the corridor which terminated in a massive sealed door, outside which sat a stern faced man at a desk.

He looked up as the couple approached, and snapped to attention.

'Good day sir.' were his only words, as the grey man handed him a small metallic disk. This was placed in a slot on the desk's surface, and two smaller disks shot out of another slot, one being handed to each of them.

'This is just a security measure to make sure that no one is ever left in this section of the ship for too long, and you'll see why later. Just press it onto the front of your tunic, and we'll proceed.'

The security man touched a key pad at is desk, and a section of the end wall slid back to reveal a small shuttle transport, waiting patiently in its tube.

They climbed in, the door hissed shut, and the shuttle shot forward with a force which took Jas by surprise, yet again.

Seconds later it did the same thing in reverse, and Jas was thrown forward in his seat, much to his embarrassment.

A short walk, a check by another security man, and they were looking down on a large chamber illuminated with a harsh white light, and packed full of equipment the like of which Jas had never seen before.

In the centre of the conglomeration was a clear space into which a deep sleep capsule had just glided in. Immediately below the watchers was a small cupola containing two operatives at a bank of instruments, who were controlling what happened in the main chamber.

The lid of the capsule opened and rotated around, exposing the recumbent form of a thick set man of middle years.

As they watched, the various pieces of equipment surrounding the capsule extended probes into the enclosure like some living entity, did what they had to, and retracted after a few moments.

'The probes have taken all the measurements needed to categorize the body, and allocate it to a particular type of environment. This is recorded on the capsule's ident tag, and it will now be stacked along with others of its kind awaiting despatch to a suitable world.'

A shield lowered itself between the main chamber, and the two operators, obscuring the capsule from view.

'This is the point when the new set of memories are implanted.' said the grey man. 'The shield is to protect us and the operators from any side effect which may spill over.'

'One of the operators will set up the pattern to suit the situation of the deportee upon his arrival to his new world, so that he feels reasonably at home there, although a little confused for a while, I suspect.'

The shield returned to its former position, and the watchers saw the lid of the capsule returned to its closed position, and the container slid out of an opening at the end of the chamber to be replaced by another capsule, which slid into the vacated space for the process to be repeated, again and again.

'There is one more thing I want to show you, and then you will be convinced beyond all doubt of the importance of your work.' The grey man turned and left the observation chamber, with Jas following almost at a run.

They entered the transport capsule again, and the grey man withdrew a tag from his pocket, placing it into a slot on the control panel.

The transport raced forward, did a side slip, and then continued for several moments in a series of jerky movements before coming to a halt. In a somewhat dazed state, Jas followed the grey man out and into a corridor.

A massively built door barred their way, the grey man paused before it, slipped a token into a slot and then it opened to reveal a dimly lit cavernous space, the contents of which made Jas gasp.

Row upon row of deep sleep capsules ranged before them, stacked in groups from floor to ceiling.

Jas felt sick, waves of nausea swept over him and his stomach tried to tie itself in knots. When the first waves of excruciating pain had passed, he was left with a dazed feeling of fear, dread, hopelessness, anger and sheer confusion.

'I am sorry to put you through that, but I want to drive home the point I made earlier. Your work, in the long run, will save an awful lot of unnecessary suffering, the like of which these unfortunate wretches are experiencing.

'You have just been exposed to what I would call a wave of mental anguish, a back wash of what they are feeling.

'No one should suffer that, no matter what they have done, but until we have a better system there is little we can do about it. I think I have made my point.'

Jas just stood there, still involuntarily shaking, the tears streaming down his face which had now acquired a pale ashen hue.

'Come my young friend, I think you have had enough for one day.' And with that the grey man led the trembling Jas back to the transport, and away from the cavern of tormented souls.

'I would like you to come to my quarters again towards the end of this shift, I am sure there a few questions you would like to ask, and I want to make sure there are no misunderstandings or mysteries left before we proceed to the next phase of this operation.'

Jas spent the next couple of hours in his private room, showering twice, and trying to forget the dreadful experience he had just had.

The feeling wouldn't go away, although the intensity had decreased to some extent. The grey man had certainly made his point, and Jas now felt even more driven to complete his work.

Later, the grey man welcomed Jas into his quarters as if nothing had happened earlier, and to him it probably hadn't. Jas gradually relaxed, the conversation skirting around the general banalities of life on the Dark Ship, until the grey man judged that Jas was in a more comfortable state of mind.

'And now for any questions you may have.' the grey man actually smiled at him.

'How well do the deportees integrate with the local population of the worlds they are sent to?' asked Jas.

'It all depends on how it is done.' the grey man replied.

'Some of the worlds we use have no humanoid life on them, though in time it is likely that it would develop. On others, where there is life, we are careful to only send down those who will physically match very closely those who are already there, and then there is usually no problem.'

'So in effect, you actually seed a planet with humanoid life if it has none of its own, but looks as if it could be sustained there?' asked Jas.

'Yes, we have no problem with that.' the grey man replied.

'You must understand how things are, or come about. The laws of physics and 'nature', for want of a better word, decree that life will come into being if the circumstances are even remotely suitable. All it needs is a soup of nutrients, usually a sea, ultra violet light, a little cosmic radiation from the local sun,   some lightning, and things get under way.'

'It begins with simple proteins being formed from some of the more complex chemicals in the water being bombarded with radiation, these then develop into more complex forms, and eventually replicate themselves, and so the very early and simple life forms come about.

'It takes a long time for the more complex things like bacteria to form, but given time, and there's plenty of that, they do, and then the whole thing accelerates at a prodigious rate, on a relative cosmic scale that is.

'Life can take on some very strange forms, some of which you wouldn't believe, but as I've said earlier, most of the intelligent life we have come across is in our form, with its many variations. What there may be in other galaxies we don't know, as we haven't been there yet.

'One day we will develop a drive which will take us out of our own back yard, and to other universes, and then we shall know. While I think of it, there is another way a planet can develop life, and that is when it gets an injection of life from somewhere else.

'Sometimes a meteorite, or fragment of a disrupted planet will contain a few spores or even more advanced forms of life, and if it lands in the right environment, will short circuit the normal development, and so speed things up a bit. To some extent, we do this when we introduce some of our deportees to an otherwise unpopulated world.'

The grey man paused to pass some refreshments over to Jas, who by now had worked up quite an appetite.

'We shall very soon be visiting our first drop off point, and you can then see first hand what we do, how we do it, and get some idea of what life is like down there on the planet's surface. You can't land as such, but the long range optics will show you all you need to see.'

'We have used this one for some time now, and I have checked the records back in time to the first arrivals. It illustrates how the races have intermingled and gone to war over what we would consider nothing, so there is plenty of data for you to peruse should you feel inclined.'

The rest of the 'evening' was spent in lighter vein of a more humorous nature, which returned Jas to a more relaxed state of mind after the shocks of the past few hours.

The next several days were spent gathering odd bits of information which Jas thought may be of use when he returned to the team back on the orbiting research station, as the Dark Ship was populated by highly trained staff of long standing, and should have a lot of data to offer on just about every aspect of the unfortunate deportees.

There were several more relaxing meetings with the grey man, the heavier topics of conversation being avoided by both, and a genial bond began to grow between them.

Jas got the impression that the grey man had not experienced a friendship of any magnitude before, and felt both pleased and honoured to be considered as such.

Slowly, as the friendship grew, a true sense of humour emerged from the grey man who was a great observer of life, and sharp witted, and he seemed the less grey for it.

The Dark Ship suddenly came alive one watch, the staff moving about much more and with an increased sense of purpose. It was nearing the time for the first depositing of the deportees.

Jas was in two minds whether he wanted to witness what he thought of as a distressful event, but the grey man had assured him that they knew nothing about it, and once they had been assimilated into the native population, they would feel reasonably at home.

The great ship swung into the solar system, reduced speed as the automatics sought out the designated planet, and went into orbit around it.

The grey man sent for Jas, and together they went to the main control room. A vast screen in front of the controls was so realistic that it gave the impression of a clear transparent window on the scene outside, and it was only when Jas commented on the 'window' that he was told it wasn't one in reality, just a viewing screen.

As the ship came around into the daylight zone again, the scene was magnified so that some of the surface detail could be clearly seen.

'It's a beautiful planet,' Jas exclaimed, 'I wouldn't mind a visit down there.'

'I don't think you would, once you had met the inhabitants.' replied the grey man with a chuckle.

Next to the vast centre screen, several smaller viewing devices were arrayed, and on one of these Jas could see long lines of capsules being loaded into a sinister looking shuttle.

The whole operation was accomplished using mechanical devices rather than personal to handle the capsules, which made the event somewhat distasteful to Jas's way of thinking, his reasoning being that they could at least have had a more humane send off than that.

Before them a large blue white planet very slowly turned, bathed in the bright light from a class seven star. Two other smaller planets were orbiting between the sun and the planet chosen for the deportees, but as the grey man said, they were of no use as the surface temperature was far too high and the atmospheres contained corrosive and poisonous gasses.

The ship swung around the planet in perfect orbit until the night side came into view.

Small centres of twinkling lights lit up the darkened areas and occasional flashes of lightning could be seen flickering between clouds and sometimes reaching out into space itself.

The shuttle completed its loading schedule, the hatches were closed and it was released from the mother ship to slowly drift away. Then the power was applied, and it glided away in a long graceful curve to begin its descent to the unsuspecting world below.

'We have the complete history of deliveries to this planet.' said the grey man. 'Also, we know a little of the planet's history.' He moved over to a panel and touched several buttons in quick succession. Another of the side screens lit up, and a picture of the planet below appeared.

'You see that large land mass low down near the southern polar ice cap, well that continent contains the only indigenous race on the planet.

'At one time the separate land masses you now see were all in one large block, but over a very considerable period of time, they split up due to plate tectonic movement, and are now scattered. Because of the conditions down there, we were able to send down several different types of people, all of which were suitable for the planet's environment.

'According to the records, these were distributed in little groups, dotted about the planet's surface. The body types were very similar, so it was just a matter of putting down groups of the same skin colour and type into different areas.

'Red skinned ones went there,' he indicated a large land mass to the left of the screen, 'and yellow ones there, black over here, white and some other pale skinned ones over this large area here. They are basically still in their original groups as far as the main land masses are concerned, but some have travelled and mixed with other races.'

Jas was fascinated, he had no idea of the complexity or scale of the operation, and was bursting with questions.

'At one time, the different groups tended to stay in their own areas, but as means of transport developed, they tended to move into each others areas, and that caused quite a bit of friction. There are records of vast wars sporadically raging down there over thousands of years, and they are still at it.

'The races have cross bred, moved from continent to continent, generally mixed with each other, and have learnt little in the process. They have polluted the waters and atmosphere, wasted the planet's resources and are multiplying at a prodigious rate. There is no attempt to control the exploding population, and soon, according to our calculations, their needs will far outstrip their resources, and then all hell will break loose.'

'But you are still adding to their numbers.' said Jas, wondering why they were still adding to the troubled planet below.

'Yes, but it will make little difference to the outcome' the grey man replied, 'A few hundred every now and again among so many billions, anyway, we are sending less now, as only the worst ones qualify for this planet and it is getting harder to find areas where the population will accept newcomers without wondering where they have come from.'

Although Jas felt saddened at the apparent cruelty of what was happening, he could see the reasoning behind it and as there was no alternative at the moment, had to accept things as they were.

Perhaps one day, if his research was completed and proved to be efficient enough, some of the misery could be spared, and everyone would be happier.

'How do you actually achieve integration with the local population?' he asked.

'We send the shuttle down on the dark side, their night time, and using long range vision equipment we can choose a site not too far from a lightly populated area. The deportee is then released from the capsule and will recover full consciousness in a few minutes, by then the shuttle will have moved on to the next location.

'The deportee comes to, which triggers off the implanted memory we have given him, and follows what ever instructions that memory contains. It's generally not long before he is accepted and is one of the locals, but it is getting more difficult to find the right situations for some of the paler skinned groups.'

'Is this the only planet you use in this system?' asked Jas.

'Yes, it is now. We used to use that one there.' indicating a pale pinkish point of light, high up in the star field.

'Unfortunately it wasn't large enough, or I should say dense enough, to hold onto it's atmosphere long enough to be really useful, and so most of the inhabitants came over to this one when the environment became uninhabitable.'

'You mean you had them all shipped out?' asked a surprised Jas.

'Oh no! Nothing like that. Don't forget the being is non destructible, and with the right implant in its memory, will obey the command of the implant when it is triggered off. It was only a matter of putting the idea of transferring to this planet when the time was right, and the job was done.

'A 'being' can move through space as easily as anywhere else, as there is no body to support, the only difference is that they are restricted to this solar system by a restraining command, and so can't get back to the Confederation.'

The great ship continued to circle the planet for several more shifts, depositing its cargo carefully in the chosen areas, picking up the latest data of the planet's progress, or lack of it, depending on view point, and then prepared to leave the solar system for the next of the rim worlds.

As the Dark Ship unloaded its unfortunate cargo of malcontents, as Jas liked to think of them, he got used to the idea of the necessity of the work and the method employed, but he was hoping for better things in the future.

The bond between him and the grey man grew as time went by and the work continued around the rim worlds, until at long last they set off for the Confederation home planets, the holding chambers empty and ready to take on their next load of human flotsam.

Research work on the stabilizing processes had gone on apace while Jas had been away, and it took him some time to catch up on the new developments.

A few of the processes needed to be refined to increase their speed of application and stabilize the results there from, but in general, the team had done very well on their own.

By the time Jas had tied up all the loose ends, there weren't many of the crew who hadn't had some gain from the processes, and many had made huge strides in their physical and mental states, raising the general tone of the whole station.

Everyone was eager to press on to new heights of mental awareness as the gains where so rewarding, with increased ability, understanding and the general feeling of wellbeing.

Several 'out reach' teams had been despatched to various planets so that the processes could be assessed for efficiency in new and different environments, and they proved successful beyond Jas's wildest dreams.

The whole thing was taking off at a frightening speed, and a new post of 'Case Confirmation Officer' had to be created to make sure that at every stage the person was stabilized and all the necessary processes had been completed to a satisfactory degree.

Jas hadn't realized just how much time had gone by since he had begun his new life, the pace of which seemed to quicken with each passing day.

It was only when he looked back that he realized the speed with which the work progressed was largely due to his increased abilities, and without such, he felt he would still be floundering at the early stages of developing the processes.

The rate with which the new system was being accepted on the various planets into which it had been introduced, only went to prove that if you have a good thing, everyone wants it, once you have shown it to be good and attainable.

Jas was at last able to sit back and relax a little as the system he had begun stabilized, and the results were being reported back to him as being repeatable and stable in themselves.

His own mental and physical state had also been enhanced beyond recognition from its former state by the very fact that he had experienced all the processes himself during the formative days of the work, as had all his close colleagues.

The greatest news he was to receive was that the grey man, unknown to him, had also been indulging in the processes and was making very good progress.

This period of comparative calm was shattered one shift when he was requested to report at the double to the grey man's office.

Wondering what could have possibly gone wrong, Jas slipped into his uniform and hurried off to see his superior.

'Good to see you Jas. I've just had some disturbing news. One of our survey ships has just returned from a section of the galaxy which we haven't explored very much so far, and reported that while doing so they were attacked very aggressively for no other reason than that they were there.

'They have gathered as much information from the area as they could, and then got out quickly.' The grey man looked a little less cheerful than he had of late, and Jas could see that he was disappointed more than angry, that such a thing should happen.

'From the report I have just received, it would appear that the four planets nearest their sun are inhabited and they have a form of space travel between them, and no doubt trade. When our ship approached the furthest planet out, it was attacked without any provocation. Small, and by our standards, fairly crude ships came out of nowhere and opened fire with solid missiles and a form of laser. The survey ships are pretty tough things, as you may well know, and it only suffered some external damage, more of an inconvenience than anything else, and it didn't stay to argue, which was wise as we don't know what else they may have had in the way of weapons.'

'One could only conclude from that,' Jas interrupted, 'that they either have a naturally aggressive nature towards any species other than themselves, or they have a very good reason to fear the encroachment of an outside force, which means they may have been attacked themselves, and in that case, we should know as much about it as possible to prevent any possible conflict in the future from such a force.'

'Unfortunately I came to the same conclusion' said the grey man. 'After some considerable thought, we have come up with three alternatives.'

One, we just leave them alone, as it looks as though it will be some time before they develop anything like deep space travel and are able to reach us, but then we will never know why they attacked us, and I think we should.

'Two, we go in and beat the hell out of them, which we can easily do, but that's against all we now purport to hold dear in the way of ethics, and so that's really a non starter.

'Three, we make them an offer they would find hard to refuse. We may have to wave a big stick in order to achieve a result, but as long as we only wave it, that should be acceptable in the long term.'

'I have thought of something.' said Jas.

'I thought you might, that's why I asked you up here in the first place.' the grey man replied with a grin.

'Here are all the reports we have received so far, go away and check them out and come back when you have formulated a plan of campaign, but I can guess what it may well contain right now.'

Jas worked long and hard into the 'night', formulating his plan, and then refining sections of it so that it was as foolproof as possible, returning next shift to the grey man's office.

'I feel we just have to make contact with them, and in order to do that with no threat or loss of life to us or them, we will have to present them with no alternative but to co-operate, although they must be made to think there is an escape loophole for them if they choose to use it.

'I suggest that we return to their system and send in a few small craft which can broadcast our message to all the people, it's not enough to just contact the leaders, as they probably have more than a vested interest in what's going on, so we must cut across that for a start.'

'We shall have to sort out all the frequencies which they use for communications, and swamp the lot, so that anyone who can pick up a transmission of any kind will receive our message. This is what I propose the message should be composed of.' and Jas gave the grey man an old fashioned written sheet, upon which his neat handwriting set out the ultimatum, for that's what it amounted to.

'Recently we visited your system and suffered an unprovoked attack on our peaceful mission ship. We have come again, not to seek revenge but to try and understand why you would want to attack when there is no threat. We also have much to offer your system in the way of technical data and trade, should you so desire to receive it. We are of the Confederation of Planets of this galaxy, a vast organization of trade and commerce, with much to offer, and no requirement for repayment of any kind except peaceful co-operation. Should you wish to remain in isolation from the greatest organization for the good of all this galaxy has ever known, then that is your prerogative, and we will withdraw, never to contact your people again. But there is one factor you must understand, and that is for our own peace of mind, your solar system will be quarantined from the rest of the

Confederation planets. You will remain in isolation, never able to leave your own solar system. We will return with one ship in twenty days of time as measured by your inner most planet for your answer. Do not attack us again, for we have the power to turn your sun into a super nova with little effort on our part, and this would extinguish all life in the entire system. This is not a threat, merely a statement of fact of our abilities. Remember, we come in peace, and should you wish it, we will go in peace, never to visit you again'.

The grey man finished reading the 'declaration', and solemnly nodded his head.

'That just about sums it up,' he said, 'I'll put it to the Council. There's one other thing, I think it would be a good idea if we applied a little of what we now know about the mind improvement system to these people, it could undercut a lot of hard work and some risks of the whole thing backfiring on us.

'Once we can get a few of them 'stabilized' as it were, the rest should follow, at least that's the theory!' He paused, 'Oh, and one other thing, in case you get any ideas about joining the mission, forget it, it's too risky.'

Jas was disappointed that he was not going on the mission, but could see the sense of it. Nevertheless, when the time came the grey man relented, with the stipulation that Jas wasn't to expose himself to any danger and that meant he couldn't contact or come near any of the new race until it became evident that they had forgone all thoughts of practical animosity.

It was decided that one of the Dark Ships would act as a base from which a smaller ship with shuttles would make the actual contact. A small scout craft was dispatched to listen in on the communications between the four worlds just in case anything could be picked up which would give the team something to go on with regard to the attitude of the new race towards the coming meeting.

The construction, or actually modifying, of several small craft to act as message transmitters didn't take long, but sorting out the transmission frequencies of the four worlds proved a little more troublesome. It was important that every possible frequency was covered so that the whole population would know what was going on, not just those in charge.

The new equipment was ready at last, and with the members of the teams well rehearsed on the parts they had to play, the Dark Ship with its accompanying small craft, left the sector and headed out into deep space to locate the newly discovered solar system.

Messages from the eavesdropping ships were not encouraging to begin with, as the degree of aggression in the intercepted transmissions indicated that the leaders of the four worlds were none too keen to lose face, or for that matter the degree of control they fancied they had over their little sector of space.

It was the fact that the general populace of the four worlds saw the sense of co-operating or getting thumped that saved the day, and a meeting was eventually arranged to take place on the world closest to the sun.

Jas and the grey man stayed on board the main ship while the smaller craft carrying the negotiation team left for what they thought might be their last flight. Contact was made, and the proposals of the Confederation laid out in no uncertain terms.

Firstly, several of the high ranking officials would have to undergo the stabilization process, and this caused the first barrier. This had been anticipated, and set up on purpose.

The team then offered to demonstrate how the processes worked and how beneficial they were so that the officials could then judge as to whether they wanted to try it themselves. This of course meant that some of the officials themselves would undergo the treatment, as there were no other personal present who qualified for the processes.

'If you can't get in by the front door, try the back door.' said Jas watching the proceedings with great interest. The grey man smiled.

As expected, the scheme worked. As soon as a few of the officials realized the gains to be had, and it was apparent to the others, there was little resistance. One or two did kick up a fuss about the rights of the individual and like limp claims, but these were soon overruled by those who saw the light, and so a stable contact was achieved.

It took a little longer for the rest of the governing bodies to realize there was now no retreating from the inevitable integration of the two peoples, but like most things, once enough momentum was gained, there was little to stop it.

The four worlds were told of the standard or degree of stability which would have to be obtained for all their citizens before full integration with the Confederation would be permitted, but by then it was far too late for them to back out, even if they wanted to.

'All in all, it went very well.' the grey man said to Jas, as they began the return journey to the research ship.

'I think a little celebration is called for, don't you?' And celebrate they did.

Shortly after returning to the research ship, the dreams of the pale grey ovoid on Mutty's world began. At first they were just simple views of the alien craft and its surroundings, but then feelings began to make themselves evident. Jas was a little disturbed when these intensified to the degree that he awoke sweating, and once he found himself trembling, not in fear so much, but in anticipation of something, but he didn't know what it was.

He toyed with the idea of telling the grey man, but thought it would be difficult to express what he felt, despite the fact that his ability to communicate was so high. No, there was something else afoot, and he would have to find out what it was before he confided in anyone.

Some time later, Jas went to see the grey man to give him the latest results of their progress on the processes, as he could find little more to improve at the level which was needed to bring about a stable civilization.

It was the upper levels which now held his interest, and as these had been mapped out, it was only a matter of researching each section to bring about the desired effect.

If everything worked out as he thought it should, and he could see no reason why it shouldn't, then mankind would be truly free as a spirit, able to have a body or not, at will, although he assumed that most people would want to keep the old system going as without a body so many of the delights of life would be missing, or would they? He wasn't sure, yet.

He had reached the state where he could leave his body under certain conditions, and be aware of his surroundings, he could see and hear and found the experience both entertaining and calming.

But there must be more to it than just that. More research was needed, and so instructions for the next stage of the exploration of the human psyche began.

As they settled down for one of their lengthy discussions, the grey man could sense that Jas had something troubling him.

'There's something else on your mind Jas,' the grey man said, 'so you may as well come out with it.'

'I will, but first I want to acquaint you with the latest run down on the processes.'

'I think we have it all buttoned up at long last, as we have had no failures for a long time, and the system is growing at such a rate on the worlds we have it set up on, that it will take care of itself now.'

'Everyone wants a piece of the action, young, old, you name it, and the word is spreading across the Confederation like wildfire. I never thought for one moment that it would be so easy, or so successful. What I call the upper levels of attainment are all mapped out, and the team have already begun work on them.

'Just to put you in the picture, the set up is like this. First you have to make people aware that a change for the better can be brought about, and this is done with a team of lecturers and demonstrators who take a well known person from the audience, and give him a quick boost in front of everyone. Although this is perhaps a little unethical, it does get the ball rolling, and once a few people are signed up, the rest follow when they see the results.

'I don't see anything unethical about that, as long as you explain what you are doing and why' the grey man said. Jas seemed a little relieved at that, and then laid out the sequence in which they introduced the processes.

'This results in the next step, the desire for change, and some are quite forceful in demanding it. That gets the show on the road, as it were. Next we improve communication to a point where there are no hang ups, which also means the person is aware of using discretion where necessary, which indicates stability at that point.

'The bad acts of the past, to others and to one's self, can lead to further similar bad acts, and this is the next thing we take apart. The person faces up to these and takes full responsibility for them, so releasing all the stored hurt and other emotions locked up in the incidents. This produces one of the biggest changes in a person at this stage. The consideration that a person is fixed in his or her abilities is then handled, and that has produced a few surprises!'

'Once past lives come into the picture, a lot of chronic ailments clear up, and then they realize that just about anything can be addressed, and they really go for it.

'A special process is used for those who will be in a position of control or power to enable them to handle it properly. It is now released to the general public as well, as it seems to benefit every one, no matter what they are doing.'

'Are you saying that even if you don't develop any of what you refer to as the higher level processes, that we now have the ability to truly stabilize the population of any world from a mental point of view, and the condition will remain that way?' the grey man asked.

'Basically yes, but there are other levels which will make the whole thing of even greater benefit. We need to know just who and what we really are, and I feel that we only have part of the story, there is more to find out and the higher levels will do that, I'm sure.'

The grey man sat back in his chair, contemplating something, but Jas wasn't sure what it was. At last he leaned forward a little, and broke the silence.

'I get the feeling that you consider your basic work is now completed, and others can carry on safely with the future developments you have outlined. Which leaves me with the conclusion that you want to do something else.'

Jas told him about the dreams of the alien craft on Mutty's world, and the strange feeling he had experienced in as much detail as he was able to.

'You are not the only one to get strange dreams, Jas. I haven't dreamt of the craft you mention, but I get dreams of something momentous about to happen that will make us change our way of thinking about the universe.'

'I don't know what it is, as it is only a feeling with no clear pictures, but it is big, and you are involved in it. We have known about the strange oval craft for some time, and I think you should visit it again. There may be something which you can pick up or understand about it now, with your heightened senses.'

After a final check to make sure things were running smoothly, the grey man made the arrangements for Jas to return to Mutty's world. After explaining to the research team the basic outline of what he was going to do, and only just surviving the party they threw for him, he boarded the craft which would return him to the enigma of the alien ship.

Mutty was more than pleased to see him again, and having been forewarned of his arrival, a reception party was organized which went well into the night.

'We have been using some of your processes on a few of the less awkward visitors we have had, and they work very well. Several have been returned to their own worlds, and have spread the word, as they say.

'It looks as if we shall all be redundant before very long, and I for one can't say I shall be sorry. I never liked what we have had to do, but there seemed to be no other way out of the problem.' said Mutty.

'Oh, and you'll see a change in Kranz. We think he may be human after all!'

The following day, when their heads had cleared a little, Jas told Mutty and Duffring about the main purpose of his visit, and it was agreed that Mutty alone should accompany Jas to the valley.

They set off shortly afterwards, Mutty bringing along the hatch opening gadget, although Jas said he didn't think it would be necessary, for some indefinable reason.

The valley looked the same, and the ovoid craft still lay nestling in the clearing on the valley floor surrounded by the ring of protecting mountains.

'I'll go down alone,' Jas said, leaving Mutty on the ledge at the exit of the tunnel which had brought them to the valley, 'just in case.'

He made his way down the never ending flight of steps which had been carved out of the living rock, and out onto the valley floor.

As Jas approached the craft, it seemed to change, although he couldn't see what the change was. There was something different about it, or was it just a feeling brought about by his heightened sense of awareness and expectation?

When he was about four metres from the ovoid, the hatch gently lowered itself down to ground level, forming an entry ramp. Jas now knew he was committed to the next series of events, what ever they were, and giving Mutty a final wave, he stepped onto the ramp and walked into the craft. As he did so, the whole ship began to change, the outer hull taking on a soft fluorescent glow, the hatch silently closing behind him.

It all appeared to be just the same as the time when he had visited the craft before, but the air had an electric feel about it as he made his way up the long corridor to what he assumed to be the control room.

The long curved bench-like object was still there, but seemed strangely different somehow, and as Jas walked up to it he could feel that something was about to happen.

What he had assumed to be a huge viewing screen at the end of the control room suddenly changed, it became transparent, and he could look out over the valley and up to Mutty who was still standing on the ledge of rock above.

Jas waved, but for some reason Mutty couldn't see him and just stood there, watching the scene below him.

Wondering what to do next, the decision was taken from him as the walls of the control room became semi-translucent and behind which could be seen a pattern of fine lines and shapes. Jas wasn't sure if he actually heard it with his ears, or if it was inside his head, but a voice spoke to him.

'Welcome, do not be afraid, no harm will come to you. We have been watching your people through the ages, and the time has now come for contact to be made between us.

You, and you alone have been chosen to act as the envoy of your civilizations, which you call the Confederation of Planets. Before this time, it was considered that your peoples were too barbaric and dangerous to be accepted into our midst, but you have made great progress in the area which made you so unacceptable.

As your people have joined together the worlds of your galaxy for your mutual good, so we have joined galaxies together.

You are invited to join us for the greater good of all, but should you wish not to do so at this period in time, then you must leave the ship, perhaps to return one day when you think the time is right.

All your needs will be catered for, you only have to go into any of the rooms onboard this ship and desire something, and it shall be provided. If you wish to join us now, you only have to place your hand in the depression on the bench before you, and the journey will begin.'

Jas knew what he must do, but hesitated for a moment. He wanted to say a proper goodbye to Mutty, who was still looking on from the ledge above, but somehow knew Mutty would understand if he didn't.

His hand moved forward, almost of its own volition and slid into the slight hollow on the bench. There was a barely audible sigh, and the alien craft silently rose from the valley floor, paused for a moment when level with Mutty who was waving with both arms, and then accelerated upwards into the inky blackness of space.

Jas stood transfixed at the bench like structure, watching the stars through the transparent forward screen wheel by at an ever increasing speed until they were just a blur, and then winked out of existence.

Mankind had just taken its next great irrevocable step forward, Jas not fully realizing just how great that step was going to be, or the part he would be called upon to play in it.

The End

**More from sci-fi-cafe.com
by David Reynolds-Moreton**

Anthology of Futures
Anthology of Possibilities
Divergence
Enslavement
Exchange Rate
Extreme Difference
Flight of the Tristan
Fully Guaranteed
Greenways
Inheritance
Light Quest
The Martian Enigma
The Power Seeds
The Seed Garden
The Single Twin
The Sweepers
The Tribe
Transplant
Of Wood, Metal and Glass